Undercover Secrets

Anna raised her head. Dr Galloway was looking deep into her eyes, penetrating her soul – commanding her. She had never, ever been told what to do by a man before. In the past, if a lover had tried to dominate Anna, she would have turned the tables on him. She would have done the exact opposite of what he wanted, just to prove who was in charge. Now, also who faced with a situation where  y along, pretending she e knew, she thought, slow he knew that she was the

By the same author:

THE SUCCUBUS
THE SEVEN-YEAR LIST

Undercover Secrets

ZOE LE VERDIER

BLACK
lace

Black Lace novels are sexual fantasies.
In real life, make sure you practise safe sex.

First published in 1998 by
Black Lace
Thames Wharf Studios,
Rainville Road, London W6 9HT

Copyright © Zoe le Verdier 1998

The right of Zoe le Verdier to be identified as the
Author of this Work has been asserted by her in
accordance with the Copyright, Designs and Patents Act
1988.

Typeset by SetSystems Ltd, Saffron Walden, Essex
Printed and bound by Mackays of Chatham PLC

ISBN 0 352 33285 9

Undercover Secrets

ZOE LE VERDIER

BLACK
lace

Black Lace novels are sexual fantasies.
In real life, make sure you practise safe sex.

First published in 1998 by
Black Lace
Thames Wharf Studios,
Rainville Road, London W6 9HT

Copyright © Zoe le Verdier 1998

The right of Zoe le Verdier to be identified as the
Author of this Work has been asserted by her in
accordance with the Copyright, Designs and Patents Act
1988.

Typeset by SetSystems Ltd, Saffron Walden, Essex
Printed and bound by Mackays of Chatham PLC

ISBN 0 352 33285 9

Chapter One

'*A* nna. Anna. Anna!'
Anna had to blink twice before she reached reality again. She turned to Suzy and smiled dreamily. 'Sorry, I was miles away.'

'Thinking good thoughts?'

'I was making my New Year's Resolutions.'

Suzy sat down beside her on the stair. 'And they are . . .?'

Anna started to tick them off on her fingers. 'I'm going to spend more time at work, for a start.'

Suzy gasped. 'You're kidding? You might as well take a sleeping bag and live at the office. You could save on rent – it's hardly worth it, for the amount of time you spend here.'

'It's the only way to get on, I'm telling you. I've worked bloody hard this year, and I've proved myself as a researcher. But if I want to break into reporting, I've got to do more. Mike's a workaholic – well, I will be, too, if that's what it takes.'

Suzy rolled her eyes. 'You'll make yourself ill if you work much harder. What else?'

'I'm going to drink less and get fit.'

Suzy tilted her head and raised her eyebrows. 'Now, where have I heard that one before?'

'I mean it, this time. And last but not least, I'm going to have some serious fun.' Her eyes glittered, showing Suzy exactly what sort of fun she had in mind. 'Starting tonight. I intend to see in the New Year in bed.'

'Oh God.' Suzy winced. 'Who's the poor unsuspecting victim?'

A slow smile spread across Anna's face. 'Rob.'

'Rob? Isn't he a bit young for you?'

From their vantage point halfway up the stairs, they both looked through the banisters at the party going on in their living room below. There were at least thirty people crammed into the small house they shared: friends, work colleagues and the medical students who lived in the house next door. Rob was one of them. He was nineteen, tall and blond, with the meaty physique of a rugby player and a desperate shyness which was rather incongruous in such a well-built man.

'I like them young.' Anna laughed. 'Young and shy is even better. Just look at him.' They both looked and, as they did, Rob glanced up at them. Embarrassed at finding two gorgeous women openly admiring him, he dropped his head and stared down at his feet, which he shuffled nervously. Anna sighed appreciatively, his innocence – and the thought of what she would do with it – making her shiver. Her wistful voice curled in the thick air like smoke. 'I bet he's a virgin.'

'I wouldn't mind playing doctors and nurses with him,' Suzy admitted. 'He is sweet. But eight years ... don't you think that's a big age gap? He's so naïve, as well. You won't have much to talk about.'

Anna shrugged carelessly. 'I wasn't planning on doing much talking.' What did age difference matter, anyway? She wanted Rob, and he wanted her. He was too bashful to either admit it or do anything about it, but she had seen the telltale signs: a blush whenever she spoke to

2

him, a guilty flutter of his pale eyelashes every time she caught him staring at her.

She checked the time. Half ten. She had an hour and a half to work on phase two of her plan. She had ogled Rob all night, burning her eyes into his face until he met her gaze, then holding eye contact for a moment before looking away. Again and again she had done this, until Rob had taken courage from her signals and set off through the dancing, laughing throng to talk to her. Then she had turned away and spoken to someone else: Mark, one of Rob's housemates, an equally good-looking young man but not half as innocent as Rob, and therefore not much of a challenge for Anna. Completely bewildered, the unsuspecting Rob had then watched helplessly as Anna flirted with Mark. No wonder the poor boy now seemed terribly confused. Anna's body language clearly spoke of her desire for Mark, as she touched her creamy-white neck and laughed generously at his poor jokes. But every now and again, she would glance over Mark's shoulder and meet Rob's doleful, puppy-dog eyes, and she would wink wickedly at him.

Stage one – harrying her prey into utter confusion – was now complete. Time to move in for the kill. Standing up, she smoothed her scrap of a dress down over her thighs.

Suzy grabbed Anna's wrist and hoisted herself to her feet as well. 'Be gentle with him,' she urged.

'Give me a break,' Anna said, rolling her eyes. 'I'm not a man-eater. I just want a little fun, that's all.'

God knows, she deserved some after the last twelve months. Years of working as a researcher on daytime TV had finally paid off, and Anna had got a job on one of the best current affairs shows on air. But doing research for *Undercover* was a lot harder than anything Anna had ever done before, and she had forsaken her social life in order to impress her new boss. She loved working with Mike, *Undercover*'s producer, but he was infuriatingly unemotional. He and Anna got on well together, and there was definitely a frisson of sexual tension crackling between them. But was Mike impressed with her dedication? A slap on the back at the office Christmas party was the only clue Anna had been given so far.

Still, she thought, there would be plenty of time to make an impression on Mike next year. Right now, she wanted to make an impression on Rob and to claim some of that fun she had been promising herself.

She slunk through the crowd to Rob's side. He was standing on his own, sipping a beer and watching with wide eyes as Anna approached. 'Hi,' she said, smiling.

'Hello.'

Anna waited, looking up at him, wondering what he would say if she said nothing.

'You've had your hair cut,' he offered hopefully.

'Yes.'

'I . . . I . . . I like it. It suits you.'

Anna looked beyond him at her reflection in the living-room window. It did suit her. She had been nervous about cutting it – her friends had always told her that her glossy black hair was beautiful. But she had wanted to look different for the party and, on a whim, she had had it cut into a short, messy bob, one side of which flopped sexily over one eye. A foot of hair had fallen to the hairdresser's floor, and Anna was amazed at the difference it made. The new style showed off the length of her neck and framed her striking features, making her wide green eyes, strong cheekbones and full lips all the more dramatic. She felt sexier and more confident than ever.

'Thank you,' she said, taking Rob's glass and putting it down on the mantelpiece. 'Come and dance with me, Rob.'

'I don't . . . I can't . . . I've never really been able to . . .'

Ignoring his stammering, Anna gently pulled him into the centre of the room. Biting his lip, Rob watched as she

4

began to move her fluid limbs to the music's insistent rhythm. While he shuffled self-consciously from side to side, Anna let herself go. She could feel the beat in her stomach and hips, and she moved instinctively. Gradually, she eased closer to Rob, until she was standing so near there was nowhere for her arms to go but around his neck. Fixing his eyes with hers, she whispered for him to put his arms around her.

He looked into her pale green eyes, then his big, warm hands tentatively touched her waist and slid around on to her back. Anna arched her spine ever so slightly with the pleasure of feeling his skin on hers, his palms only separated from her by the flimsy satin of her black dress. They stayed like that for a while, Anna gyrating ever so slightly, keeping up the pretence that she was dancing. Then she turned within his arms so she had her back to him. Resting her small hands over his, she crossed them around her slender waist, imprisoning herself within his thick forearms. Leaning her head back on Rob's shoulder, she sighed with genuine pleasure. Behind her, Rob's body felt so hard, so strong. And yet she knew he was putty in her hands.

Suddenly, she pushed out of his grasp and went to the stairs. She was intensely aware of the silky brush of material on her thighs and the slight sway of her hips as she climbed. Pausing halfway up, she turned. And with a silent half-smile, she gave Rob the invitation of his life.

'Anna? It's Mike.'

Anna sat up on the edge of the bed. 'Mike?' At the other end of the telephone, he sounded breathless. 'Are you OK? Is something wrong?'

'Anna, I'm at the office. I want you to come into work as soon as possible.'

Slightly confused by the amount of champagne she had drunk, Anna thought about this for a minute. 'I'll be back at work on Monday, Mike.'

He sighed impatiently. 'Are you drunk?'

'No. But I will be soon. It's New Year's Eve, you know. What the hell are you doing in the office? Don't you have a home to go to?'

'Anna, I've got a lead. This could be a big story, but it's sensitive stuff and it needs investigating thoroughly. I want you to do it. I need you to come into the office.'

All of a sudden, Anna felt perfectly sober. 'I'll be there in fifteen minutes,' she said.

'Where are you going?' Rob asked plaintively.

Anna looked regretfully at his smooth, hairless torso; at his thick wrists, handcuffed to the bed, and at the magnificent erection rising from his crotch. 'I'll be back as soon as I can,' she promised, grabbing her coat.

Anna hailed a taxi on the corner and arrived in Soho fourteen minutes later. The streets were full of party-goers emerging from the trendy pubs and wine bars and staggering towards the clubs. Anna let herself into the office and closed the door on the revelry. She had been planning and looking forward to her party for weeks, and now here she was, back at work at just gone eleven on New Year's Eve. If she wasn't so ambitious, she would have been annoyed. But Mike's calling her was the confirmation she had been praying for. There was a fist of excitement clenching in her stomach at the flattering thought that he had picked her from their team to carry out this investigation. Smiling to herself, she climbed the stairs to Mike's office.

With the lights out and only his desk lamp alleviating the darkness, Mike was standing behind his desk, staring out of the window at the noisy street below. Anna hesitated at the door, unable to resist the opportunity for an appreciative glance over his body. He was dressed scruffily, as always, but there was something appealing about a man who didn't care how he looked. There was definitely something appealing about this man. And

Mike didn't really need to care; whatever the state of his creased shirts and mismatching trousers, he always looked darkly handsome. He was an Australian of Italian descent – a big, serious man with short, dark brown hair which stuck up untidily in sympathy with his clothes. He had dark eyes, dusky skin and a constant rash of stubble on his angular jaw and dimpled chin. He also had a wonderfully tight bottom, which was a constant source of delighted whispering amongst the female staff in the company.

Anna took off her coat and hung it on the hatstand. 'Mike?'

He swivelled on his heels, opened his mouth to speak, then paused. 'Wow,' he said, looking Anna up and down and flickering his thick eyebrows appreciatively. 'You look . . . Did I drag you away from something?'

'My party. Remember? You were invited.'

He looked blank. Parties meant nothing to Mike. He probably hadn't even looked at the invitation. 'You've had your hair cut,' he said. 'It looks great.'

Anna held his gaze. The fist tightened in her guts; there was that sexual tension again, obvious in his dark brown eyes. 'Thank you, I –'

'Anyway, we haven't got much time, so let's get down to work. Take a seat, Anna.'

Anna sat down. Mike revealed the reason she had been summoned to the office, pacing distractedly and ruffling his hair as he spoke.

'This afternoon, I had a phone call from an old friend of mine. His daughter, Jane, ran away from home a week ago. Jane came back today, told her father where she'd been, and he called me straight away.

'I drove over to their house to see them. Jane's a beautiful girl, but she's immature for nineteen, and she's easily led. Her father and I suspect she was almost led into something quite sinister. Luckily she had the sense to realise it herself, and she got out of it while she still could.

'Jane still lives at home with her parents. Just before Christmas she had a massive row with her father and decided to move out. But where could she go? She had very little money of her own, and no one who could put her up. She saw an ad in the paper. The MS Institute of Research was asking for young people with no direction in life to attend their open day – get this – on Christmas Day. Successful candidates would be offered interesting work and free, luxurious accommodation. It sounded ideal.

'So Jane went to the open day. She was pleasantly surprised to find the Institute was more like a health club than a lab, and that all the scientists she saw seemed to be young and attractive, happy and very friendly. So she was pleased when she was selected to go through to the next stage. She had an interview with a Dr Galloway, who introduced himself as the Institute's founder and director.

'Galloway, according to Jane, is mesmerising. In her interview, he asked her all sorts of personal questions about her sex life. Jane answered some of them – she says he was trying to hypnotise her, but that sounds like Jane exaggerating, to me – then suddenly something clicked in her mind. She asked Galloway why he needed such personal information. He got defensive, saying the Institute is a very special place. With only one empty position on his research team, and twelve candidates, he needed to be sure Jane was the right choice.

'But that didn't really explain why he should want to know which was Jane's favourite sexual position. Jane started asking him questions, about the work she would be doing at the Institute if she was accepted. Galloway wouldn't tell her much, but he explained that the Institute carries out ground-breaking genetic-engineering studies, vital to the development of the human race. Jane would start off working in the kitchen or the laundry, but eventually her job would be to assist one of the scientists, recording his research data and helping him with experiments. That sounded harmless enough, and fairly interesting too, and at that stage Jane was still furious with her father. She decided that life at the Institute would be a far better option than going home. She told Galloway that she wanted the place.

'Galloway told her that if she was prepared to shun the constraints of society, she would discover a new existence filled with endless possibilities. Life at the Institute would broaden her horizons and open her mind. Well, that rang alarm bells in Jane's head. She is sure that Galloway could tell she was worried. She thinks that's why he asked her to do what he did – he was testing her, seeing how far she would go to gain her place at the Institute.' Mike paused, grimacing as he seemed to be searching for the right words.

'And?' Anna prompted. 'What did he ask her to do?'

'He . . . er . . . he . . .' Mike swallowed hard and looked down at his paper-strewn desk. It was the first time Anna had ever seen him embarrassed. 'He asked her to . . . you know . . . touch herself.'

Anna's brow furrowed slightly. 'You mean . . . masturbate?' She winced with disgust. But she also recognised a minute but undeniable fragment of depraved excitement lurking in the back of her mind. What sort of man was Dr Galloway? What sort of man would ask such things in an interview situation, and why? He sounded like someone who liked to control people, who liked to play games. Someone like Anna. 'Galloway wanted her to masturbate for him?' she asked again.

Mike nodded. 'Jane didn't tell that bit to her father, but she told me. Galloway never laid a finger on her, and Jane said she never once felt she was in danger. But she said – how did she put it? – he made her feel helpless.

9

She's worried that other girls will fall for Galloway, and be drawn into whatever sick game he's playing.'

'Well, we've certainly got an interesting story on our hands,' Anna said.

'We have.' Mike placed his palms on the desk and leant forwards. 'But that's not the real story. The real story is in whatever's going on behind the Institute's closed doors. What do you know about genetic engineering, Anna?'

As his searching eyes bored into hers, she felt she should know something. 'Erm . . . well, the subject raises a lot of moral questions.'

'Yes.' Mike jabbed a finger towards her. 'Spot on. Genetic engineering is a very touchy subject within the scientific community. Very few labs are given licences to carry out gene experiments, and they all have to document their studies very carefully and publish the results in the medical journals.' He sat down in his high-backed leather chair and clasped his hands on the desk. He had an expression Anna recognised: bright-eyed, intense, edgy. 'So why doesn't the MS Institute of Research publish any of its findings?'

Anna sat forward in her seat, electrified by the tension in Mike's voice. 'Because it's doing something it shouldn't.'

Mike began to shuffle papers, looking for something. 'Maybe the Institute hasn't got a licence, in which case Galloway's breaking the law. If so, that's one hell of a risk to take. What is it that makes that risk worthwhile? It's always the same thing, Anna.'

'Money,' she butted in.

Mike smiled, obviously pleased that Anna was on the ball. 'Money,' he agreed. 'But is it money from a drugs company? Or a foreign government – a fascist dictatorship perhaps?' Mike's voice grew raspy as he jumped to dramatic, newsworthy conclusions. He found the piece of paper he had been searching for. He narrowed his eyes, squinting in the darkness as he stared at it. 'Just what is that creep Galloway up to, that has to be kept so secret? Chemical weapons? Experiments on animals?' He lowered his voice. 'Experiments on humans?' He passed Anna the newspaper cutting. 'I want you to go, Anna. I want you to play along with Galloway's games. I want you to get into that Institute, and to stay there until you find out what's going on. This could be the biggest story *Undercover*'s ever done.'

Anna's fingers trembled slightly as she read the cutting out loud. ' "Eighteen to thirty? No direction in life? Nowhere left to go? Then come to the MS Institute's open day. We will show you a new way of life, where your work is rewarded and your mind is opened to new possibilities." ' She looked up at Mike. 'This open day – it's tomorrow.'

Mike nodded. 'It seems these recruitment drives are always held at odd times of the year, on days when most of us have better things to do. Jane said that the others who turned up the day she did were all the same: drifters, travellers, hippies, people running away from something. Holding interviews on Christmas Day and New Year's Day is obviously a ploy by Galloway. He wants to attract people with no family lives, no ties. Why, Anna?'

She turned down the corners of her mouth and shook her head. She didn't have a clue why but, the more Mike told her, the more desperate she was to find out.

'The Institute's somewhere in the Lake District. If you want this job, Anna, we'll have to leave soon. But I want you to think about it very carefully.'

There wasn't much to think about. Anna was hooked. 'But why me?' she asked. 'Shouldn't someone with more experience do this? Kevin, perhaps, or . . . or Julie?'

Mike shook his head. 'They're experienced, but there's always a faint chance they'll be recognised from being on telly. I want you to do this, Anna, and not just because you won't be recognised. I think you're the best man for the job. You're thorough, hard-working, and you can look after yourself. You're also the best-looking woman on the production team. I mean ... I don't mean that to sound sexist, but Galloway obviously likes his staff to be attractive, for whatever reason. He won't be able to resist you.' Mike's eyes drifted down Anna's body. 'Especially if you wear that dress.'

'I'll wear whatever you think is right.' Anna basked in his longing. Her pussy twitched, partly with the warmth of his gaze, partly with anticipation for her first job as a reporter. 'Thanks, Mike, for giving me a chance.'

'You deserve it,' Mike said nodding. 'You're one hell of a researcher. Don't thank me yet, though. Neither of us can be sure of what you're getting into. I'll be honest, you could be in danger.'

'I can look after myself.'

'I know you can.' Mike smiled fondly at her. 'You remind me of me.' He picked up a file and handed it to Anna. 'All the information you need is in here. I'll drive, so you can read it on the way. I've given you a new identity, which you'll have to know inside out and back to front by the time we get to the Institute. There's a letter in there from an imaginary fiancé, breaking up with you. He's one of the reasons you're seeking a new life at the Institute. You'll have the letter in your bag, just in case they do some snooping around of their own.'

Mike had thought of everything. That was his job. 'You have been busy.' She looked up at him. 'What would you have done if I'd said no?'

'I knew you wouldn't.' Mike leant back in his seat and watched Anna for a moment, as if weighing her up. 'But there's one thing I don't know about you, Anna. How far will you go?'

'What do you mean?'

'You'll only have one chance to get into the Institute tomorrow. If Galloway fancies you, and I think we can

12

safely assume that he will, then you're likely to get to the interview stage. But what then, Anna? What if you find him repulsive when he starts asking you personal questions? What if you freeze when he asks you to touch yourself?'

Anna smiled to herself, thinking of how she had manipulated poor Rob, and the lover before him, and the one before him. Anna enjoyed being single and being in control. She was as capable of playing games as any man. 'I'll do whatever it takes to get into that Institute, Mike. Men like Galloway don't frighten me. He may think he's testing me, but I'll be the one in control.'

'So you won't mind flirting with him?'

'Flirting is something I'm very good at,' she said.

'Show me.'

Anna raised one eyebrow. 'Sorry?'

'Show me. I want to be sure of this, Anna, and I want you to realise what you'll have to go through, tomorrow. I'll be Galloway. Show me how you'll flirt with him.'

Anna slowly nodded. 'OK.'

As Mike talked, pretending to be Galloway and telling Anna about the Institute and its work, a tingle ran up the back of Anna's spine and down her bare arms, making the hairs stand up. Her excitement was like flaky pastry, layer after layer of sweet pleasure. There was Mike's deep, gravelly voice. There was the thought of meeting Galloway tomorrow, knowing she had to impress him and knowing she would have the upper hand. There would be the tense, thrilling buzz of infiltrating the Institute and betraying its secrets. And tonight there was Mike, wanting her, using this role-play as an excuse to come on to her. Well, she would show him. He wanted flirting; that's what he would get.

She leant forward. Resting her elbows on the desk, and her chin on her laced fingers, she gazed into Mike's eyes. Unblinking, she looked from one eye to the other, then slowly she moved her gaze on to his mouth. As she watched his lips moving, her own lips parted slightly. When Mike's voice faltered, just for a second, she noticed and looked up. Smiling slightly and innocently, she blinked.

Mike continued talking. Anna dropped one hand on to the desk and, with the other, began a journey over her neck which was designed to distract Mike's attention. Slowly, absent-mindedly, as if totally caught up in what he was saying, her fingertips trailed around the back of her head. She played with her hair for a moment, curling a lock around one finger. Then her touch moved back across her throat and down to her shoulder. As if she was aching there, Anna spread her hand over the lower slope of her neck and gently squeezed. As she did so, the delicate strap of her dress slid from her shoulder. Keeping her eyes fixed on Mike's, Anna left the strap dangling provocatively and sat back in her chair.

'So,' Mike said, shifting in his seat and quite obviously enjoying this game as much as Anna was, 'that's all I can tell you about the Institute. I would like to offer you a place here, Anna, but I need to be sure you're the right candidate for the position. May I ask you some personal questions?'

Anna crossed her legs high up. Her short dress rode up her thighs. She folded her arms in her lap, surreptitiously pulling her skirt upward by another all-important couple of inches. Without a downward glance, Anna knew that the top of her stocking was now clearly visible. 'Fire away,' she answered breathily.

'How . . .' Mike salvaged his attention from her thigh and retrieved his line of thought. 'How many lovers have you had, Anna?'

She raised her chin, meeting his challenging stare. 'Not enough.'

'What is your favourite sexual position?'

'I'll show you,' she said, slowly standing up. Her heart pounded noisily as she took a step towards Mike's desk.

Holding his eyes with hers, she gradually leant forward and placed her hands next to his elbows. Her back was straight, parallel to the desk, her legs apart and her sex throbbing. At that moment, she forgot about everything else and wanted one thing only: Mike's body behind hers, his hands grabbing her waist, his cock sliding into her wet pussy.

Mike couldn't stop himself. His mouth gaped and his grateful eyes fell down the front of Anna's dress. Anna knew exactly what he could see; it was what she had seen when she had bent to the mirror to put her lipstick on, earlier that evening. It was what Rob had seen as she had knelt over him, cuffing him to her bed – her breasts, full, pale and perfect, dangling seductively, her dark nipples wide and pouting.

'Jesus,' Mike murmured.

Anna raised the three-inch heels of her strappy black shoes another inch from the floor. Pushing her torso further forward, she brought her face a breath away from Mike's. He hesitated for a second, looking up at her, blinking uncertainly. Then he kissed her, his tongue urgently forcing its way inside her mouth, his lips crushed to hers. His hand slipped beneath her dress and cradled one pert breast, while his other buried itself in her hair. Softly moulding his fingers to her wonderful shape, Mike groaned quietly with pleasure. 'Jesus, Anna,' he whispered, when their faces parted for air. 'I want you so much. I've always wanted you. But we work together . . .'

His voice had doubts, but his body had none. He stood and moved around the desk. With two strides he was behind Anna, his hands on her waist. 'We shouldn't,' he grumbled, ruffling up her dress to expose her naked behind. 'We can't, it's hopeless, we've got to work together, oh Jesus,' he gasped. 'You've got no knickers on.'

Anna languidly arched her lower back. She felt her

pussy lips parting. Mike's hands were on her arse, and she almost cried with longing as they slowly moved downward. With his palms on her cheeks, he delicately opened her sex with his thumbs. 'We shouldn't,' he sighed. 'I swore I'd never sleep with anyone I worked with . . . It's bound to cause problems . . .'

Anna straightened up, pushing his hands away. 'Let's not do it, then.' She turned to face Mike. 'If it's going to cause problems, we should just forget it.' Inside, she was burning, but outside she was as cool as ever. Her expression was blank, giving away nothing.

Mike's expression gave away everything. He couldn't forget it, no matter how unwise it was for him to sleep with a colleague. He gave up the half-hearted battle and kissed Anna's long neck, smothering her skin with his lips. He grabbed her breasts, squeezing them together beneath the soft satin of her dress. Leaning his pelvis into hers, he pressed his erection against her hip.

Anna slipped her hands between their urgent bodies and fumbled with his flies. Sliding a hand into his boxer shorts, she curled her fingers around his long, thick penis and brought it out of the dark warmth. Pulling away from Mike, she hitched herself up on to the edge of the desk.

Anna watched as Mike's head bowed. There was silence apart from his heavy, rapid breathing, and Anna savoured the stillness. She loved that moment: the final, heart-stopping instant of anticipation, the point of no return, the slow-motion, tension-saturated second before the searing pleasure. With tremulous fingers, Mike pushed her dress up over her thighs, then over her hips. His palms slid downward again on to her legs, and then gently pushed them apart. Looking down, his eyes feasted on the dark triangle of hair pointing the way to his pleasure. His hands moved around behind Anna. Holding her buttocks, he eased her closer to his rearing cock.

Then they were together, the sharp edge of the desk biting into Anna's flesh while his penis thrust deep inside her. Mike fucked her with long, deliberate strokes, his head bowed in worship of her sex and his hot fingers grasping her tightly. Anna grasped him too, wrapping her calves around his legs. But it was no use; he was pulling at her, urging her sex further on to his prick, and any minute now she would fall off the table. So she lay back, pressing her torso on to the cold wood and lifting her legs. She rested her ankles on Mike's shoulders, digging in with her heels as her feet pointed with pleasure. As he thrust, Mike turned his face to kiss and bite Anna's calf. He held on with one hand while the other stroked up and down her stockinged thigh. Anna saw him, lost with rapture inside her silken pussy, and she lost herself. She pushed the low neckline of her dress down over her breasts. Exposing the swollen white mounds, she pinched her engorged nipples until the pain shuddered down into her belly and mingled with the champagne swilling around in there. Keeping one nipple trapped between her fingers, she reached down with her other hand. Her clitoris was throbbing with desperation, and a few seconds of pinching and rolling in time with Mike's last, grunting thrusts was all it took. As they came in close succession, shuddering and groaning loudly, the sound of their climax was accompanied by delighted whooping, clapping and cheering outside in the streets.

Anna began to laugh. Not only had she managed to see the New Year in as planned, but the whole of London was applauding.

It wasn't until they were in the car, on their way up North, that Anna remembered Rob. 'Oh shit,' she whispered, fumbling in her bag for her mobile. After ten rings, Suzy answered breathlessly.

'Suzy? Having fun?'

'Anna! Where are you?'

17

'I'm on the M6.'

'Anna, are you all right? What's going on? No one knew where you'd gone.'

'I'm fine. I'm working on a story.' She paused, telling Suzy in the short silence what she would have liked to tell her in words, had she been alone. 'I'm with Mike.'

'With Mike. Oh, I see,' Suzy said, in a suggestive tone of voice. 'Thought you'd make a start on your New Year's resolutions, did you? Tell me, which one are you working on? The putting in extra hours bit, or the having fun?'

'Both. Listen, I'm on my way to check out a story. I can't tell you anything else, but I wanted to let you know I won't be coming home tonight.'

'OK, sweetie. I'll see you when I see you. Take care.'

'Do me a favour, Suzy.'

'Sure.'

'Go into my bedroom, and ... er ...' She glanced at Mike. 'Look after Rob for me.'

It was Suzy's turn to pause tellingly.

'Suzy?'

She giggled. 'Don't worry about Rob. He's in safe hands.'

Chapter Two

*T*hey arrived at the motel at five in the morning. Exhausted, Anna stumbled into bed and slept. A minute later, or so it seemed, Mike woke her up. He was still sitting in the chair, still fully dressed.

'Don't you ever sleep?' Anna muttered, holding her pounding head as she sat up.

Mike's eyes flickered as the sheet fell from Anna's breasts. 'I couldn't risk not waking up in time. It was better to stay up.'

Anna shook her head in disbelief. Easing her heavy limbs out of bed, she walked across the room to the bathroom, passing Mike on the way.

'I need a shower,' she moaned. In the mirror, Mike appeared behind her, looking more sexily rumpled than ever. 'Do you want to join me?' she mumbled hopefully.

He shook his head. 'Well . . . of course I do,' he said regretfully, his dark eyes taking in her nakedness. 'But we haven't much time. I want to test you on your new identity. We can't afford any mistakes, Anna.' He turned away from her. Resting his forehead against the tiles, he let out a long sigh. 'Christ, I'm nervous about this.'

Anna turned on the shower and stepped in. 'Nervous?' she shouted above the spray. 'What about?'

Mike watched through the glass as she soaped her breasts. 'I'm having second thoughts about sending you off into this alone. If anything happens to you . . .'

'Nothing's going to happen,' Anna said cheerfully. She was sure of that. No matter how mesmerising Dr Galloway was, Anna would handle him.

Half an hour later, Anna set off alone for the Institute. Mike's old VW Golf had been cleared of anything relating to him. The debris left in there now was purely anonymous: sweet papers, newspapers and crumpled tissues. Anna's bag had been emptied of credit cards, driving licence and anything else with her name on, and her head had been filled with her new identity. Anna Johnson was twenty-seven, like Anna. But unlike Anna she had no family, no job, no life to speak of.

Following Mike's directions, Anna exited the quiet motorway. After twenty minutes on an empty dual carriageway she was almost lulled back to sleep and nearly missed her next turning. Spotting the sign just in time, she took a left on to a smaller road. This one wound dramatically upward, taking Anna further into the Lake District's snow-topped hills. She hadn't been to the Lakes for a couple of years, when one boyfriend had insisted she accompany him on an outdoor-pursuits holiday. Anna hadn't been keen – as far as she was concerned, there was only one outdoor pursuit worth pursuing – but she had fallen in love with the splendour of the area. Now, in winter, the countryside looked very different. The lushness had turned stark, the greens and blues darkened to browns and greys. The views were even more stunning than she remembered.

In those majestic surroundings, the Institute was like blasphemy. A huge, white building perched forbiddingly on top of a small hill, it peered down threateningly through blackened windows. As Anna approached up the long driveway, the first bud of nervousness popped open inside her. There was nothing welcoming about the Institute at all; in contrast to the open-armed tone of the newspaper ad, the architecture bluntly said, 'Keep Out'. The complex was surrounded by a tall, barbed-wire fence with closed-circuit cameras on every corner. Their beady, prying eyes swept around in all directions, both into the compound and out into the grounds. Anna hoped the cameras weren't quite so rife inside; they would hamper her investigation.

Someone was watching her approach from within the building. A gateway opened up in the fence to allow her inside. Following the track up to the front of the building, Anna parked Mike's Golf with the other cars. Hugging her coat around her against the bitter wind, she rang the bell by the Institute's front door.

Inside, it was a different matter. Despite the blackened windows, the interior was flooded with light. The large hall was bright, sunny and airy, and filled with smiling faces and gentle, friendly voices. A young, strikingly handsome man in a white lab coat greeted Anna with a perfect smile.

'Welcome to the MS Institute of Research. We're very pleased to see you. In a few minutes you'll meet our founder, Dr Galloway. In the meantime, please help yourself to refreshments and make yourself at home.' He motioned to a table in the corner of the hall, where a very pretty girl, also dressed in a lab coat (although hers was short and a little too tight), was serving drinks. She smiled sweetly as Anna approached.

Mike's information had been correct. Every staff member, both male and female, was good-looking. It was a feast for the eyes – at least, it would have been, if they hadn't all been so deliriously and suspiciously happy. Real people didn't walk around beaming like that.

There were a dozen or so 'real' people in the hallway

too: the open day's applicants. Mike's information about them was accurate as well. If you could judge by appearances – and in this case Anna suspected she could – then they were all drifters and loners as predicted. There were a couple of men with long, straggly hair and grubby clothes; student types with pierced faces and dyed hair; and others, who wouldn't fit neatly into categories but whose vacant stares and slumped shoulders suggested they were either on drugs or running away from something.

The drinks-server poured Anna a fruit juice and asked for her name. 'We're very pleased to meet you, Anna,' she simpered, as she wrote her out a name badge. 'And what is the reason you've joined us, today?' Her smile was blank. Anna thought she looked like an extra from *The Stepford Wives*.

I've come to blow the lid off whatever's going on here, Anna thought. I've come to wipe that vacuous smile off your pretty face. 'I . . . things haven't been going too well for me,' she murmured. 'I'm looking for a new start.'

'A new start for a new year,' the woman said chirpily. 'Well, you've come to the right place.'

The man who had opened the door clapped his hands. 'Ladies and gentlemen, if you will follow me please . . .'

The motley crowd of visitors shuffled behind him through the double doors at the far end of the hallway. They were shown into a small conference room with rows of chairs facing a low stage. Anna took a seat in the front row and glanced around her. Again, this room was bright and cheerful, decorated in sunny yellows and with plenty of fresh flowers and soothing greenery. Was this all fake, like the grinning welcoming committee; a ploy to make the outsiders feel at home? Or was Anna reading too much into the pleasant surroundings?

Her attention was diverted by the arrival of a middle-aged man, the first person over thirty she had seen so far. From then on, her attention – and that of everyone else in the room – was transfixed.

He stepped up on to the dais. 'Good morning, ladies and gentlemen. I am Dr Galloway. I would like to take this opportunity to welcome you to the MS Institute of Research, and to thank you all for coming.'

Anna took a slow, deep breath. Already her pulse was quickening. Jane was right; he was mesmerising. Everything about him reeked of control. His gestures were slow and deliberate, as if they had been carefully planned out and rehearsed before they were executed. His outfit was immaculate: a slate-grey suit beneath an open lab coat, the grey matching his piercing eyes. His hair was dark brown with hints of silver at the temples, the streaks so perfectly placed they almost looked unreal. He was of medium height for a man, just a little taller than Anna, but he seemed to dominate the room with his presence as he spoke. And his voice ... his voice was deep, rich and slow. Anna wanted to coat her body in that voice, and then have him lick it off.

His speech was innocuous. He reeled off fact after fact about the Institute, without actually telling his small audience anything. But he did it in such a way that the listeners felt they were being given a privileged insight into a new world. He made the Institute sound like a secret, wonderful club, which had been built on his pioneering vision. And they could all share in that vision, if they chose. He almost sounded like the high priest of a religious cult, except that Galloway didn't worship a god. Galloway worshipped science and progress, and, Anna suspected, power.

He was certainly enjoying holding the audience in his thrall. His words were empty, though. Anna was more interested in his eyes; they told a lot more. As he talked, making vague allusions as to what the scientists actually did there, his eyes were never still. They darted restlessly around the room, pausing for a moment to stare at a member of the audience before moving on again. He was searching for something. What?

Whatever it was, he found it in Anna. Eventually, his attention worked its way from the back row to the front. Without faltering in the flow of his speech for an instant, his grey gaze drifted quickly down Anna's stockinged legs to her strappy, black, fuck-me shoes. Then his eyes bored into hers, and they stayed there until, five minutes later, he finished talking. Unflinching, Anna returned his attention. She might have been imagining it, but she didn't think so; by the time his speech ended, there was a slight, knowing smile playing at the corners of his eyes and lips.

She felt his eyes still following her as she was ushered with the others into another room. Watching her all the time, Galloway trailed behind the small group as one of the staff took them on a tour of the ground floor. What they were shown was wonderful: an Olympic-size pool, steam rooms, indoor tennis courts, a small cinema, television rooms and a reading room with a huge window providing an awe-inspiring view of the distant lake and mountains. But the more Anna saw, the more strange it all seemed. Why did the Institute need to attract outsiders? Why was it trying to impress a bunch of strangers with its superb facilities? And why weren't the visitors shown the parts of the Institute in which they would be working – the kitchens, the laundry, and most important of all, the labs?

The tour ended, and the group was taken to yet another light, tastefully designed room. This, they were told, was one of the Institute's cafés. A buffet was laid out for them. They should help themselves. The staff would be on hand to chat and answer any questions they may have.

The visitors began to pick at the food, separating into twos and threes as people always do in unfamiliar situ-

24

ations. Anna purposely remained aloof. Standing alone, she hugged her coat around her as if she was cold.

'Would you like something to eat?'

She turned. Dr Galloway was smiling at her side. But unlike the vacant, emotionless smiles of his staff, there was meaning in his expression. His eyes echoed his thoughts, and Anna's heart jumped as she realised her first objective had been completed. Galloway was obviously attracted to her.

'I'm not really hungry,' she said quietly.

He motioned to her arms, wrapped tightly across her waist. 'It's warm in here. Are you cold?'

Anna shook her head and laughed shyly. 'I feel a bit silly. I came straight from a party.' She opened her short black coat slightly, revealing her short black dress beneath. 'I'm not really dressed for a research institute.'

Galloway's eyes slowly, greedily moved over her. As with his speech, he took his time. It was the perfect dress to show off Anna's good figure, and Galloway's reaction confirmed it. He savoured the thinness of the straps on her bare shoulders. He savoured the beginning of her cleavage and the shape of her pert breasts, tantalising beneath the clinging fabric. He savoured the inward arch of her slender waist and the feminine generosity of her hips.

Raising a hand, he touched the collar of her coat, moving it so he could look at her name badge. 'Well, Anna, would you like to tell me why you came here, straight from a party?'

'It's . . .' She dropped her eyes momentarily. 'It's a bit personal.'

'Tell me anyway,' he urged, his voice so smooth Anna wanted to bathe in it. 'I like to know why people come to the Institute.'

Anna sniffed with the memory of the 'party'. She had thought about it so often since Mike had given her the story, she almost believed it. 'It wasn't a very good party.

Not for me, anyway. My ex-fiancé was there, with his new girlfriend. She was going to be my bridesmaid,' Anna said bitterly. 'To cap it all, I went into the kitchen, looking for my new boyfriend, only to find him . . .' She hesitated, biting her lip with the memory. 'He was fucking someone else. Under the kitchen table.'

'I don't believe it.'

Anna glanced up quickly. Was that it – her cover blown? How on earth could he tell she was lying?

Galloway rested his warm hand on Anna's cheek. 'Why on earth would anyone cheat on someone as sexy and beautiful as you?'

She swallowed with relief. Her lips parted, but no words came out. She looked up into Galloway's eyes, knowing that Jane's warning was right. Women could be drawn in by this man; made to do things for him. Made to feel helpless.

But his questioning wasn't over yet. 'Why aren't you with your family?' he asked. 'It's New Year's Day, a time for big roast dinners and walks with the dog, and falling asleep in front of the television.'

'I don't have any family,' Anna whispered. God, her acting was so good she could even feel a tear welling up in her eye, right on cue. 'My parents died in a car crash last year. I'm an only child.'

'What about friends?'

'Friends?' she spat. 'One of my friends stole my fiancé. The other one grabbed my boyfriend.' Her jaw hardened. 'I can do without friends like those, thank you very much.'

'Calm down.' Galloway stroked her cheek. 'You're safe here, Anna. You're amongst real friends now.'

She doubted it, but she smiled anyway.

'Do you have a job, Anna?'

She shook her head. 'I've had loads of jobs. I've been a secretary, a receptionist, a waitress, a nanny . . . I'm afraid I never stuck at any of them. I just didn't find them very fulfilling.' Her eyes glazed. 'My life's come to a dead end. I need a change,' she said wistfully.

'Anna, I can offer you a fulfilling job, a beautiful place to live, and a new set of friends who will accept you for who you are. I can offer you the chance to change the course of your life for the better.'

Anna looked unsure. 'What's the catch?'

Galloway let go of her cheek. 'You need to have an open mind,' he challenged.

Slowly, Anna let a faint smile show on her lips. 'I already have an open mind.' She flickered her eyebrows, ever so slightly.

Galloway noticed, and put his arm around her shoulder in reply. 'In that case, come with me,' he purred. 'We've a lot to talk about.'

This room was different from the others: it was starker, more businesslike. The walls were white, and there were no pictures or plants. There was a big oak desk between two dark-red leather chairs and no other furniture. There were no windows, but there were three doorways: the one they had come in through, and two on the left-hand wall. Behind the desk, covering most of the back wall, was a gilt-framed mirror. It didn't take much to work out that this was a two-way mirror. Cold fingers of nervous tension gripped Anna's neck as she wondered how many people were sitting watching her in the adjoining room.

Dr Galloway took Anna's coat and hung it on the hook on the back of the door. Motioning her into the chair in front of the desk, he sat down opposite her and got a file out of the drawer.

'Right, Anna. You've heard all about the Institute and what we do here.'

She nodded. Oh yes, she thought, I now know exactly as much as I knew yesterday. The Institute conducts 'ground-breaking genetic research, vital to the development of the human race' – whatever that means.

'I think we have established that you are interested in a new life, here, with us. Now, we must establish whether we are interested in you.'

He began to ask Anna questions, noting down her answers in his file. Name, date of birth, address, next of kin; Anna reeled off her answers from the file she had open inside her head. Galloway asked about the jobs she had done and her qualifications. He asked about her medical history, illnesses she had had, and vaccinations. He promised her she could never fall ill at the Institute. 'We're even safe from the common cold, here,' he smarmed. 'As you will see, there are many benefits to living in a controlled environment.'

How controlled? Anna wondered.

Galloway continued. Her height and weight were noted; her eye colour, hair colour, the condition of her nails and teeth. Whatever he wanted her for, he was leaving nothing to chance.

'Right,' he said, clasping his hands and leaning back in his seat. 'Now, Anna, I'm afraid I must ask you some rather personal questions.'

What a surprise. 'Fire away,' she said.

'How many sexual partners have you had, Anna?'

Anna looked up at the corner of the ceiling, working it out. There was her ex-fiancé, the cheating boyfriend, the boy who had taken her virginity, multiplied by ten for good measure. 'About thirty,' she said at last. 'Or maybe it's thirty-one . . .'

'My, my.' The doctor seemed satisfied with her answer. 'You have been busy.'

Anna shrugged. 'I enjoy sex.'

'I'm pleased to hear it.' A smirk twitched across his lips. He was liking her more with every minute. 'And what is your favourite position for intercourse, Anna?'

Anna's lips parted as she pretended to be taken aback by the question. Galloway was testing her, just as Jane had said. And looking at him, feeling his eyes burn ferociously into hers, she thought she knew why. If she answered these deeply personal questions, she would show her keenness to enter the Institute and her willingness to be under Galloway's control. There was no possible reason he could need to know about her sex life, other than to feed his depraved mind and test her tolerance. Galloway fancied her; she had given plausible reasons for wanting to escape life and begin again at the Institute. She had passed the initial tests and this was the final hurdle. If Anna faltered now, as Jane had done, she would have been gently guided to the door; she was certain of it.

But Galloway didn't know that she knew. She was one step ahead of him; she was in control of this bizarre game. 'I like to be fucked from behind,' she said, raising her chin defiantly. Sitting back, she crossed her legs high up. Her dress rode up over her thighs, and as she folded her arms she surreptitiously pulled it an all-important couple of inches further. Without looking, she knew the top of her stocking was now clearly visible, a black band in dramatic contrast to the creamy paleness of her upper thigh.

Unlike Mike the night before, Galloway didn't notice what she had revealed for him. Either that, or he was purposely ignoring the display. His gaze remained steadfast. 'And why do you like to be fucked from behind? What makes that position so good for you?'

Anna licked her lips. 'The deep penetration,' she said slowly. 'I like to feel . . . full with a man's . . .'

'Cock.' Galloway finished the sentence for her. They stared at each other in silence for a moment. Anna's breathing grew deeper. Beneath the low neckline of her dress she felt her bare breasts rising and falling, and swelling under his attention. 'I'd like to see you touch yourself,' he said at last. 'Touch yourself for me, Anna. Show me.'

Anna sat forward on the edge of her seat. Watching

Galloway's face, she slipped one strap from off her shoulder. The material covering her breast fell, exposing the pure curve beneath. Anna pushed the strap further down her arm until her breast was naked, peering out at Galloway. Then she began to caress her tender skin, smoothing her hand over the ripe mound of her flesh, cupping her breast, squeezing it. With one fingertip she circled the large, sensitive arc of her areola until she felt the soft skin stiffen. Bowing her head, she watched her nipple darken with desire. She pinched the protruding tip, as if she was punishing herself for her obvious arousal.

'That's very good,' Galloway said. 'Now, touch your pussy with your other hand.'

Anna raised her head. Galloway was looking deep into her eyes, penetrating her soul – commanding her. She had never, ever been told what to do by a man before. In the past, if a lover had tried to dominate Anna, she would have turned the tables on him. She would have done the exact opposite of what he wanted, just to prove who was in charge. Now, she was faced with a situation where she had no choice but to play along, pretending she was willing to submit. If only he knew, she thought, slowly uncrossing her legs. If only he knew that she was the one who was really in control.

Then Galloway began to speak, dousing her in the intoxicating stickiness of his voice. 'That's it, Anna. Lift your dress for me. Slide it up over those pretty thighs. Do as I say, Anna. Open your legs for me. Show me your panties.' Effortlessly, it seemed, he kept his handsome features composed as Anna obeyed. It was as if he saw this sort of thing every day. He was totally cool. 'It feels good, doesn't it, to do what I say? You don't have to think any more, Anna. Just do what I tell you. Let yourself go. Show me your panties. You know you want to.'

Anna gasped as she realised he was telling the truth.

He was voicing her own thoughts; the ones she had been vainly trying to push back into the recesses of her brain. But hearing him say those things was like a flash of revelation. It did feel good, to do what he said, to let herself go, not to have to think. But it was shocking to admit to herself that, investigation or no investigation, she actually wanted to masturbate for this man. For an instant – a long, blinding, earth-shattering instant – she was not in control. She was so out of control, she felt light-headed.

And then the instant crashed to the floor, and suddenly Anna had the upper hand again. 'You've no panties on,' Galloway said, shock quivering in his throat.

Anna's clitoris throbbed in triumph. It was satisfying to see him taken aback. But as quickly as she had taken command it was seized from her again. Galloway got to his feet. Turning his back on Anna, he looked into the mirror.

'Well, gentlemen, I think we've found our new recruit.'

Galloway went through the doorway first, holding it open for Anna. She stepped through in some trepidation, and turned to find it was as she had suspected: on the other side of the mirror, a panel of eight scientists sat behind a long table. Every one was wearing a white doctor's coat. Every one had a notebook and pen in front of them on the table. And every one of them had watched through the glass as Anna had been 'interviewed'.

'Come and meet the selection team.' Galloway took Anna's elbow and steered her across the wide, empty room to one end of the table. Walking along its length with Galloway, she was introduced to each of the doctors, and she tried to memorise their names in order to tell them to Mike later. It was difficult, though. These men were older and not quite as pretty as the staff she had seen downstairs but, like Galloway, each was compelling in his own way. And they all stared, quite openly, at Anna's body. She might as well have been a naked slave, being offered like a gift. They were treating her like an object, looking her up and down, inspecting her for flaws.

'You won't see much of these doctors,' Galloway explained. 'These men are the Institute's patrons, decision-makers and top scientists. They are leaders in their respected fields, and as such they are extremely busy. The men you're meeting here are in demand all over the world. We are very lucky they find the time to show such an interest in our recruitment days.'

Not so lucky for me, Anna thought, feeling distinctly uncomfortable at their avid attention.

'You'll be pleased to know you've passed the interview stage,' Galloway continued. 'Now, Anna, if you wish to gain entry to the Institute – to your new life – you must undergo a medical.' He gently grasped her shoulders and turned her to face him. 'Are you happy to have a medical, Anna? If not, you can leave now. You don't have to do anything you don't want to.'

His voice was low and quiet. It was as if he was Anna's confidant; they had shared the ordeal of the 'interview', and they had found an understanding. Now, they were friends. She could trust him – that was what his tone of voice implied. But Anna wasn't fooled. She knew this was all part of the elaborate act he was putting on for her benefit.

'Anna? Do you want to go on? Or do you want to leave?'

She wanted to leave. These men were giving her the creeps. Or perhaps she was feeling the aftershock of submitting to a man, for the first time in her life. Whatever the reason, she had no option but to hide her unease and go through with whatever was necessary. 'I'll have the medical,' she said.

At some unseen signal, a door at the back of the huge room opened. A petite, striking woman, with pale skin and dark auburn hair cut dramatically short, strode purposefully across the floor.

'May I introduce Joan, my wife.'

Joan stuck out her hand and gave Anna's a cursory, no-nonsense shake. 'Full examination?' she asked her husband. Galloway nodded and took the empty seat at the table, giving Anna a reassuring wink.

Behind Anna, lurking silently like a beast about to pounce, was a medical bed. Joan wheeled it forward into the centre of the room, placing it beneath the large cluster of ceiling lamps so it seemed to be in a pool of light. Then, moving back to Anna, she told her to raise her arms and pulled off her black satin dress in one swift movement.

Anna was so taken aback she didn't know where to look. The doctors, sitting only feet away, knew precisely where to look, though: at her pert, naked breasts, her brown nipples and her black bush of luscious pubic hair. Kneeling, Joan supported Anna's weight as she slipped off her shoes. With quick fingers, she unfastened Anna's suspenders and rolled down her stockings. Before Anna knew it, she was totally naked.

Joan pulled a tape measure out of her white coat pocket and unfurled it like a weapon. Directing Anna to bend her arms, to move this way and that, she measured each joint and limb. As she called out her dimensions to the watching doctors, Anna wondered why they would need to know the size of her wrists and the width of her neck. She had no idea; all she knew was that this woman was going about her well-practised tasks without a thought for Anna's embarrassment. Anna enjoyed being an exhibitionist in the privacy of her own bedroom, with her lovers. This was a different matter.

And yet, at the same time, there was a germ of excitement growing inside her. It was exactly the same excitement she had felt during that moment of clarity in Galloway's office, when she had realised she was out of

33

control – and realised it felt good. In a strange, bizarre twist, her own humiliation was becoming a turn-on. Her shame in front of these men was working like an aphrodisiac. She hardly dared admit it to herself, but it was undeniable: her pussy was wet.

Startled, Anna jumped as Joan squeezed one of her breasts, and then the other. 'Nice firm tits,' she commented to the panel. Manoeuvring Anna by the shoulders, she turned her so her back was to the audience. 'Bend down and touch your toes.'

Anna complied, feeling her hamstrings stretching as she did so. She also felt her face heating up. The doctors now had an extremely intimate view of her arse. Her pussy lips were open. They would see her moistness, glistening from between her swollen, fleshy lips. They would see her clit, burning red with desire. And they would know what she was so ashamed of: that this examination was becoming as thrilling as it was embarrassing.

Anna heard the snap of rubber gloves being put on. A second later, something cold and greasy was rubbed into the delicate skin around her anus. Anna shuddered and held her breath as her arsehole twitched in response, the nerve-endings sending panicked signals to her brain from beneath Joan's fingers. Anna guessed what was coming next. Hanging upside down, she could see the eagerness in the face of the scientist sitting directly opposite her. Still, it was a shock when Joan slid her long forefinger deep inside Anna's arse. She bit her lip to stifle her cry. It came out as a faint, strangled whimper. Joan moved in and out, in and out, and the backs of Anna's legs began to tremble. 'Tight anus,' Joan said, her voice as rasping as Galloway's was smooth. 'Normal reflexes – she's trying to expel my finger. She's enjoying it, though. I'd say she's had anal sex before. Stand up, Anna.' Joan's finger was gone. She peeled off her surgical glove and dropped it to the floor. How strange for a doctor to do that, Anna thought, her mind choosing to fixate on this tiny incongruity instead of the incredible weirdness of the situation.

Joan rolled on another glove and patted the bed. Anna climbed on and lay down on the clean white sheet as directed, with her head propped up on the pillows and her feet facing the scientists' hungry eyes.

Joan moved Anna's legs so that her knees were bent and her legs wide apart. Anna wanted to shut her eyes, to shut out what was coming next. She wanted to close down her senses and stop her pulse from racing so frighteningly. But Galloway's words echoed in her mind, taunting her. Open your legs, Anna. Show me. Let yourself go. You know you want to.

She did want to. She wanted Joan's long, probing finger inside her. She wanted the doctors to watch her beautiful pussy being invaded. She wanted them to see, and smell, and taste her pleasure. She wanted to spread her thighs wide for them, to let each one into the secrets of her sex.

Anna groaned and arched her throat as Joan slipped into her warm cunt. A solitary finger eased effortlessly in, lubricated by Anna's readiness. 'Squeeze my finger,' Joan commanded, and Anna did, clutching greedily to try to trap the pleasure within her. 'Tight vagina, strong inner muscles,' Joan said. 'Excellent lubrication.' Joan withdrew the first finger and pushed in again, this time entering Anna with two. With the next stroke it was three, gently stretching Anna's sex.

Anna's body, subjected to such intense examination, was beginning to free itself from self-consciousness. Allowing her desire out into the open, Anna lifted her pelvis from the bed. She pushed her hips up slightly to meet Joan's thrusting hand, moaning pathetically with the strength of her need. She felt dizzy as Joan invited the scientists to approach the bed and inspect her for themselves. Yes, she screamed inside. Look at me. Touch me. Fuck me.

They didn't fuck her. Instead, they formed an orderly queue behind Joan, as if they were waiting for dinner. Joan stepped aside, relinquishing her hold on Anna's pleasure, and the first doctor loomed over Anna's prone body. With searching hands he grabbed her breasts and squeezed them, hard. He pinched her nipples. He put one hand on one shaking inner thigh and his other hand over her mound. His thumb slipped inside her gaping pussy, filling her with a fraction of relief. Then he stepped aside, mumbling his comments, and the next doctor took his turn. Standing at the end of the bed, he held on to Anna's ankles and bowed his head to her crotch. His nose pressed to her hole and he took in a deep breath. Anna looked down her body at his face, eyes shut in rapture. Fuck me, she begged silently. Why won't you fuck me?

He moved away and another doctor took his turn. As Anna lay there, helpless, she watched with wide eyes as her body was scrutinised. Fingers poked in and out of her vagina as if she were a medical specimen. Her pussy was licked with one flick of a doctor's tongue. He then proceeded to try to describe her taste to the others, while Joan conscientiously wrote down his remarks. Her breasts were praised for their shape and pertness as if they were separate beings in their own right and nothing to do with the naked woman lying in front of them.

Then it was Galloway's turn. He walked slowly up to the bed, Anna following his every movement with desperate eyes. This is it, she thought. He's the boss; he would be the one to take her, to plunge his penis inside her and induct her into the Institute. In a moment her body would be filled with his, and she couldn't wait. Her need for relief was becoming unbearable.

But, for a cruel eternity, Galloway didn't even touch her. Putting his hands behind his back, he circled the bed. Stopping when he saw something of interest, he bowed over Anna to inspect closer. He took a good look at her nipples, her neck and her open lips. He peered into her eyes and spent a long time at the end of the bed, staring inside her open sex. Just like before in his office, when she had crossed her legs to show him her stockings, he was oblivious of Anna and concerned only with following his secret agenda. Then, all of a sudden, he reached between her legs and rubbed her clit between finger and thumb.

Anna's body jerked with shock, and she cried out. Immediately, Galloway removed his touch, straightened up and nodded at the others.

'She's perfect, gentlemen. Are we all agreed?'

The panel murmured, making positive noises.

Galloway clapped his hands together. 'Conference room, five minutes.' And, with that, the others filed out.

Now, Anna begged. Do it, now.

'You may get dressed again,' he said, as the door closed, leaving them alone.

Anna didn't move. She couldn't.

'Put your clothes on, Anna.'

As he walked back to the table, she propped herself up on her elbows. Looking between her spread thighs, she threw Galloway a sultry smile. Two could play at this game. 'What if I don't want to put my clothes on?'

He didn't look up from his notebook. 'Then you'll get cold.'

'But . . .'

'But what, Anna?'

He remained engrossed in his notes. Confused, Anna slunk off the bed and retrieved her clothes. Standing in front of him, she waited like a naughty schoolgirl for him to finish writing.

Finally he put down his pen. His smile was like silk. 'Well, Anna, you've passed with flying colours. I'm pleased to be able to offer you a place at our Institute. You have been accepted on the basis of a one-month trial, which is as much for your benefit as it is for ours. Seeing as you have nothing to go home to, you can start here immediately.'

Anna thought of Mike, waiting for her at the motel. 'Oh.'

'Is there a problem?' Galloway's tone turned chilly. 'I thought you would be pleased.'

'I am,' she insisted. 'I'm really pleased. But I have a few things I need to sort out first.'

His eyes narrowed. 'Such as?'

Anna looked down at her outfit. 'Well, I'll need to get some more clothes, for one.'

'Uniform is provided. You don't need to bring anything with you.'

'Well, that's great, but there are a few other things I need to do.' Anna concentrated on her body language, trying not to fidget or blink – telltale signs of dishonesty. 'I rent a flat. I'll have to tell the landlord I'm leaving, and move my stuff out. I'll have to find a home for my cat. I'll have to settle my bills and tell the telephone and electricity companies that I'm moving out. Then there's the –'

'You won't come back.'

Anna's brow twitched nervously. 'Sorry?'

'You're a beautiful woman. You're also a smart, rational woman. You'll get back to the outside world and you'll wonder what on earth you were thinking of. You'll meet some man who'll make you believe that life out there –' he waved dismissively towards the black window '– isn't so bad, after all. And you'll forget all about this place. If you go now, Anna, you won't come back.'

'Oh, I will,' she promised. I'll come back and get to the bottom of your warped mind games. 'Nothing could keep me away from here, believe me. But I do have to tie up my loose ends. You don't want me to get in debt for unpaid rent, do you? Or to let my cat starve to death?'

'No, of course not. I just don't want you to forget what

38

brought you here today. Sometimes, in the cold light of day, people have second thoughts.'

'Not me. I'll be back as soon as I can.'

Galloway got up and moved to Anna's side. He put his gentle fingers to her neck and smiled with what seemed like genuine concern. 'You're right for the Institute, Anna. And the Institute is right for you. We want you here, with us.'

I know you do, she thought. I just don't know why. But I will find out.

'Thank God you're back. I was getting worried.'

Anna practically leapt past Mike into the room. She had been on a high since she had left the Institute. She had turned the radio on in the car and sung at the top of her voice all the way back to the motel, trying to expel some of the exhilaration bubbling up inside her. Her voice had sounded strong and clear, booming powerfully above the noise of the engine. With every breath she took, she seemed to refuel her body with simmering energy. She felt empowered by her sense of achievement at securing her place in the research centre. At this moment, she knew she could do anything.

'Mike, it was amazing,' she said, jumping around. 'I've never done anything so exciting in my life. I feel fantastic.' She paused as she caught sight of herself in the mirror. She looked like she had just had sex: flushed, breathless, glowing. 'I was born to do this job, Mike. I'm bloody brilliant, I tell you.'

Mike slumped down on the edge of the bed and scratched his stubbly chin. 'I've been going out of my mind here, not knowing what was happening, wondering whether you were OK.'

'OK? You should have seen me, Mike. I gave such a convincing performance, I even managed to produce a tear when I was talking about my poor "parents".'

'And Galloway? Was he what we expected?'

'Oh, yes. Jane's information was spot on. He is mesmerising.' Anna failed to hide a secretive smile.

'Do you like him?' Mike asked, suspicion in his voice.

Anna tried to find the words to describe how she felt about Galloway. She shouldn't like him; after all, she knew he was up to something which was possibly quite sinister. But she couldn't help admiring the man. He was audacious. Anna was someone who had always liked playing games, and in Galloway she recognised a masterful opponent. She wanted to get to know him better. The way he had acted with her was bizarre, creepy even; but she found him intriguing rather than repulsive. 'He's an enigma,' she said wistfully.

Mike got his dictaphone from his bag and turned it on. 'Tell me everything,' he urged.

Anna told him everything, prancing excitedly around the room as she spoke and illustrating her narration with wild gestures. It was thrilling to reveal the fruits of her first investigation, and her excitement was mirrored in Mike's taut features. But there was something else there in his tired face. Anna couldn't quite put her finger on it, until she began to tell Mike about the 'interview'.

As it emerged that Galloway had, as expected, asked Anna to touch herself, Mike's envy became obvious. His cheeks colouring faintly, he lowered his eyes to the grubby carpet and gritted his teeth. 'And how did that make you feel?' he asked accusingly, his face set hard. 'Was it revolting, having that pervert leering at you?'

'Not really.' How could she possibly explain that Galloway's leering had been a thrill – a warped, twisted thrill, turning everything Anna had ever felt completely on its head? 'It sounds strange, but it was sort of enjoyable.'

Mike looked up quickly, his expression a mixture of confusion and jealousy. 'Enjoyable? You're right. That does sound strange.'

'Galloway is an amazing man. He makes you feel

like . . .' She squinted with the effort of vocalising her vague ideas. 'Like he knows what's going on inside your head before you do.' Anna put her hand on Mike's knee. 'But I was in control, remember. I was one step ahead of him. I knew what was coming. That was what made it enjoyable, feeling we'd got one over on him. Knowing that what I was doing was a means to an end, a way of getting ourselves inside that Institute.'

Mike nodded, begrudgingly accepting her explanation. 'So, what happened after that?'

Anna went on to describe the selection panel and her incredibly thorough 'medical'. Now, Mike's jealousy metamorphosed into something altogether different. 'So you were lying there on the bed, naked? How? How were you lying?'

Anna showed him. Mike watched from his seat on the end of the mattress as she lay down in the middle of the bed. Bending her knees, she opened her thighs. Mike was unable to resist a glance at her naked pussy.

'Oh, Jesus,' he gasped. 'You lay there like that? And they all . . .'

'They all lined up to touch me.' Anna watched as Mike's mouth opened and closed without emitting a sound. 'This is turning you on, isn't it?'

Mike replied with a silence that was an emphatic 'Yes'.

This was more like it. Anna was back with what she knew and loved; the ball was in her court, and she was in control of the game. 'The first one touched me here.' She demonstrated. 'Then he put one hand here –' she rested her own hand on her stocking top '– and he put his thumb inside me.'

'Jesus H Christ.'

Anna went through the doctors one by one, hinting with her fingertips as to what each one had done to her. By the time she had finished her account, there was an unmistakable bulge growing in Mike's baggy chinos. And growing inside her was the sharp, desperate lust for release she had felt when the panel had finished with her. Recounting the story to Mike had re-awakened that desire, and now she had to have relief.

She sat up and reached into Mike's lap. Turning the dictaphone off with one hand, she lightly squeezed his erection with the other.

'What are you doing?' he whispered huskily.

'You're turned on, I'm turned on . . .' Did that explain it clearly enough?

'We should be getting back to London. We've a lot of work to do before –'

His voice ended in a strangled groan as Anna delved between his legs and rubbed his balls. 'Lie down,' she commanded.

Mike climbed up on to the bed. Kneeling by his side, Anna unbuckled his belt and unzipped his trousers. She got rid of his shoes, socks, trousers and boxer shorts and threw them to the floor. Then, sitting astride him, she unbuttoned his shirt and ran her hands over his warm, hairy chest.

'Anna –'

Whatever he was about to say, he didn't get the chance. Anna lifted herself above his rearing cock, paused for a second to open her damp pussy lips and ease his purple plum inside her, then slammed herself down on to him. Pushing the low neckline of her dress down, she lifted her breasts out and squeezed them together. She threw her head back and yelled with relief. She took what she wanted, and filled herself up with it.

Mike's cock was glorious. Trapped beneath her raging lust, his body was mouth-wateringly hairy and heavy. His dark eyes were clouded with gratitude and awe as he looked up at her bouncing breasts and her pink, pleasure-flushed neck. His thick fingers reached for her buttocks beneath her skirt and grabbed greedy handfuls of her flesh. Carried away, his moaning grew louder until it was as unrestrained as Anna's.

Here was a man she could spend some time with, she thought. What more could she possibly want? He was clever, ambitious and sexy, and had a heavenly cock that fitted perfectly into the heaven of her pussy. So why did she imagine it was someone else's cock, filling her; someone else's voice, curling around her neck and making the hairs stand on end? Why, when she closed her eyes, did she see Dr Galloway?

Chapter Three

*F*our days later, Anna drove back to the Institute. She was in Mike's car again, to keep appearances consistent with her first visit. This time though, Mike wasn't waiting in a motorway hotel room; he was back at the office, a phone call and more than three hundred miles away.

Concealed in the car were the tools of her trade, the means she would use to expose whatever was going on at the Institute. There was a dictaphone for keeping notes and recording conversations; a miniature camera the size of a credit card, bought from a surveillance shop; a digital camcorder; and a mobile phone for keeping in contact with the office. Hidden in her head were Mike's home and mobile numbers, in case of emergencies, and the number of a colleague of Mike's who lived only twenty miles away – in case of a more urgent emergency. As the gate opened for Anna, she decided she would leave all the technology hidden in the Golf until she had settled into the Institute. She could always come back to the car to fetch what she needed, when she needed it. First, she had to find out whether there were as many cameras inside as there were outside.

Anna had phoned from a call box to let Dr Galloway know when she would be arriving. He and his wife greeted her at the door.

'Anna,' he beamed, opening his arms. 'We're so pleased to see you again.'

Cut the act, she wanted to say. Somehow, his joy at her return was far more creepy than anything he had done at the interview. Anna summoned a smile to hide her sudden nervousness. 'I'm pleased to be here, Doctor Galloway.'

'Call me Peter,' he said, putting a fatherly hand to her shoulder.

'O ... OK,' she faltered, slightly put off by the glare Joan was giving her husband. Peter was making it blatantly obvious just how pleased he was to see Anna again, looking her up and down like he had done at the open day.

'Come along,' Joan urged, interrupting Peter's leering. 'I'll show you to your room.'

Peter followed as Joan bustled Anna into the lift. From the ground floor, which Anna had seen at the open day and which was more like an exclusive health club than a research centre, they went one floor up. Anna hadn't been shown this part of the building at the interview, and it was a big contrast to the friendly, warm colours of the floor below. As they walked along spotless corridors their shoes squeaked on the lino. Harsh fluorescent bulbs lit the way and bounced off the white walls, making them seem slightly grey. An unending row of closed, numbered doors lined one wall, reminding Anna of a hotel. A hotel that had been stripped of soul and colour. Why, when the ground floor was so inviting, were the living quarters so stark and unwelcoming?

'The living quarters are fairly bare,' Galloway explained, reading Anna's thoughts. 'No one actually spends much time in their rooms, except for sleeping.

45

We're either working or we're downstairs, enjoying ourselves in our wonderful facilities.'

'You'll find everything you need downstairs,' Joan added. 'You'll probably remember that we have a fully equipped health and leisure centre, as well as a library, television rooms and three dining areas. One specialises in traditional English food, another in European cuisine and the other one serves American-style food.'

'We cater for all tastes here,' Peter said, rubbing his oily voice into the back of Anna's neck.

'Food is available from six a.m. until midnight. If you're hungry outside those hours, there's a bar by the pool which stocks all kinds of snacks.'

Anna was surprised. 'There's a bar here?'

'It doesn't serve any alcohol, Anna.' Joan pursed her lips disapprovingly at the very thought. 'I hope that won't be a problem.'

'No, of course not.'

'Drinking and smoking are not permitted in the Institute,' Joan continued. 'We provide the best medical care in the world for our staff. The only thing we ask in return is that our staff treat their bodies with respect. So, no alcohol, nicotine or other substances.'

'I don't smoke anyway,' Anna shrugged. 'And I hardly drink at all,' she lied.

'Alcohol is a depressant,' Joan lectured. 'It destroys the brain cells.'

Behind her, Peter muttered suggestively, 'We don't need alcohol to have fun, do we Anna?'

Abruptly, Joan stopped in front of door number seventy-two. With a warning glance at her husband, she opened the door and invited Anna inside.

The room was small, light and pristine. There was a single bed along one wall, a window opposite the door, and on the other wall a narrow wardrobe and a desk and chair. It was completely devoid of any decoration except for a small mirror over the desk, and reminded Anna of a hostel or a brand-new prison cell – except that, as she noticed with a quick flick of her inquisitive eyes, there wasn't a lock on the door. They wouldn't be able to lock her in and she wouldn't be able to keep them out.

'This is your room, Anna.' Joan stepped inside after her and went to the wardrobe. 'Bathrooms are shared, one between every four bedrooms. You'll find yours next door but one, room seventy.' Joan brought out a hanger from inside the wardrobe. Holding it up, she beamed at the new recruit. If the smile had not been so completely fake, Anna would have taken it as the first sign that Joan was happy for her to be there. As it was, the falseness was almost disturbing, because it made Anna wonder what was hiding behind it. 'Take off your clothes, Anna. It's time to put on your new uniform. Time to start your new life.'

Peter moved further inside the open doorway as Anna put her bag down on the bed. Kicking off her shoes, Anna unzipped her jeans and dropped them to the floor. Feeling both Peter and Joan's eyes boring into her, she shrugged off her jacket and pulled her jumper over her head. Standing in only her underwear, she held out her hand for the hanger.

Joan's grey eyes – a paler version of her husband's – gave Anna a disdainful once-over. 'Take that tacky underwear off too, please. Only regulation underwear is permitted, and it must be white underneath your day uniform.'

Anna reached behind her back to unfasten her black lacy bra. But before she could, Peter's warm fingers were there.

'Here. Let me help you with that,' he said smoothly. He unhooked the bra and slid the straps from Anna's shoulders.

'Thank you,' she murmured, blinking guiltily at Joan. Joan glowered at her husband's interfering fingers, wanting to singe them with her narrowed eyes. Her thin lips were pressed tightly together in disgust as Peter 'helped' Anna with her panties, too, sliding them down over her hips. There was so much tension in the room Anna didn't know where to look.

'Fantastic,' Peter whispered, as his fingers brushed over Anna's buttocks and down the backs of her shapely legs. He stood up and held the crumpled scrap of her knickers up to his face and breathed in. He breathed out again in a sigh of delight.

'Give me those,' Joan snapped.

With laughing eyes, Peter handed Anna's tiny black panties over to his wife. As he turned and went back to his vantage point in the doorway he gave Anna a lascivious wink.

She couldn't believe what was going on. Peter was openly teasing his wife. Joan was obviously furious at Peter's undisguised desire for Anna's body. What the hell sort of marriage did these two have?

Joan dropped Anna's knickers into one of the two bins beneath the window. She opened a drawer inside the wardrobe and beckoned Anna closer. 'We cannot risk bacteria being brought into the labs. The clothes you came in must all go into the bin. They will be burnt. The other bin is for your dirty laundry which is collected daily. From now on, you will wear only those items provided for you by the Institute. The white dresses are for working in, and they're worn with these.' Bending down, she produced a pair of white trainers. 'The other dresses and the tracksuits are for wearing during leisure time.' Inside the wardrobe, Anna saw two navy tracksuits, black and red dresses in the same style as the white one Joan was holding, and a pair of knee-length black leather boots.

Joan jerked her head towards the drawer, and Anna picked out a white bra from the neat piles of red, white and black. 'Stockings and suspenders are in the drawer below, and panties in the one below that.'

'No panties,' Peter chimed in. Anna and Joan both turned to look at him. One side of his mouth was lifted in a sneaky leer. 'Anna doesn't wear them.'

Peter stared at his wife, challenging her to argue. Joan stared back at him, fury in her eyes and colour edging her high cheekbones. Caught between them, Anna felt distinctly uncomfortable. Trying to diffuse the situation, she lunged for the bottom drawer. 'Well, actually, I do usually wear knickers –'

'But not today,' Peter insisted.

With a toss of her cropped auburn head, Joan turned her back on her husband. Anna folded her arms and fixed her eyes on some indeterminate point outside in the grounds. Ignoring his wife's anger, Peter offered Anna his help again. Taking her bra from her, he fed her arms through the straps and fastened the hook between her breasts. His fingers lingered over her skin, brushing the insides of her arms, the cups of her shoulders and the undersides of her breasts. The bra was a simple, seamless one, the same type Anna often wore under close-fitting tops; it had silky cups which were so sheer they left her wide nipples provocatively obvious and her shape completely natural. Anna watched as Peter got out a pair of fine stockings and a white suspender belt. Kneeling, he told Anna to lift her right leg so he could roll one almost invisible nylon over her ankle. Anna had to reach for his shoulder to keep her balance, and as she did, Dr Galloway smiled to himself. With both stockings on, their lacy tops pulled up by the suspenders, he sat back on his heels and admired the darkness of her pubic hair against the white frame of her underwear. 'Fantastic,' he said again.

With that, Joan sprung into action. Spinning around, she grabbed Anna's shoulders and turned her to face her. She whipped the uniform from the hanger and thrust it towards Anna. Anna hurried into it, keen to hide her body from the Galloways and try to stop the tension from flooding the small room.

Roughly, Joan buttoned up Anna's dress. 'It's a bit tight,' she scowled.

Anna looked down at herself. Her new uniform was a short white cotton dress, like a nurse's. It had a revere collar, short sleeves, a hem which ended halfway down her thighs and buttons all the way down. The neckline came to a deep V in her cleavage, giving a hint at the inner curves of her breasts. Joan was right about it being tight; it hugged her hips and upper thighs, and the buttons were pulling under the strain of holding her full breasts.

'Honestly, I can't trust you to do anything properly,' Joan hissed. 'No doubt you were so busy looking at her tits, you took her measurements down incorrectly.'

Peter shook his head, his mouth twisting sadistically. 'No, dear. I wrote them down accurately. But I left instructions for Anna to be given a dress which was slightly too small for her.' Peter sidled past Anna to his wife. He slipped his hand around her narrow waist. 'You can see more of her body, that way. Those sexy hips . . . those pretty legs . . . those lovely tits . . .'

Anna felt her naked pussy clench beneath her dress. And not just because Peter was looking at her as if he owned her. Anna got an almost sexual buzz from the thought that the tension between the Galloways could be a weak link she could work on. Peter was making no secret of the fact that he wanted her. It was cruel, what he was doing to his wife. Perhaps Anna could play on this; perhaps she could inflame the situation and get Joan to turn against her husband.

But for now, the situation was diffused before the flame had a chance to take hold. Peter took his wife's pointed face in his hands and kissed her on the lips. 'Come on, darling, we've got to show Anna the rest of the building before the meeting.'

50

Joan's hard features softened slightly. 'You'd better give her a security bracelet.'

'Oh yes, I'd almost forgotten about that.' Peter let go of his wife and delved inside his pocket. He pulled out a narrow strip of what looked like black plastic, and moved towards Anna. 'This goes on your left wrist.'

Anna held up her hand. 'What's it for?'

'It's a security pass. There's a thin metal band embedded in the bracelet which emits a silent pulse. This is picked up by sensors in the doors, and will allow you access to the sections of the Institute you'll be working in. We don't often get intruders here, Anna, but these bracelets are designed to stop unauthorised access. They also work as a key to the front door and to the gate.'

Anna looked down as the black band was snapped into place around her narrow wrist. She felt like a prisoner, being tagged.

The laboratories were on the second floor. If anything odd was going on at the Institute, it wasn't immediately obvious. The high-ceilinged, clinical rooms looked just like any other labs. There were microscopes, computers, racks of test tubes and petri dishes, fridges, labelled jars and stainless-steel work surfaces. The only thing which stood out to Anna was that each of the twenty labs they walked past was empty.

'Where is everybody?' she asked, as they peered through the glass into yet another deserted room.

Peter glanced at his watch. 'They'll all be assembling in the lecture theatre. There's a meeting at two.'

'Do you have any questions so far?' Joan asked her.

Peter had mentioned the security band opening the front door and the gate. Anna wanted to know if the staff were allowed out – it might be useful to be able to go into the village – but she didn't want to raise suspicions. 'I was wondering, do any of the staff go walking in the mountains around here? I'd really love to see some of the countryside, get some fresh air, you know, having lived in London for so long . . .'

Joan glanced nervously at her husband, but Peter didn't hesitate. 'This isn't a prison, Anna. After working hours, your time's your own. You're free to walk in the grounds, but until you've completed your trial period here we would prefer it if you didn't venture outside the fence. It's purely for your own safety, you understand. You're in our care now.'

Anna tried to look grateful.

'If you pass all the tests satisfactorily, and I'm sure that you will, then at the end of the trial period you will be free to come and go as you please. You can drive into the village or go walking in the mountains, provided you're accompanied by another staff member. Again, this is for your own safety. But I think you will find that very few of our staff feel the need to go out. We've got everything here, you see. We expect you to work hard, but in return you will enjoy a fulfilling and rewarding social life.'

'Fulfilling' and 'rewarding' were very pleasant words. Talk of 'tests' was a little more ominous. 'What does my trial period involve?' Anna asked, making her voice slightly higher in a bid to sound innocent. 'Do I have to take any exams?'

There it was again, that flutter of eye contact between Joan and Peter. 'There are no exams here.' Peter laughed. 'No pressure. But you will be assessed constantly during the next four weeks. This is a very special place, Anna. We can only offer you a permanent position here once we're certain you fit in.'

'I'll try my best,' Anna promised.

Peter's eyes smiled knowingly. 'I'm sure you will.'

The three of them continued to the end of the corridor and turned the corner. A bell rang just as they arrived at wide double doors. 'Time for you to meet your colleagues,' Peter said.

With a flourish, he opened the doors. Anna walked in

behind him, followed by Joan. In single file they went to the front of the huge, brightly lit lecture theatre. There were three chairs waiting for them, and Anna was motioned to the middle one. Sitting centre stage, sweat began to prickle her skin. Stretching out in front of her were rows of tiered seats. As Peter's hypnotic voice commanded everyone's attention, Anna counted up: ten seats per row, ten rows of seats. There were a hundred people sitting in that room. A hundred pairs of eyes, fixed on her. A hundred white uniforms. And, as far as she could see, only a quarter of those uniforms were short, white dresses like hers. Every one of those dresses was a little too tight.

Anna's eyes scanned the room while she listened to what Peter was saying. All the women there were very attractive. There were all types: blondes, brunettes, red-heads; all shades of skin from creamy white to darkest brown; voluptuous and skinny frames. But why so few women compared to the men?

The men were all attractive, too. Their uniforms were not quite as revealing as the women's; they wore pristine lab coats over blue shirts and dark trousers. As Anna looked out at the audience, each person whose eyes she met gave her the overly friendly welcoming smile which was beginning to get on her nerves. Why were they all so sickeningly nice? She knew she looked quite sexy in her crisp white uniform, but was that any reason for one hundred young, presumably sane people to sit and grin at her?

Peter finished speaking and sat down beside Anna. Joan took over, reading out work schedules and rotas from a clipboard. Her voice was dry and monotonous and would have been hard enough for Anna to concentrate on even without Peter distracting her.

He leant towards her and whispered, 'I like you in that uniform.'

Glancing quickly at him, Anna found his gaze nestling

down her cleavage. She tried to keep calm and to hide her emotions, but his attention in front of all these people was embarrassing. Anna looked down into her lap at her hands.

'Everyone's staring at you, Anna. They're staring at that top button, and willing it to burst open.'

A blush began to warm her cheeks.

'They're staring at that tight little dress, and wondering what you're wearing underneath.' He rested one hand on her thigh. His palm burnt her with lust through the pure white of her stocking. 'You and I know, don't we, Anna? We know there's nothing underneath.' He pressed his lips on to her ear. 'Nothing but your sweet, wet pussy.'

Anna swallowed hard and clenched her inner thigh muscles together. This was too much, even for her. She loved to tease and shock, but it was a different matter to be teased and shocked by someone else, especially by an older man with penetrating eyes and a voice that seemed to stroke her sex. How did he know she was wet?

Dr Galloway curled his hand around her leg, slipping his fingertips between her tightly closed thighs. Mortified, Anna felt the attention of a hundred people following the path of his hand as it moved downwards to her knee. Pulling at her, he parted her legs an inch.

'Show them,' he breathed. 'Show them what you showed me in your interview. Show them that you've got no panties on.' He squeezed her knee. 'You know you want to.'

She didn't want to. Anna closed her eyes as he eased her legs further apart. Safe in the darkness behind her eyelids, she could have pretended it wasn't happening, were it not for the gasps in the audience.

Peter's hand left Anna's knee, and she opened her eyes again as he stood up. 'Don't move a muscle,' he commanded under his breath. He moved behind her chair as Joan sat down again. 'And now, ladies and gentlemen, I would like to introduce you to our new recruit.' Sitting there with her legs apart – not wide open, but wide enough to show a shadow of dark pubic hair – Anna found it hard to breathe. Putting his hands on her shoulders, Peter spoke over her head into the audience. 'Everyone, this is Anna. Anna comes to us, like most of you, disillusioned with the outside world and its constraints. She is twenty-seven, and looking for a change of direction in her life. I'm sure you will all want to join me in welcoming Anna to the Institute.'

As one, the audience murmured their approval that Anna had been chosen to join them. She felt her blush spreading down her throat as a wolf whistle echoed in the high ceiling, and several people laughed as the sound reverberated around the room.

'Simon, was that you?' Peter asked.

All eyes momentarily left Anna and turned to Simon. He was sitting in the back row, grinning along with all the others. 'I was just being friendly,' he said, and there was more laughter.

'Perhaps you'd like to come down here and give Anna a personal welcome.'

Simon's eyebrows flickered and his eyes slowly lowered from Peter's to Anna's. Then they lowered further, exploring the parts of Anna's body which were visible. Judging by the look on his face, he was delighted with what he found. He hesitated for a long moment, his lips apart as he stared between her thighs. Then the man sitting next to Simon nudged him in the ribs, and to a chorus of encouraging whistles and cheers he stood up.

Anna's body began to tremble as she watched him come down the gently sloping stairs to the front of the lecture theatre. He was very attractive: tall, with floppy dark blond hair, warm brown eyes and long limbs. But that didn't make it any easier to sit there and wait for him to approach, with her legs apart in welcome.

Hoping Peter wouldn't notice, she edged one foot back

towards the other. 'Don't,' he hissed, gripping her shoulders to emphasise his point. 'I told you not to move.'

Wide-eyed and helpless, Anna looked up as Simon walked towards her. 'Hello, Anna,' he said, in a friendly Northern accent. 'I'm Simon. Nice to meet you.'

She smiled uncertainly. 'Nice to meet you, too,' she croaked. But before the words were out, Simon was on his knees in front of her. With a swift, fluid movement, his hands flowed over her knees and up under her dress. He pushed her thighs wide apart; so far apart that the tendons in her inner thighs strained in protest and the skirt of her dress rode up over her crotch. Now, there was no mistaking what she may or may not be wearing under her uniform. Wincing, Anna glanced down in horror at the sight of her lush black hair and her plump, open lips. The curls on either side of her gaping sex were slick with longing; a bizarre longing, borne not out of sensual foreplay but shame and humiliation. Her pussy was overflowing with desire, but she wasn't at home, in bed with a lover; she was in a research centre, with a hundred strangers peering into her secret self and a doctor controlling her movements.

Her hands flew to cover herself. Unsure of where to turn for help, she looked out into the audience. Those sitting in the centre of their rows had their view hidden by Simon, and they were leaning to one side, straining to share the intimacy Simon was enjoying. On Anna's left, Joan was eyeing Anna's crotch disapprovingly. Peter was bowing forwards, his face at her shoulder. 'Please,' Anna whispered, turning to him to save her. 'Please . . .'

She wasn't quite sure what she was asking him to do. All she knew was that she wanted this stopped, before she fainted with humiliation. But Peter ignored her pleading, and Simon gently uncrossed her hands and moved them away from her pussy.

As he dipped his head, all rational thought was swallowed up. Anna shuddered as Simon's tongue unfurled inside her and lapped at her juices. Behind her, Peter tightened his grip. It was as if he were reading her thoughts, sensing that she was desperate to push Simon's head away, close her legs and pull her dress down to hide her shame.

But Anna could not have moved, even if she had wanted to. As well as the pressure on her shoulders, Simon was gripping her knees tightly. And then there was the real reason Anna was there; her investigation. She had to go through with this, she told herself. It was vital she did whatever was expected of her. She had no choice.

There was another reason, too, for allowing this to happen; the reason she dared not think about too deeply – the one which made her clutch desperately to the sides of her seat. It was insane and incomprehensible, but as Anna watched Simon's sandy head tilting and pushing with effort, her helpless shame began to slowly twist inside her guts and turn into something else. It was just like in her interview: Anna was completely out of control, and enjoying it. The realisation split her in two like a spear of lightning. One half of her was utterly mortified at being exposed like this. The other half was lapping it up with as much fervour as Simon was lapping her up.

His lips and tongue were skilful, licking the smooth inner edges of labia, sucking on her tender folds of flesh and then diving deep inside her. Her mouth open with silent shock, Anna looked out into the rows of seats. The hundred staff members were watching her more eagerly than ever now, their smiles fading as their hands twitched in their laps.

Pausing for a second to glance up into Anna's face, Simon began working on her throbbing clit. Suddenly, Anna lost all control of her mind and body. Her senses blurred into one, and her entire being was distilled into the tiny nub of flesh that was being so wonderfully nibbled and tongued. Letting go of the seat of her chair, she lifted her trembling fingers. Tentatively, as if her touch might wake him to reality and put a stop to the flow of pleasure coming from his mouth, Anna rested her hands on the back of Simon's neck. Feeling his muscles strain to give her more pleasure – more tongue, more lips – drove her wild. She either forgot about her audience or forgot to care. She dropped her head back, looking up into Peter's eyes. She spread her thighs still wider, and pressed on her feet until her hips lifted from the chair. Shameless now, she pulled on Simon's head and thrust her sex further into his face. Her fingers twitched and dug into him as he found the spot. With a sublime, earth-shattering mixture of lips, teeth and tongue, he sent spasms of ecstasy shuddering through Anna's body. She cried out. The sound flew up to the ceiling where it echoed for a moment. The audience replied with applause.

Simon's hands slid up to her hips and he pinned her down into her seat. He didn't stop licking at her pouting sex until her climax had whirled through her body and subsided. Feeling her surrender to the pleasure, he finally let her go and sat back on his heels.

His grinning mouth was shining with Anna's juices. 'Welcome to the Institute, Anna. I think you're going to like it here.'

'Thank you,' Anna whispered, her voice a faint breeze after the storm. 'I'm sure I will.'

Chapter Four

*I*t was her first test; a test she had to pass. Just like in her interview, Anna was being teased and provoked. And just like in her interview, she got the feeling that her reactions were being scrutinised. She was on a month's trial and this was the first step in her assessment. It was important she succeeded.

Anna paused in her typing and glanced up at Dr Galloway. For the umpteenth time that morning, she caught him openly staring at her thighs. Her desk was positioned directly opposite Peter's, giving him an uninterrupted view of her legs which he was quite obviously relishing. He looked up just as she did, his grey eyes full of lust. Embarrassed, Anna blinked several times as she focused on her work again. It was ridiculous that, after her baptism of fire in the lecture theatre the day before, something as relatively innocuous as Peter's leering should cause her to blush. But there was something unnerving about Dr Galloway and the game he was playing.

It was a game, Anna was sure of it. Galloway was pushing her for a reaction, keeping his cards close to his chest while he waited for Anna to show her hand – or any other part of her body she may care to display. The next time she caught him, she promised herself, she would respond. She would finish the section she was typing, then look up again. If he was still staring at her, she would ... She didn't exactly know what she would do. Something. Anything to take this game on to the next level.

Concentrating with every fibre of her body, Anna forced her eyes to stay on the computer screen. It was almost impossible, as she could feel the heat of Galloway's eyes, like lasers, searing into the curves of her flesh. Her legs wanted to fidget, but she managed to hold them still and let him look. At last she finished typing, sent the page to print, and sat back in her seat.

Anna met Galloway's smiling eyes. He seemed to be challenging her. Perhaps it was time she picked up the gauntlet. She laughed nervously as she spoke. 'What are you doing, Peter?'

Galloway raised one thick eyebrow. 'What do you mean, what am I doing?'

'Well, it's just that you said you had a lot of work to do this morning. But you seem to be spending most of your time looking at my legs.'

Galloway put his pen down, rested his elbows on his desk and laced his fingers. 'Are you questioning whether I am working hard enough, Anna?' His voice was stern, but there was amusement in his eyes.

'N – No,' Anna stuttered. 'It's just that –'

'Do you mind my looking at your legs?'

'Well ... no.'

'Then may I remind you, Anna, that you have work to do as well. I suggest you concentrate on that, instead of worrying yourself about what I am up to.'

'Y – yes, Peter.' Admonished, Anna plucked the sheet of paper from the printer and added it to the pile she had already produced. She turned back to the computer, but before she resumed her typing she couldn't resist one last surreptitious glance at Galloway. He was still looking at her, but with admiration in his expression now, as well as lust.

It was quite a strain to ignore his staring. Anna's eyes were being pulled like magnets towards Galloway's, and it was a real effort to stop them from straying. But she concentrated on her word-processing, working through the notes Peter had given her. It was her first proper day, so it wasn't surprising that she had been given a fairly simple task to break her into her new job at the Institute. She had to type out work rosters for each of the labs, detailing the names of staff and the code numbers of the experiments they would be working on for the next week. For her own part, Anna would be working in Peter's office for her first week; he had told her that there was lots of secretarial and administrative work he wanted her to do, and besides, it would give her a chance to get to know him better. How much better? Anna wondered, as his attention settled over her lap like an itchy blanket.

She finished printing out the laboratory schedules and began on the next sheaf of notes. There were rotas for everything: laundry duty, cooking, cleaning and even security work. It seemed that the Institute was completely self-contained; there were no outside contractors, which was more than a little surprising. No wonder the staff was so big, Anna thought.

She waited for the final sheet to whirr out of the printer. 'I've finished these, Peter,' she said quietly, not wanting to interrupt him now that his eyes had finally returned to his work.

'Bring them here,' he said, without looking up. 'I'd like to check them.'

Anna stood beside him and handed him the rosters. Slowly, he worked through them, nodding to himself. As she stood there in silence, Anna noticed his hands. They were big, with long fingers and dark hairs on their backs.

She liked looking at men's hands, and she liked Peter's. They were sensual hands. She wondered how they would feel cupped to her breasts, then sliding down, over her waist, on to her hips, down . . .

'There's a mistake here.' Peter slapped a sheet down in the middle of his desk and jabbed his finger accusingly at it.

'Is there?' Anna asked. Peter's handwriting, like every doctor's, was heavily slanted and straggly. But Mike's scrawl was just as bad, and since she had begun working for him she had become an expert in deciphering the indecipherable. She was also an excellent speller, and had double-checked everything before printing. She was certain she hadn't made a single error. 'Where is it?'

'There.' Peter wafted his hand dismissively towards the page. 'Second column.'

His desk was very wide, and very deep. 'I can't see it from here,' Anna said.

'Then lean over the desk and have a closer look.'

Anna's brow furrowed as she wondered what on earth this was all about. But as she obeyed him, it became obvious. Placing her hands on the cool, lacquered oak, Anna bent her torso over the desk in order to get a look at the paper. As she leant forward Peter sat back. There was method in Galloway's madness; by getting Anna to bend over like that, he rewarded himself with a view up her dress as it rode up at the backs of her thighs.

'I still can't see any mistakes,' Anna insisted breathily, her skin prickling.

'You're obviously not looking hard enough, then,' Galloway said, his voice low and syrupy.

Anna pored over the rota. She was right; her typing was perfect. But Peter wanted her to continue searching, so she did.

'Still not found it?'

Anna shook her head.

'Really, Anna, you must do better than this. I cannot

abide sloppiness.' Sitting forward again, Galloway pushed the offending sheet of paper a few inches further away. 'I demand perfection from you, Anna, as I do of all my staff. Now, have another good look.'

Anna put her elbows down on the desk and pushed her body further over until her eyeline reached the paper. She felt her hamstrings pulling slightly. She felt her dress riding higher, until she was sure the tops of her stockings were exposed. The back of her knee twitched as one of Galloway's fingers began a path up the rear of her thigh.

'I still can't see it,' she whispered, as his touch slipped over her stocking top and upwards, following the taut line of one suspender as it rose beneath her dress.

'Keep looking.' The warmth of his wide palm spread over her buttock. Beneath the flimsy white cotton of her knickers, Anna could feel goosebumps forming. 'We'll stay here all day, if necessary, until you find that mistake.'

Anna closed her eyes. She could happily stay there all day, with his fingers and eyes on her panties. What was it about this man, she wondered, that made her want to do these things for him? How did he manage to make her feel like it was her duty to show him her body? And, even more amazing, why didn't she find herself repulsed by him?

It was quite the opposite. As his fingers edged towards the cleft of her arse, a shudder of cold pleasure ran up Anna's spine. Her mouth opened as one finger moved along her crack. Even with her knickers shielding her skin from his, when he touched her anus there were miniature shocks of delight. Continuing down, he brushed over her plump labia. Anna was sure she could feel her sex lips swelling as he passed over them, reaching for him from within her underwear and her pubic hair like the silent, sucking mouth of a sea anemone.

'Found it yet?'

'No,' she breathed. But she had found something much

more interesting – that whatever warped mind game Peter had in store for his new recruit, she was going to enjoying playing it.

'How's the new girl coming along?'

Peter looked up from his lunch. 'Anna? Oh, she's wonderful. Isn't she, darling?'

At the other end of the long dining table, Joan winced with delight. 'She's perfect,' she agreed. 'I've been watching on the monitor while she's been working with Peter.' She shook her head slightly in disbelief. 'Do you know, I don't think I've ever seen a new recruit take to our training methods quite so willingly.'

'Is that true?' one of the doctors asked Peter.

'Oh, yes.' He nodded, his eyes narrowing slightly. 'She's very keen. There's something different about Anna. I can't quite put my finger on it.'

'I bet you've had your finger on it quite a few times already, if I know you,' another doctor sneered enviously.

Peter looked around the senior scientists' private dining room. The selection panel had gathered for lunch to discuss, amongst other things, the success of their latest recruitment drive. 'I think she's ideal for us. She's certainly willing. She does whatever I ask her.'

'But?' Dr Jeffries prompted. 'There is a "but" coming, isn't there?'

'Yes.' Galloway eased himself up from the table. Walking over to the window, he stared out. He didn't see the splendour of the distant snow-capped mountains though, because his eyes were glazed. 'I have a funny feeling about Anna.'

'I bet you do,' someone sniggered.

Peter ignored the schoolboy innuendo. 'I have a gut feeling. And my gut feelings are usually right.'

Struck by the seriousness in her husband's voice, Joan

put down her knife and fork. 'What is it, darling? What's worrying you?'

'I don't know.' His eyes clouded like the grey sky. 'But she's been working for me for three days now, and she hasn't hesitated for a second, no matter what I've asked her to do. Her interview was the same story. Don't you think that's odd?'

'I think it's wonderful,' said Jeffries.

'Oh, she makes my job very easy,' Galloway nodded. 'Too easy. It almost spoils the fun. It's usually quite a struggle to break in our new staff members, as you all know.'

'She does seem very eager,' Joan said, looking around the table. 'Did you see her in the lecture theatre?'

A murmuring hum went round the room. 'She was shameless,' Dr Sullivan admitted. 'Most of the new girls run out, or cry out, or do something, but she just sat there and let it all happen.'

'She enjoyed it,' said another.

Dr Jeffries shrugged. He didn't see the problem. 'Perhaps Anna's an exhibitionist.'

'Perhaps.' Peter turned back to face the room. 'Perhaps she's a spy.'

Shock silenced the table. Everyone stopped eating. The doctors glanced nervously at each other.

'Peter, do you really believe that?' Joan got up from her meal and went to her husband's side. She eased him back into his seat and put a comforting hand around his neck, lightly squeezing his tense muscles. 'Don't you think you could be getting a little paranoid?'

Peter looked up at his wife. 'Maybe you're right. Maybe I am feeling a little nervous. It's probably just a coincidence that Anna turned up now, when we're about to embark on the next phase. But there's so much riding on our work here. I don't want to risk anything going wrong. There's too much at stake for all of us.'

The doctors muttered in agreement. 'So get rid of her, now,' one of them said.

'That would be the easiest thing to do. But we've got to think of the consequences. What if she is a spy? Industrial espionage isn't uncommon in our business. But if she is working for one of our rival labs, asking her to leave now is only going to convince them that we're close.' Peter reached around his neck and held Joan's hand. 'And if she is genuine, then Joan's right. She's perfect. We'd be getting rid of a fresh research subject and a willing participant in our other activities.' He winked wickedly at his colleagues. 'Don't forget, gentlemen, the other reason we set up this Institute.'

Dr Sullivan made a suggestion. 'We should keep her out of the way of anything . . . sensitive. No security or lab work. Assign her to the kitchen or the laundry, and keep her there until we're sure about her.'

Peter huffed. For one of the world's leading genetic engineers, a genius in his field, Sullivan was surprisingly stupid. 'When you think there's a rat in the ranks, Sullivan, what do you do? Ignore it? Or set a trap? Anna will be working on our most sensitive material, I'll make sure of that. That way I can keep my eye on her. If she's interested in what we're doing here, we'll soon find out.'

The doctors nodded in approval. 'What's the plan, then?' asked Sullivan.

Peter pulled on Joan's arm and sat her on his lap. He put one hand around her waist and the other on her thigh. 'We'll continue with the month's trial. I'll follow the usual training procedure, and see how she reacts. She'll work with me until the end of the week. When I've finished with Anna, I'll give her to Simon. He'll be able to find out whether she has an ulterior motive for being here, or not. If anyone can get her to confide in them, it's Simon.'

Joan looked lovingly at her husband. 'Let's hope she

has nothing to confide. It would be a shame to lose someone so willing.'

Peter's skin warmed with the familiar look of restrained excitement on his wife's face. 'You like Anna, don't you?'

Joan nodded.

'Will you be watching this afternoon?'

She nodded again, quickly, her eyes glittering. 'What will you do to her?'

Peter's hand slowly travelled up Joan's leg and into the warmth of her crotch. 'Anna's a little different. So I've something a little different in store for her.'

'What?' Joan urged, shuddering as Peter's hand squeezed between her inner thighs.

'Wait and see,' he purred.

Anna was already sitting at her desk when Peter returned to the office. 'Nice lunch?' he asked, settling back into his leather chair.

She looked up from her work and smiled sweetly. 'Yes, thank you.'

Beneath the heaviness of the food in his belly, Peter's guts twitched. Anna was his favourite type of woman: a wide-eyed beauty with the ability to look both deliciously innocent and wickedly corrupt. Innocent women were lovely; so were corrupt ones. But it was rare to find both qualities in one woman. Anna, as he had said to his wife, was different.

In silence, except for the quick sound of her fingers on the keyboard, he watched her for a long time. Her face was radiant, the grey glow of the computer screen doing nothing to dull the translucent perfection of her skin. She was quite obviously aware of his staring and was enjoying it; her body language made that clear. It was almost as if she was posing for him. Sitting up straight, her breasts jutted eagerly towards him, straining to escape from the tightness of her dress. Slowly, deliberately, she uncrossed and re-crossed her legs, and Galloway was sure that she was relishing the faint sound of her stockings rubbing over each other, just as much as he was. Occasionally she would glance up at him, and a secret smile would dance at the corners of her full lips.

Galloway was excited by the thought that Anna might be an industrial spy, sent from another lab. If that was the case – if her mission was to infiltrate the Institute – then he could probably ask her to do almost anything, and she would comply. She would have to. The sense of power rushed through his veins and put him on a high.

'Made any friends yet, Anna?'

She looked across at him. 'Well, no one in particular. But everyone seems very nice. They've all made me feel very welcome here.'

'Especially Simon.'

She seemed embarrassed at the memory of her ordeal in the lecture theatre. She blinked several times and her cheeks flushed faintly. There it was again, Galloway thought; the contradiction that was Anna. Shameless and yet ashamed.

'Well . . . I . . .' She was lost for words.

'You didn't expect quite such a warm welcome, did you?'

She shook her head, relieved he'd answered for her.

'We like to do things a little differently here, Anna. You may have noticed that already.'

'Well, yes.' She blinked again, and the embarrassment was gone. She gave Peter a knowing look.

'Am I right to think that you're enjoying your work here so far?'

Her lips parted. Oh, Galloway thought, how he would love to slide his angry cock between those pretty lips. How he would love to fill that mouth –

'Yes,' she answered, interrupting his silently raging desire. 'I'm glad I came.'

'So am I.' He fidgeted in his seat, readjusting himself

as his penis began to thicken. 'And is my wife behaving herself?'

Anna was puzzled. Her dark eyebrows flickered with confusion. 'Joan? What do you mean?'

Peter laced his fingers behind his head and sighed, looking up at the ceiling. 'Joan has ... problems. She finds it hard to deal with her emotions. She is an accomplished scientist – a woman with a brilliant analytical mind. And yet she has no control over her insane jealousy.'

Anna pushed her hair away from her face and tucked it behind her ear. 'What is it she's jealous of ... if you don't mind my asking?'

'No, I don't mind, Anna.' He sighed again, as if the weight of the world was pressing down on his shoulders. 'She's jealous of you.'

Anna's eyes widened. 'Of me? What have I done?'

'Nothing.' Peter tutted. 'Joan is jealous of every new recruit we get here. She accepts that the Institute needs to expand, and she knows we need more staff in order to do that, but she just cannot accept that we need to recruit women as well as men. She'd rather we had an all-male staff, but like I keep explaining to her, that just wouldn't be healthy.' Peter slumped forward dramatically, banging his elbows down on to the desk and dropping his head into his hands. 'She makes my life hell. She's furious that I've asked you to do some typing for me, but what does she want me to do? Whoever I ask to do my secretarial work, she isn't happy. There's no pleasing her.' He was silent for a moment. Then, as if he had just realised what he'd said, he looked up. 'Oh, I'm sorry, Anna. I shouldn't burden you with all this.'

'It's all right,' she soothed, getting up from her seat. She moved around her desk and stood in front of Peter's. 'Is there anything I can do to help?'

Oh yes, Peter thought, his eyes falling quickly over her body. You could take off that sexy little dress, for a start.

You could plant your luscious arse on my desk and spread your milky white thighs for me. You could let me lick your pussy like Simon did, until I feel you coming beneath my tongue. You could wrap your pretty ankles around my neck, push your mound into my face, wet my lips with your juices, beg me for more . . .

Peter swallowed hard, his erection throbbing now at the thought of what he would ask her to do next. This wasn't written in the training manual. This wasn't usual. Would she fall for it?

'Well,' he said quietly, his eyes lowered. 'There is something you could do for me, Anna. But I'm afraid to ask.'

'Peter?'

He slowly lifted his gaze, as if he was ashamed to meet her eager eyes.

'Peter, what is it? I'd like to help, please.' She searched his eyes. 'Peter, I'll do anything.'

'Well,' he winced, pretending he was frightened to let the words out, 'I don't quite know how to put this.'

'Just say it,' Anna urged.

'When Joan's furious with me, she won't . . . she doesn't . . .' Peter glanced down into his lap. 'And I get very frustrated and, when I'm frustrated, I can't concentrate on my work. And working with you, Anna, makes it even harder.'

If she noticed the double entendre, she didn't react to it. 'Would you like me to relieve some of your . . . frustration?' she breathed huskily.

'Oh, Anna,' he whispered gratefully, holding out his hand. He could hardly believe it as she walked around to his side. He put his arm around her waist and looked up at her, smiling to thank her. 'If only you knew how much this means to me.'

If only you knew, he continued silently. If only you knew that Joan is watching on the monitor, lapping up my lies, her fingers busy between her slender legs. If only

70

you knew that my cock is bursting for you, and that the thought of my wife watching, and wanting you as much as I want you, will make me want to flood your lovely mouth with my come. If only you knew what else is in store for you here.

Peter's arm slid from her waist. One greedy hand gripped her buttock and squeezed lasciviously. His other hand parted his white lab coat and unfastened his trousers. He had no underwear on, as usual, and Anna's eyes were drawn to his cock as he unfurled its length from the darkness of his groin.

Peter pulled on Anna's arse and slowly she got to her knees. Tentatively, she rested her hands on Peter's thighs. With a subconscious movement, the tip of her tongue ran across her pouting lower lip. She stared at Peter's long, thick penis, mesmerised, it seemed, by the sight of it rearing from his trousers. Peter touched her chin, raising her eyes to his.

Her green eyes were wide, looking up at him with such innocence he almost lost control and slammed her head down into his lap. Gritting his teeth, he slowly moved his hand round to the back of her neck. Gently, he brought her lips closer to the head of his cock. His cock wept a silvery tear in anticipation.

Peter dropped his head back and groaned as her lips sucked greedily at the end of his penis. Her mouth was soft and wet and warm, her lips strong and her tongue urgent. Her fingers delved into his trousers and felt for his hairy balls, lightly squeezing until his buttocks twitched with pleasure. Tangling his fingers in her dark, silky hair, he pushed her further down on to him. She sucked him in as far as she could, until most of his penis was inside her. Then she began to raise and lower her head, flickering incessantly with her tongue between hungry sucks, and driving him mad. He was torn, not knowing whether to look down at her head bobbing and the way her hair brushed his lap, or up into the centre of the ceiling at the light fitting, where the tiny concealed camera was sending images of his pleasure to his wife.

A moment later his dilemma was solved. Without knocking, Joan opened the door. Leaving it wide open, she stalked into the office, right up to Peter's desk.

'Where's Anna?' she snapped, her eyes glinting with evil delight.

Anna froze. With an urgent hand, Peter pushed at her shoulder, moving her into the footwell of his desk. She was the perfect accomplice; with one silent backward movement, and without taking her lips from his cock, she settled her body into the narrow hole. Peter opened his thighs wide, pressing his feet and knees against the sides of the footwell. Anna crouched between them, out of sight – or so she thought.

Peter grinned at his wife, making sure to keep his voice calm for Anna's benefit. 'Anna's on an errand, darling. I sent her down to the kitchen with the rosters.'

'Hmmm.' Joan bit down on her thin lips, stifling the laugh that was trying to escape. 'I don't like that young woman, Peter.'

'You shouldn't be so hard on her.' He smirked. 'She's very efficient.'

'Oh, I'm sure she is.' Joan's eyebrows flickered suggestively.

Peter slipped one hand beneath the desk. Reassuringly, he stroked Anna's hair. In response, she grasped his penis in one hand and slowly licked from base to tip. Peter shivered at the feeling.

'Are you all right?' Joan asked, almost giggling.

'I'm fine, darling. I just wish you'd give Anna a break. She's doing a good job.'

'Is she?' Joan put her hands on the desk and leant right forward. Straining her neck, she could just see a glimpse of Anna's black hair in her husband's lap.

'Oh yes,' he said, struggling not to groan as Anna sucked hard on his erection. Recovered from the shock of

72

nearly being caught *in flagrante*, she now seemed to be savouring the forbidden naughtiness of her task. Her head was bobbing eagerly, her mouth pulling on his swollen prick as if she were trying to uproot it. Working silently and diligently, she was bringing Peter closer to climax with every second. It was almost as if she were turning the game on its head, wanting Peter to give himself away.

'Well,' Joan hissed, sensing that her husband was losing control and wanting to get back to the monitoring room to watch, 'there's a long way to go before Anna's trial period is over. We'll see whether you're as happy with her in a couple of weeks.'

'Oh, I will be,' Peter promised, flinching as Anna's tongue poked the eye of his penis. He squeezed his eyes tightly, holding his breath. He could feel hot pleasure about to bubble over in the tight sacks of his balls. 'Anna puts a lot of effort into her work,' he mumbled.

'Just make sure she does,' Joan said, pausing at the door. 'I won't have her thinking she'll get an easy ride, just because she's pretty.'

'No, dear,' Peter grumbled.

Joan slammed the door behind her. Peter let out his breath in a long woosh of relief. On the brink of orgasm, he grabbed Anna's head and pulled her down on to him, holding her still. His buttocks clenched spasmodically and he jerked into her mouth, thrusting his cock between the moistness of her lips. With an agonised moan, he felt his come spurt into her throat. Bent over him, Anna gulped hungrily.

Peter rolled his chair back to let her out of her hiding place. She was breathing fast as she sat up and wiped the back of her hand across her mouth.

'Jesus, Anna,' Peter whispered, holding her flushed cheek in his hand. 'That was close. I almost came when Joan was standing just there.'

'I know,' she said smiling.

73

He shook his head slightly. 'You're wicked.'

Her smile deepened, echoing in her lovely green eyes. 'I know.'

After dinner, Anna went for a walk. She told her new 'friends' that she needed a breath of fresh air, and said she would meet them in the television room in fifteen minutes. They seemed happy with her story. Pausing at the front door, Anna heard the latch release as the sensors picked up the signal from her security bracelet.

Outside, the sky was clear and sprinkled with stars. A frost was on its way, and Anna could see her breath clouding in the night air. She hugged her arms across herself and walked briskly around the side of the building, ignoring the prying eyes of the cameras on their fence-top perches.

There was only one camera around the back, where the car park was, but still it would be difficult to get to her car without being seen. Watching in the shadows, Anna studied the camera's silent choreography for a few minutes. Sweeping slowly over the rows of empty cars, the lens moved from left to right, taking about thirty seconds. Anna's car was parked in the corner furthest away from it, on the far left. She reckoned she had about ten seconds when the automatic eye couldn't possibly pick her up.

She waited, her heart pounding. If someone did spot her, she only had a very poor excuse prepared. There was a hairbrush in the glove compartment; she had come to retrieve it. She fervently hoped she wouldn't have to rely on such a weak reason for being there.

The camera made its slow journey to the right, and Anna slunk from the corner of the Institute to the passenger door of the Golf. Fumbling with the key, she couldn't fit it in the lock. Sweat crept cold across her skin as she wasted precious seconds. Then she was in, flinging herself on to the seat, and huddling down just in case the camera could pick up movement in the darkness of the car park.

She opened up the glove box. She got out the hairbrush, a screwdriver and a slender pen-sized torch. Holding the torch between her teeth, she dipped her head towards the opening. Moving as quickly as her nervous fingers would allow, she unscrewed the ceiling of the compartment.

Reaching inside the flap, she felt for the smooth rectangle Mike had hidden in there. She found it and pulled it out. Flipping the keypad open, she dialled Mike's number; one of the direct lines to his office, the one he was keeping open for Anna's calls.

Anna heard Mike's phone ringing, and she put the keypad back in its hiding place. Her mobile phone's receiver and microphone were concealed in the car stereo's speakers. That way, she could sit in the car and talk, without holding a handset to her ear. If anyone was watching, it would be possible to explain that she had been talking to herself, or singing.

The ringing stopped. 'Anna?'

His voice sounded urgent and flustered. But then, it always did when he was working on a big story. 'Hello, Mike.'

'Christ, Anna. I've been so worried about you. I thought you weren't going to ring.'

'It isn't easy to get to the car,' she said. 'There are cameras outside. I haven't seen any inside, though, which should make things easier.'

'How's it going?' Mike asked. 'Tell me about Galloway.'

Mike drummed his fingers on the desk as Anna told him about her first few days at the Institute. His cheeks grew hot as she told him about the very personal welcome she had been given, although Mike couldn't work out whether he was blushing with embarrassment or anger.

What the fuck was Galloway playing at? The man was warped. And Mike was stupid. He should never have sent Anna there, alone. It was too much to ask of her, a rookie on her first job.

Anna seemed oblivious to the enormity of her task, though. Her voice was rushed and breathless as she told Mike about the work she had done for Galloway. There wasn't much of interest to them, she said, apart from a mailing list with names and addresses of the Institute's sponsors and patrons, the people who funded the 'research'. Anna had copied the list on to a floppy disk, which she was keeping in her desk in Peter's office.

'Be careful,' Mike warned.

'Oh, it's all right,' she insisted. 'I've got it all worked out. If anyone asks about the disk, I'll say I've made a back-up copy in case the hard drive fails. Peter doesn't know anything about computers; he'll think that's wonderfully efficient.'

'Don't underestimate Peter Galloway,' Mike said, rubbing his forehead.

'Don't worry about him,' Anna said, satisfaction in her voice. 'I've got him just where I want him.'

'What do you mean by that?'

Anna told Mike that Galloway had been coming on to her, and that he was having problems with his jealous wife. 'It's the perfect situation for me to manipulate,' she said, her voice tight with excitement. 'I can get on Peter's side by giving him sexual favours. Then I can go to Joan and cry on her shoulder about the awful things her husband's asked me to do. She'll be angry with him and sympathetic to me. A wronged woman just loves to confide in another woman. I may be able to get her to compromise her husband.'

Mike closed his eyes. 'For God's sake, Anna, be careful. Don't do anything unless you're sure.'

'Mike, I wish you'd stop worrying. Everything's under control.'

76

Why did he find that so hard to believe? Perhaps it was the fact that Anna had been welcomed to the Institute with oral sex. Perhaps it was the fact that Peter was behaving in a way that would get a sexual-harassment charge slapped on him the minute he stepped into the real world. Perhaps it was the suspicion – an idea that chilled Mike to the core – that Anna was enjoying herself.

'Anna, don't lose sight of what you're there for, will you?'

Mike could hear the indignation in the silence that followed. 'Think there's a chance I'll forget, do you? Think I'll get taken in by Galloway's perverted behaviour? Think I'll be so busy enjoying being treated like a sex object, that I'll forget to do the investigation?' The microphone was very sensitive; it picked up the annoyance in her sigh. 'Honestly, Mike, I'm twenty-seven, not seventeen. I can handle Galloway. He's only a man, after all, with his brain in his trousers like all the rest of you.'

'Sorry,' Mike murmured. Perhaps his discomfort lay in the fact that he was just the tiniest bit jealous. Thinking of Anna doing those things for Galloway, without question, was not an idea he should dwell upon unless he fancied a bout of insanity.

'I'd better go now,' she said. 'I'll ring again as soon as I can.'

'Don't leave it too long, please. I know you can look after yourself, Anna, but we still don't know what we're dealing with here. I can't sleep unless I know you're all right.'

Anna said goodbye, and Mike put the phone down. He left his hand on it for a moment, as if he could feel Anna through the plastic and wires. It was only the first week of her stay at the Institute, and already he was going mad, wanting her to return to the office.

Absent-mindedly he rubbed his head, trying to re-arrange his thoughts so that they made sense. He wasn't sure – did he want her back because he feared for her safety or for more selfish reasons? Caught up in his work, which he loved passionately, *Undercover* had been his only mistress for the last year. And now, having sworn he would never again fall for someone at the office, he couldn't stop thinking about Anna. But was it her abilities as a reporter that occupied his thoughts, or her breasts, full and perfect; her neck, long and pale and arching with pleasure; her green eyes half-closed in ecstasy . . . her full lips on his skin –

The shrill sound of the phone ringing brought him back with a jolt. 'Mike Bailey.'

'Mr Bailey, my name is Professor Philipson, from the University College Medical School. You left a message with my secretary.'

Mike shuffled about on his desk, looking for the relevant piece of paper. 'Yes, thank you for calling back, Professor.'

'This ex-student you are researching, Peter Galloway. I'm afraid I can't give you an awful lot of help.'

'Oh.' Mike wasn't too surprised; after a whole day of phone calls, faxes and e-mails, practically every line of enquiry had drawn a blank.

'Peter only did a year at the university before we had to ask him to leave. So you see, I didn't have much chance to get to know him. Sorry I can't be of more assistance.'

'He was asked to leave?' Mike sat up straighter. 'Is that common?'

'Oh no.' The professor laughed. 'It's never happened before. But Peter was quite an unusual young man. I caught him making LSD in the lab, at night. He was selling it to the other students on campus. Made quite a lot of money for himself, before he was found out. It was a shame. He was a brilliant student and he threw it all away. Ruined several people's lives, as well as his own.'

'How?'

The professor sighed, obviously disturbed by the

memory. 'Galloway put something in the LSD – a chemical that wasn't fully tested. It was renowned for its hallucinogenic effects, but no one really knew about the possible side effects until Peter came along. Three of his victims suffered irreversible damage to the part of the brain which controls memory. They had to give up their studies.'

Mike felt twitchy as he picked up the scent. 'Did Galloway go to prison?'

'I'm afraid not. The police didn't have enough evidence to convict. This chemical he used, you see, it doesn't show up in blood samples. Peter was a very clever young man. Clever, and lucky.'

Mike nodded to himself. 'Do you know where he eventually got his doctorate from?'

The professor laughed. 'I don't think you understand, Mr Bailey. When a student is thrown out of medical school for something as serious as that, his misdemeanour is put on the computer records for all to see. Peter would not have been accepted into any other university. The British Medical Council placed a ban on him ever becoming a doctor.'

The warmth of discovery settled warmly around Mike's neck. 'Thank you, Professor. You've been most helpful.'

Mike could feel his heartbeat quickening as he put down the phone. He picked up a newspaper clipping, an old one from a regional paper with a photo of Galloway coming out of church on his wedding day. Mike's eyes narrowed as he stared at the oily smile and the laughing grey eyes. 'I'll get you, Galloway,' he promised. 'Your luck's about to run out.'

Chapter Five

'*T*here you are, Anna. You remember Simon, don't you?'

Simon turned his head as Anna came into Peter's office. He stood up and smiled at her. She smiled coyly back; it was quite obvious she did remember him.

'Hi,' he said.

'Come and join us, Anna.' Galloway motioned to the empty chair next to Simon's. The two men waited for her to take her seat before resuming theirs. 'Now, let me just have a look at my schedule for the week.'

While Galloway studied the open file on his desk, Simon turned to Anna. 'How are you enjoying it so far? Are you settling in?'

'Oh, well, the work's fine,' she said, nodding, 'and everyone's very friendly. I like it here.'

'I knew you would.' His smile deepened into a grin at the thought of how she had liked it in the lecture theatre. Simon, as one of Peter's favourites, was often given the enviable job of welcoming the new recruits. But very few actually allowed themselves to enjoy the experience. Anna, as Peter had explained in some detail over breakfast, was different.

'I hope Peter's treating you well.'

Anna hesitated, her eyes flickering to Peter's bowed head. 'Very well,' she said, as Dr Galloway looked up and their eyes met. When she turned back to Simon, her cheeks were slightly pink.

'I hope you don't mind, but I'm going to tear you away. If Peter will let me, that is.'

Peter slammed his file shut. 'Yes, Simon, you can have her. But don't work her too hard. This is only Anna's second week, you know.'

'I'll be gentle with her,' Simon assured, his brown eyes oozing warmth.

Anna looked quizzically at Peter. 'Simon's assistant sprained her wrist yesterday evening, playing tennis,' Galloway explained, lying smoothly. 'Until she recovers, she's not allowed to do any typing. Simon is currently involved in some essential research programmes which need documenting. The work's simple enough, but it needs someone accurate and conscientious. You're ideal, Anna, since you so rarely make mistakes. And your working for Simon will save us switching round all the rosters.'

She nodded. 'But what about your work? What about the filing you wanted me to do?'

'It'll wait. What Simon's doing is far more important. His need is greater than mine.' Peter smirked.

'The work's quite tedious I'm afraid,' Simon warned, as if Anna had a choice in the matter. 'Every experiment I do has to be catalogued and the data has to be fed into the computer. You'll have to check and double-check everything you type. And then you'll have to go back and check it again.'

'I'm sure I can cope with that,' Anna said.

'You'll also have to wear regulation underwear,' Peter added.

Simon watched as Anna's beautiful lips opened and then paused with confusion. 'I . . . I am,' she said. 'You know I am.'

'Show us, please, Anna.'

She glanced at Simon and then back to Peter, her dark eyebrows dipping slightly. 'But . . .'

'Don't be shy, Anna.' Peter's grey eyes bored into her. 'Simon's already seen your pussy. You're not going to shock him, you know. You're going to work in the lab today, and we must be sure you're wearing the correct uniform.'

Simon watched Anna's expression as it changed from bewilderment to knowing resignation. She wasn't taken in by all the 'regulation' nonsense – who would be? – but she wasn't fazed, either. Slowly standing up, she looked down at her fingers as she unbuttoned her dress.

Simon's gaze drifted longingly down her body as it was gradually revealed. She was gorgeous: a slim waist, feminine curves, nicely proportioned legs and high, full breasts. Her large, dark areolae peered provocatively above the low-cut lace of her bra. She had on sheer hold-ups with lacy bands at the tops, the creamy colour almost matching her skin. Pushing their way out from beneath the edges of her matching skimpy panties were wispy tendrils of black hair. Simon blinked slowly as he looked at the triangle of satin covering her pussy, remembering how sweet she had tasted and how good she had felt, pushing up into his face – and wanting his mouth there again.

He looked up at her face. Her head was bowed, her eyes eagerly fixed on Peter's. Looking through her long, thick eyelashes at him, she waited for his approval. There was a strange mixture in her expression: a mixture of humiliation at having to reveal herself, and pride in what she had revealed. It was an incredibly sexy combination.

'All right, Anna, you can put yourself away now.' Peter winked at Simon as she buttoned up her dress again. 'I'm satisfied that you're dressed correctly. Simon?'

'Oh, completely satisfied,' he said.

* * *

'What are you doing?' Anna asked, looking away from the computer screen.

Simon laughed quietly. 'Do you really want to know? I mean, you don't have to pretend to be interested, if you're not.'

'But I am interested,' she urged. 'I always loved science at school. I never took it any further, but it always fascinated me.' She leant her elbows on the table and rested her chin on her hands. Squeezed between her elbows, her cleavage deepened dramatically and drew Simon's attention for a moment. God, she was lovely.

'I'm doing gene research,' he said, putting his test tube in the rack. 'Do you know what a gene is?'

'Vaguely.'

'Well, explained simply, it's the part of a cell where the information about our make-up is stored. When we're conceived, when any living creature is conceived, our cells divide and replicate. Our genetic make-up is copied again and again. Every cell in our bodies contains the full set of genetic information which goes to form who and what we are. In turn, this information has been copied from our parents and ancestors. So, for instance, I've inherited my mother's hair-colour gene and my father's eye-colour gene.' And you've inherited fantastic tits, he thought to himself.

'So, are you researching something in particular?'

'I'm trying to isolate certain genes. At the moment, I'm doing a study to find the gene for asthma. Asthma affects about one person in ten in this country.'

Anna thought about this for a moment. 'So, what do you do, once you've isolated the gene?'

'Eliminate it.' Simon waited for her reaction. Slowly, it lit up in her eyes.

'You could do that? You could get rid of asthma?'

'That's what we're aiming for. The technology isn't quite there yet, but we're not far off. Once we know what the gene looks like, and how it works, we're hoping to begin work on what's known as gene therapy. We'll attempt to take the asthma information out of people's genetic make-up. It's a bit like looking for a computer virus. You go into the program, search for the defective codes that are causing all the problems, and alter them until the program runs smoothly again.'

She looked stunned. She shook her head slightly. 'That's incredible. To think you could wipe out asthma, just like that.'

Simon was gratified to see her so impressed. It was good to be able to tell someone about his studies, for a change. The only downside to working at the Institute – and it was a small, selfish one – was that he would never receive the recognition he deserved. But then again, who needed awards and interviews in the medical journals? There were different rewards at the Institute.

'Could this gene therapy be used on anything else?'

'Oh, yes.' Simon nodded eagerly. 'Any disease that's hereditary. Any allergy. Anything that's contained in the genes can be engineered.'

'That's absolutely amazing,' she gasped. 'Think of all the diseases that could be wiped out . . . all the millions of people that your research could help . . . Simon, this is so exciting!'

'It is, isn't it?' He walked towards her, pleased to be able to share the buzz he got out of his work. 'Just think, Anna,' he said, raising his clenched fists for emphasis, 'the possibilities are endless. People's lives could be changed for the better, for ever. In a hundred years' time, asthma will be part of history.' He ran his fingers through his floppy hair, pushing his long, heavy fringe out of his face. 'I love this job, Anna. I love having the chance to make a difference.'

'Well, I can understand that,' she said. 'It must be so satisfying to know that what you're doing is going to help so many people.'

He perched on the corner of her desk. 'It is. And now you're a part of that, too.'

She seemed pleased, her eyes wide and shining. 'How long have you worked here?' she asked.

'I've been here ever since Dr Galloway founded the Institute, three years ago. I was the same age you are now, with no direction in life and a job I hated.'

'Doing what?'

'I was working in the same field, genetic engineering. But I was working on fruit and vegetables.'

She arched an eyebrow. 'You were? What on earth for?'

He rolled his eyes. 'I was part of what was known as the "Tomato Team".' He grimaced at the memory of it. 'We worked for a lab which was owned by a supermarket chain. Our job was to isolate the genes controlling redness, growth rate, susceptibility to bruising, resistance to insects...' His voice trailed off and his eyes glazed. 'The aim was to create the perfect tomato – one that was bigger, redder and more juicy than ever before. God, it was boring. Coming here was the best move of my career. Of my life, actually,' he added, thinking of the extra-curricular perks.

'Really?'

He waved his hand around the spotless laboratory. 'This is a scientist's dream, Anna. A lab to myself and the best equipment money can buy. I'm charting unexplored territory here. I make breakthroughs every day. But do you see anyone breathing down my neck? Do you see a senior scientist telling me I can't possibly do it like that, because it's never been done before?' He shook his head, realising once again what an amazing opportunity he had been given. 'This is the only place I've ever worked where I've been left to my own devices. If I want to try something new, I try it, even if it is crazy. Because Peter Galloway understands that science is like art. The artist has to be creative, to learn to think on different levels, to challenge himself. And only by following his instincts can he create a work of genius. A work of perfection.' He slapped his hand down on the table. 'Perfection, Anna, that's what we're searching for.'

Anna seemed taken aback by Simon's sudden burst of evangelical zeal. 'It's nice to see someone so happy in their work,' she said at last.

'It doesn't happen often,' Simon agreed. 'Most of us go through life doing uninspiring jobs for ungrateful bosses. We're lucky, Anna. The Institute is a very special place.'

She smiled warmly. 'I can see that.'

Simon got to his feet and went back to the bench where he'd been working. Anna returned to her task, entering data into the computer. For the first time since she had started work in the lab the previous day, she seemed to drop her act and relax.

From time to time, Simon glanced across at her. She was a hard one to figure out. She was friendly and outgoing, and yet she seemed the tiniest bit reserved, as if she was holding something back. She worked hard; she laughed along with his jokes; she did everything that she possibly could to fit in. But behind her smile, he suspected, there was something on her mind. Yesterday, when he'd asked her about her family, she had been reluctant to talk. And yet, according to Peter, she was neither reluctant nor reserved when it came to playing along with his games. She had certainly responded to Simon's gentle flirting.

Still, he thought, that was no reason for Peter to suspect her of ulterior motives. Simon had wolf-whistled at her in the lecture theatre, and then knelt between her legs and made her come. That would be reason enough for any woman to assume that he liked her. The Institute attracted lots of young people like Anna; people with no family ties, no career success, and more often than not a problem they were running away from, whether it was the law or a disastrous relationship. Whatever Anna's reasons were for being there, Simon was convinced they were innocent. Her eagerness to please could simply be put down to her desire to pass her trial and stay on at the Institute.

He glanced up at her again and their eyes met. She was smiling slightly, secretively.

'What is it?' he asked, flattered to find her watching him with such an alluring expression on her face.

'I was just thinking.' She laughed. 'My interview was quite ... unusual.' Her eyebrows flickered suggestively. 'I was imagining you, in your interview, and wondering whether Joan gets the job of selecting the male recruits.'

'I didn't have an interview,' Simon said. 'I was head-hunted.'

'Oh?'

'All the scientists here were head-hunted when Peter founded the Institute. He scoured the world, looking for the right people. A lot of the doctors here are leading authorities in their fields.'

Anna tucked her hair behind her ear. 'It was stupid of me, I suppose, but I assumed everybody came to an open day, like I did.'

'Most of the staff did. But not the scientists. It's highly specialised work that we're doing here. Peter had to be sure he was getting the right quality of staff. He poached three of us from my old company.'

'Did you know straight away that this was the job for you?'

'Oh, yes. When Peter told me I'd have the chance to make history – well, you don't turn down opportunities like that every day. But it wasn't just the job that attracted me. The perks were tempting, too.'

'Such as?'

Such as things you couldn't begin to imagine, he thought to himself. 'Such as, having the freedom to explore new possibilities.' The vagueness of his answer amused him. He laughed to himself, and moved on before she could question what that meant exactly. 'Such as having attractive female assistants. Coming to lunch?'

Anna tapped a couple of buttons on the keyboard and stood up, straightening her uniform. 'Are your assistants always female?' she asked.

'Always female, always attractive.' He held the door open for her. 'Some more attractive than others.'

As she approached, Simon moved into the doorway, leaving Anna little room to get past. Clocking what he was up to, she paused, meeting his eyes. Holding his gaze in a way that would have made some men weak at the knees, she brushed purposely close to his body. The tips of her breasts just touched him as she squeezed through the gap. Then, without a backward glance, she set off down the corridor, her hips swaying slightly as she walked.

Simon let out the breath he'd been holding in, and he silently thanked his lucky stars. Following her, he watched her glorious arse as she slunk down the passageway. And he thought of the colleagues he'd left behind at his old job.

Right now, they would be on their way to lunch in the canteen with their lab technician. Without a doubt, he would be male, adolescent, dedicated and dull. Meanwhile, Simon was on his way to a gourmet lunch with Anna. And to think his colleagues had scoffed at him when he'd handed his notice in.

'Suckers,' he said to himself.

By Friday afternoon, the atmosphere in the laboratory was simmering away nicely. Simon had developed a flirtatious rapport with Anna which they were both enjoying. They laughed a lot. They talked about films and books and music, and discovered that their tastes were very similar. Simon took every opportunity to brush past Anna when she was working, especially when she was poring over his notes, leaning over the bench. By the end of the week he was being blatant, hesitating as he pushed by her, savouring the wonderful feeling of his cock rubbing against her taut buttocks. And she was playing along, just as Peter had predicted.

A bond was beginning to form between them. Simon, as much as he would have loved to, didn't allow himself to do more than tease her. It was important that Anna liked him, as a friend and a potential lover; it was important that their relationship was different from the one Anna had with Peter. Peter could play the domineering boss, which was what he did best. But Simon had to reach Anna on a different level. So when she was sitting at the computer, her beautiful breasts almost bursting the top button of her dress, and what he wanted most in the world was to unzip his trousers and rub his erection between her tits, he didn't. He smiled or winked at her, and kept his lurid thoughts to himself. He would have her later, when the time was right; when Peter said that he could.

Right now, it was time to test Anna's curiosity. Simon handed her a dossier of notes; her workload for the afternoon. Anna's reaction to what was inside would be interesting.

Less than a minute later, she glanced up. Her pretty green eyes were serious. 'Simon?'

He looked up from his computer. 'What is it?'

She seemed uncertain, her mouth opening and closing as she glanced down again at the notes. 'Well . . . can I ask you something?'

'Of course you can.'

She swallowed, as if she were nervous. 'These results I'm putting on to the computer . . . this experiment . . . I don't understand the reason for it.'

'The reason for what?'

She picked up a sheet of paper and read from it. '"Study to isolate and replicate the gene for eye colour."' She stared at the words for a moment, as if they might explain themselves. Then she peeled her attention away and smiled half-heartedly at Simon. 'Why on earth would you want to find the gene for eye colour?'

He shrugged nonchalantly. 'Why not? We study genes, Anna. We need to gather as much information on all the different gene types as possible, to make sure our research is complete.'

'But why would you need to replicate eye colour?' Her smooth brow furrowed. 'In what situation would you need to do that, Simon?'

She was smiling, but her voice was tighter and more urgent than usual. Simon shrugged again. 'I don't know, Anna. Not every experiment has a reason.' He bowed his head, focusing back on his work.

'Doesn't that bother you?'

'What?'

'That you're doing experiments without knowing what they're for?'

'Why should it?'

'Well, it seems odd, as well as being a waste of your time.'

He kept his eyes on his work. Please shut up, he was thinking. Please don't be a spy. 'No experiment is a waste of time, Anna. Everything has its use. If not now, perhaps in the future.'

'Hmm,' she said – not the sound of someone convinced.

'I found the eye-colour gene by accident,' Simon told her. 'I decided to do some work on it. Like I told you, we're allowed to follow our own agendas here. So I took some time to look at the gene, to find out everything I could about it. In the future, if anyone needs that information, it's held on our database. Or at least it will be, when you get round to entering it.'

'Sorry,' Anna said, going back to her word-processing.

'It's all right, Anna. It's good that you show an interest.'

* * *

'You heard all that?' Simon closed the door behind him. 'What do you think?'

Without lifting his attention from the monitor, Peter motioned for Simon to sit beside him. 'What do you think, Simon?'

Simon sat down in front of the bank of screens. He looked at the one Peter was staring at. The tiny camera hidden in the laboratory light gave a bird's-eye view of Anna, sitting at the desk. She was just as he'd left her, typing away. Simon shook his head and sighed. 'I don't know, Peter. She was certainly concerned about the eye-colour experiment. But does that make her suspect? I mean, anyone with half a brain would be curious to know why we wanted to duplicate eye colour.'

Peter's eyes bored into the screen. He leant in closer to the image. 'She's a spy,' he said, under his breath and almost to himself. 'I just know it.'

'I'm not so sure. I mean, this trap we're setting for Anna is all very well, but it's not exactly a controlled experiment, is it? None of the new recruits ever step inside a lab until they've done their first month. By that time, they know all about our research programme. You've thrown Anna in there straight away, and given her one of the most sensitive jobs in the Institute. I'm telling you, Peter, anyone would be interested if they saw those experiments. Anna's new to this place. If you had just arrived, and you were going to live and work here, don't you think you'd be keen to know what we were up to?'

Lost in his thoughts, Peter shook his head slightly. 'Anna's not like the other recruits.'

'No, she isn't. But the fact that she's asking me questions doesn't mean anything. You can't compare her to the others, because the others go through the normal training procedure. Anna's an intelligent woman. You're showing her things she wouldn't normally see until her trial period was over – and you're expecting her not to

91

be interested?' He tutted. 'I don't know how you're going to find out anything this way.'

Peter turned to Simon, anger glinting at the edges of his grey eyes. 'Are you questioning my judgement? Do you think I haven't thought this out properly? I've got it all planned, believe me. Now that we've aroused Anna's curiosity, we're going to take it a step further.'

'We are?'

'You are. You're going to become her confidant. You're going to tell her that you've got worries about the research, too.'

Simon nodded, a bubble of warm admiration expanding in his chest. Peter was so clever, so masterful. 'Shall I . . . fuck her?' he asked hopefully.

'No. No fucking.' Peter broke into a wicked smile at the sight of Simon's disappointment. 'This woman is used to fucking. You will make love to her.'

'Yes, Peter.' Simon got up to go.

'Wait.' Peter stopped him, grabbing his wrist. 'Let's leave her alone for a while, see what she does.'

Simon sat down again. He tried to concentrate on the television, but it was difficult, with Peter's fingers tight around his wrist. Galloway's presence was almost over-powering and, as Simon's thoughts tangled, it was impossible to tell whether it was Peter's cruelty or Anna's softness he wanted more.

Anna felt like she was being watched. She wasn't, she was certain of it – she'd had a good look around the lab during the past week, and there definitely weren't any cameras there. But a strong sense that she wasn't alone, combined with her increasing paranoia, kept her in her seat after Simon left the room.

She continued with her work, her fingers running on autopilot while her mind occupied itself with other things. There would be lots of mistakes in her typing, but she could always go back and correct them later. Right now she had to use the opportunity of being alone to figure out what to do next.

This eye-colour thing was very worrying. Simon's explanation hadn't washed with her. If there had been a legitimate medical use for locating the gene, Simon would have said so. He'd been very keen to explain the benefits of the asthma experiment.

Anna wondered what other pointless research had been done here. Studies designed to help mankind control diseases and allergies were admirable; but studies into eye colour? She could only think of one possible reason for those. And, if her hunch was correct, then Mike had been right when he'd said this was potentially the biggest story the *Undercover* programme had ever investigated.

She kept glancing at Simon's notes, to keep up appearances should anyone be watching or walking by. But she'd given up on her work now, and was trying to find a way into the computer's records. She saved the database she was working on and clicked the mouse on to the computer's main menu. Quickly, she scanned the options. 'Records' seemed to be the obvious choice.

She clicked on to the icon and waited while the screen dissolved and reappeared. Then there was another menu. Under the main title of 'Records' were several sub-headings: personnel, suppliers, purchase orders, work schedules, accounts, lab results.

Lab results – that was the one she wanted. She clicked on to it and waited again, her heartbeat beginning to quicken. The screen turned blue and flashed a warning: 'The MS Institute of Research. Confidential Lab Records. Authorised Access Only. Do you want to proceed?'

She almost laughed out loud. A question like that, to an investigative journalist, was like a red rag to a bull. She took the Yes option.

'Shit,' she hissed, as the computer asked for the password. In the centre of the screen were two words, one beginning with M, the other with S. After the M, three empty spaces winked intermittently. There were six after the S.

A buzz of nervous energy made her hand shake slightly. If her hunch was right, then there was a very small, almost infinitesimal chance that she could guess this password correctly. But it was still an infinitesimal chance. And, if she was wrong, she would probably freeze the computer, and leave herself with a lot of explaining to do.

Gulping down her fear, she carefully typed in her guess. The screen did nothing. She pressed the ESCAPE button; the screen still didn't react. 'Christ,' she whispered, trying to stay calm. She had got it wrong, and the computer was not going to let her get away with it.

That's it, she thought. It's all over. Simon will come back in and find me snooping. I'll be marched to Peter's office, then expelled from the Institute. Mike will be furious, and my career will be over before it's begun.

Get out now, her instincts screamed at her. Go now, before Simon gets back. Get into your car and go. Her palms began to prickle with sweat. She felt her body rush with adrenalin. Her muscles tensed as she got ready to run.

Then, just as she was about to go, the disk drive whirred and its tiny green light flickered on and off. Seconds later, the screen changed again. She was in.

Anna didn't waste time congratulating herself, although she could have jumped up on to the table, danced with joy, and given herself a huge pat on the back for being so ingenious. Instead, she glanced again at Simon's notes, just for appearances, before diving into the records.

The heat of satisfaction quickly turned cold. As Anna searched through the list of experiments, she found that there were few with any obvious benefits. There were details of studies into various allergies and into several

94

hereditary diseases. These made sense. But the majority of the research that had been conducted at the Institute did not. Her worst suspicions had been confirmed and even exceeded. An icy shiver rippled down her neck as she realised that her hunch had been right.

Faint footsteps squeaked down the corridor outside. Calmly, Anna exited the Institute's records and returned to the page she had been working on when Simon had left. Without missing a beat, she picked up her typing where she'd left off, just as the lab door opened. She finished the sentence before glancing up at Simon.

He smiled as he came towards her. Anna smiled back. An extraordinary feeling encased her body; it was almost like the intense, impenetrable calm after the rush of orgasm. Anna felt completely safe, completely in control. The old maxim 'Knowledge is power' flashed across her brain and she realised how true it was. The knowledge she had about the Institute could be enough to close the place down for ever.

'Did you miss me?' Simon asked, standing at her side.

'I'm supposed to be working, aren't I? Not thinking about you.' She laughed gently, pretending to be flattered by his attention.

'I've been thinking about you,' he said. 'I've been thinking about what you were asking me, before.'

Anna was taken aback by his sudden seriousness. 'You . . . you have?'

Simon's eyes darted around shiftily. When he spoke again, his voice was lower and quieter. 'Anna, I've never said this to anyone. But those eye-colour experiments . . . They've been puzzling me, too. I lied when I said I'd found the gene by accident. Peter asked me to locate it, but he wouldn't tell me why.'

Anna didn't know what to say. This was almost too good to be true – a discovery and an accomplice coming forward, all in one day. 'What are you trying to tell me, Simon?'

'I'm not sure. Until you came along, I hadn't really thought much about it. I suppose that's one of the pitfalls of enjoying your job so much – you can lose sight of what's going on in front of your eyes. But what you said before was right. Some of the studies I've done . . . Well, there's no reason for them I can think of.'

Anna tried to play it cool. She needed to find out what Simon knew, but he mustn't know why she was so interested. Not yet. 'I'm sure there's a logical explanation for everything.'

'Maybe. Maybe not.' He glanced up nervously as someone walked past the lab's windows. 'Look, we can't discuss it now. Will you come to my room, tonight?' His brown eyes filled with worry. 'I need to talk this through with someone.'

Anna almost felt sorry for him. Whatever was going on, it had obviously been playing on Simon's mind for some time. 'Sure, I'll come,' she said. 'What time?'

'Late,' he said. 'I don't want anyone to see us together.'

'Ashamed to be seen with me?' she joked, trying to soothe his tension.

His smile returned. 'Anna, no one in their right mind would be ashamed to be seen with you. You're lovely. You know that I want you. I think I made that pretty obvious in the lecture theatre.'

He raised his hand and gently touched his fingertips to her cheek. The tension dissolved from his face as he watched his touch move up her cheekbone, down her face, and over the edge of her jaw to her neck.

'I . . . I'd better get on with my work,' Anna said reluctantly, even though work was the last thing she wanted to do. But there were people walking past the lab all the time, and what if Peter walked past? She didn't want to jeopardise the relationship she was building up with him.

'Don't let me stop you,' Simon said. 'Go on,' he urged,

nodding towards the computer. 'Back to work. Just ignore me.'

Perching on the edge of her desk, he grabbed the back of her chair and swivelled her round until she faced the screen again. Anna poised her fingers over the keyboard and looked at the notes she was working from. But Simon's fingers were back at her throat, distracting her, and she never saw a word. Suspended in soothing pleasure, and still intoxicated by the thought of the breakthrough she'd made, she sat completely still as Simon's fingertips drifted downwards. With a touch as light as an insect's wing, he discovered the gentle curves of her cleavage.

Anna looked up at him. She wanted to bathe in the soft, caressing heat of his desire as his eyes fluttered down into her cleavage. Moving over the collar of her dress, he slid his hand on to the swell of her breast. Anna felt her chest rising and falling as her breathing deepened. She rested her hand on top of Simon's and pressed his palm into the yielding softness of her flesh, wishing the white cotton of her dress would dissolve, so she could feel his skin on hers.

'Get on with your work,' he whispered.

Anna took her hand away. She raised her chin determinedly and focused on the screen. But it was no use. The words and figures seemed to blur as Simon moulded and squeezed her breast. Her flesh was so pliable in his fingers; her nipple so hard as he pinched its tip beneath the material.

'Oh,' she breathed, as the faint pain twitched through her body. The next thing she knew, Simon had deftly flicked open the top button of her dress, and with the back of his hand he pushed aside the collar. Anna saw him blink slowly, sleepily, as he took in the beauty of her breast. She had on a glossy, sheer bra which held her in a natural shape. Her nipple was dark and obvious beneath the pale, translucent fabric. Simon sighed with appreciation, and lightly scratched her engorged areola.

Moving through a dream, Simon slid from the edge of the desk and got to his knees. He turned Anna's chair to face him and knelt up in front of her. Pushing aside the other half of her neckline, he revealed her other breast. His breath was loud and slow as he cupped his palms to her curves, pushing them together.

'Oh God, Anna,' he gasped, dipping his head. He kissed the deep furrow of her cleavage, and the inner slopes of her breasts. Easing his fingers beneath the edges of her bra, he pulled the cups over her mounds and freed her swollen breasts. Anna looked down at their tips as they turned from pink to brown and pointed at Simon. Her lips parted and faint sounds of pleasure came out as Simon's mouth fixed to an areola. Anna arched her upper back slightly, pushing her breasts up to his face. She held the back of his head and felt his soft, sandy hair move over her fingers. Her head tilted and her pussy clenched as Simon tenderly nibbled and sucked at her. Simon's head rolled from side to side as he switched his attention from left to right. His tongue – that wonderful tongue – hungrily licked all over her: in the creases beneath her breasts, around her nipples, up along the inner arcs of her cleavage. His hair brushed her skin, awakening every pore to pleasure.

'Oh God,' he said again, pausing as he sat back on his heels to admire her. 'You taste so good,' he said breathlessly. 'I want to taste every inch of you. I want to eat you up.'

You can do what you want, Anna thought. Your tongue is heaven. Eat me.

He heard her thoughts and lunged for the remaining buttons. He pulled her dress open, then her thighs. Leaning into her quivering body, he kissed a path from her cleavage to the taut curve of her belly. Then he reached the edge of her panties, and he kissed all over her hidden mound and nipped at the material with his teeth. His gentle biting caught her labia, and she shuddered.

He pressed his tongue over her pussy, making the dampness of her tiny panties even damper. Anna cried out quietly, tortured with frustration and desperate to feel his warm mouth on the warm mouth of her sex. Reaching down, sliding her hand against his face, she roughly pulled her knickers aside in invitation, straining the flimsy material to breaking point at her hip.

Her muscles twitched. Ecstasy rose in her throat. She threw her head back in a soundless scream, a plea for mercy; but she didn't want mercy. She didn't want this to ever stop: his tongue inside her, his lips pulling on her clit, his eagerness, her thighs spread wide open for him, her body imploding with depraved delight. Out of the corner of her eye, she was vaguely aware of shapes passing the window: doctors on their way to other labs. They would glance in casually as they passed, and they would see her as they'd seen her in the lecture theatre – wantonly exposed, lost in sensual delight. Not only did she no longer care, but she actually wanted them to see. She wanted to show them her body, splayed wide with lust. For now, thoughts of knowledge and power and incriminating evidence were swallowed up along with her honey. For now, there was no investigation, no programme, no Peter or Mike. There was just Simon, his tongue, and her pleasure, spiralling out of control.

Anna squirmed impatiently in the car seat as she waited for Mike to pick up his phone. 'Come on,' she muttered. She had so much she was dying to tell him, she'd burst in a minute if he didn't hurry up.

At last, the ringing stopped. 'Hello?'

'Mike. Thank God you're at home. I tried the office, but you'd already left.'

'What is it? Are you all right?'

She rolled her eyes, irritated by his concern. 'Of course I am. I've just got a lot to tell you, that's all. I thought for a moment you'd got yourself a life and gone out for a drink, or something normal like that.'

'I was about to go out. But I always keep my mobile switched on. You remember the number, don't you?'

'Yes, of course I do.'

'What is it, then? Repeat it to me, Anna, just to be sure.'

Sighing, she told him his mobile number. 'Happy now? Can I tell you my news?'

'Go on.'

'Are you sitting down?' She paused dramatically. 'I've had the most amazing week. I was sent to work in one of the labs with one of the Institute's best young scientists.'

'You were?' Mike butted in, worry tingeing the edges of his gruff voice. 'Why?'

'Simon's assistant sprained her wrist and she couldn't type up his notes. Anyway, listen. This guy was telling me all about the experiments he's been doing. It's incredible stuff, all very noble. He's been looking into ways of engineering people's genes to cure asthma.'

Mike whistled. 'Is that possible?'

'Apparently it will be, soon. So, Simon's telling me all about how they aim to wipe out diseases and allergies for ever, and I'm thinking, wow, this is wonderful!'

'Sounds too good to be true,' Mike grumbled. 'If that is what they're really involved in, why keep it a secret? That would be the biggest medical breakthrough of the century.'

'Exactly what I was thinking,' she said. Her pulse was tripping over itself. Her words wouldn't move quickly enough from her brain on to her tongue. 'And then, this afternoon, I was given a file full of notes on another experiment to type up.' She hesitated, her blood rushing noisily in her ears as she wondered whether Mike would jump to the same conclusion she had. 'An experiment to find and copy the gene for eye colour.'

Mike was silent for a moment, as Anna had been when she'd first seen the words on paper. 'Eye colour,' he repeated to himself. 'What on earth would they want to do that for?' He spoke quietly and steadily, and Anna could hear his brain following the path she was laying for him.

'I asked Simon, but he wouldn't tell me. I had a suspicion, but to be honest I thought it was a bit far-fetched. I needed to find out some more about the other research they'd been doing. And, luckily, I was left alone for about five minutes. I managed to break into the computer records.'

'You're kidding me. Anna, please be careful.'

Anna huffed frustratedly. 'Mike, I thought you said I was the best person for this job? How come, all of a sudden, you've no faith in me? Credit me with a little intelligence. I wouldn't have done it if it was a risk.' She winced slightly at the sound of her lie. It had been an enormous risk, hacking into the computer. She could have jeopardised the whole investigation. But at the same time, Mike was going to have to let her get on with her job. He was going to have to trust her.

'Anna, the only reason I'm worried about you is that I found out some information about "Dr" Galloway. He isn't a doctor, for a start.'

A chill crept stealthily over Anna's skin as Mike told her what he'd learnt. Slouching down in her seat, she hugged herself, trying to eke a little warmth out of the familiar comfort of her arms.

'Now do you see why I'm concerned?' Mike asked, when Anna didn't react to his revelation. 'For all I know, Galloway could still be experimenting with people's minds – with your mind.'

'Actually, I think he's moved on to something even more sinister than drugs,' Anna said. 'When I went back

101

into the lab records, I found out that research into hereditary diseases and allergies only forms a tiny part of their work. Most of the experiments they do are pointless. Pointless, that is, unless the Institute's staff are involved in something which would raise the biggest ethical and moral questions of our time.'

'What sort of experiments?'

Anna tried to keep her voice steady. She wanted to scream with the exhilaration of her discovery. 'Mike, they've done research into the genes that control eye colour, hair colour, hair loss, height, weight, gender, sexual orientation, behavioural patterns, intelligence, athletic prowess, aggression, genital size ... the list goes on and on. Now, why would they need that information, Mike? What could they possibly need it for?'

There was barely restrained excitement in Mike's deep voice. 'You think ... you think they're trying to –'

'They're trying to clone humans. It's been done with sheep, and Galloway's taking it a step further.' Anna leant eagerly towards the speaker where the phone's receiver was hidden, as if that could bring her closer to Mike. 'I'm sure of it. Why else would the Institute be such a secret? "Dr" Galloway is conducting research that's morally and ethically corrupt. That's why.'

The pragmatist in Mike – the part of him that sniffed out potentially expensive libel cases – elbowed its way to the fore. 'Now hang on a minute, Anna. I'm convinced that Galloway's up to no good, but ... cloning? That's one hell of an accusation.'

'What else would he be compiling all this genetic research for?'

'Just because they've done these studies doesn't necessarily mean they're going to use them.'

'So why is the Institute named after Mary Shelley?'

'What?'

'The MS Institute of Research. The "MS" stands for Mary Shelley.'

Mike paused. Anna could sense his thoughts colliding. 'As in . . . the woman who wrote *Frankenstein*?'

Anna smiled at the incredulity in his voice. 'I had to guess what the initials stood for to get into the records. I guessed right.'

Mike's breath wooshed noisily down the phone line. 'Jesus, Anna. That's eerie.'

'I've got a gut feeling about this, Mike. Galloway's trying to compile all the information he needs to clone a human. And I'll get the evidence to prove it. The man's obviously mad. He's got to be stopped.'

Mike was quiet for a while, probably already thinking – as Anna was – of what a coup this was going to be for the programme. When he spoke again he was abrupt and businesslike, using a tone of voice Anna had heard so many times before as he'd paced around the office. 'Right. I'll carry on doing all I can at this end, checking out anyone who's ever worked with Galloway. I'll see if I can find out what he was up to before he set up the Institute. And I'll try and talk to the detectives who investigated the LSD case. What's your next move?'

Anna told Mike about Simon. 'He could be a useful ally,' she said. 'I'm going to his room, tonight. He's got something on his mind and he wants to discuss it.'

'Anna, I know you don't want me to, but I'm going to say it again anyway. Be careful.'

'I will.'

'Anna?'

'Yes?'

'Brilliant work. Well done.'

His praise warmed her, and she smiled. She wished she could touch him, wished she could see the thrill in his eyes. She felt a pang of longing in her stomach as she realised how much she liked him. She and Mike were perfect for each other: both intelligent, ambitious and driven by their work. But they were good together on another level, too, and something stirred deep inside her guts as she thought of the night they'd had together before she'd left for the Institute. As he said goodbye she closed her eyes, trapping his voice inside her mind. She longed to feel the heaviness of his chest bearing down on her as she lay beneath him. She longed to feel his thick limbs wrapped around hers, to smell the maleness of his skin and to hear him groan with effort.

But for now she had to put Mike out of her mind. There was another man waiting for her.

'Simon?' she whispered hoarsely outside room twenty-seven, tapping lightly on the door. 'Simon!'

The door opened and he appeared. Poking his head out, he looked up and down the dark corridor. Smiling nervously, he pulled Anna inside.

Simon's room was just like Anna's, bland and functional. As she stepped inside she looked around, but there was nothing to see – no clues to his personality. Still, Simon's personality was not the one in question here. It was Galloway who was the lynchpin and Simon, she suspected, was simply a pawn in Galloway's grand scheme.

He sat down on the bed and looked up at Anna. For a moment there was silence, as they both admired the sight of each other out of uniform. Simon had on a tight white T-shirt and the navy tracksuit pants which were part of the male staff's regulation clothing. He looked as if he spent most of his leisure time in the sports centre: beneath his clinging clothes he was lean and coated in just the right amount of muscle. His top was stretched tightly across his well-defined chest and his nipples were poking stiffly under the taut cotton. His dark-blond hair was ruffled and slightly damp, as if he was not long out of the shower. He looked clean and fresh, and real – the only real man in this strange, fake place.

Anna had on the black version of her usual tight-fitting dress, with matching underwear beneath and knee-length black boots. She looked sexy, she knew, and the way Simon's eyes flittered over her said the same thing. The corners of his lips twitched upward along with his eyebrows. He patted the space beside him.

'What did you want to talk to me about?' she asked, sitting down.

Immediately, as if it were a reflex, Simon clamped his palm over Anna's mouth. She flinched, and her eyes widened with surprise. Simon put a finger to his lips and shook his head.

Anna nodded her understanding, and slowly he took his hand away. Shuffling closer to her along the edge of the bed, he leant into her. His breath was hot in her ear. 'We can't talk freely,' he whispered. 'The walls are thin. If anyone found out I'd been discussing my research with a new recruit, I'd be in big trouble.'

Anna was puzzled. She put her mouth to Simon's ear. 'Why did you ask me here to talk then, if we can't?'

'I had no choice. This is the only place we can be alone together. We'll just have to be very quiet.'

Anna nodded.

'We'll have to sit very close together.'

Anna nodded again, noticing the faint glimmer in his brown eyes. She suspected Simon would have wanted to sit close to her whether they had had to whisper or not. She copied him as he turned to face her. Their knees touched as he leant into her shoulder and brought his mouth right against her ear.

'You look lovely,' he said softly.

As he stayed still, poised by her ear, Anna studied the back of his neck. His hair was shorter there, and blonder. His neck looked warm and strong. His closeness was irresistible, and she slid her hand around the back of his head. 'Is that what you wanted to tell me?'

'No. But you do look lovely. You know you do.'

Her fingers tingled where she held him; the same place she'd held him earlier, in the lab, as his head had rolled in her lap. Anna closed her eyes and concentrated on what she was really there for. 'So what did you want to discuss?'

He took a long deep breath, as if he too was caught up in the memory of before. 'What you were saying today, about that experiment. It worried me.'

Her fingers ruffled upward into his hair. 'The eye-colour thing?'

'Yes.' He put his hand to her shoulder and brought his head even closer to her. His lips touched her ear. 'I'd been wondering about it myself. Why on earth would Peter ask me to replicate that particular gene? It just doesn't make sense. But I'm afraid, until today, I'd pushed the whole subject to the back of my mind. I'm so happy here, you see. I didn't want to have to think about anything which might ... well, which might bring my work into question.'

Anna shivered as his mouth tickled her.

'But then you started asking the same questions I'd been mulling over in my head. And all of a sudden I couldn't ignore them any more. I'm worried, Anna. I feel I'm being used. You're right – I shouldn't be doing research unless I know what it's for.'

She pushed her fingertips up through his hair, massaging his scalp, trying to soothe him. 'I'm sure there's a good reason. Why don't you ask Peter?'

'I already did. When I left you alone this afternoon, I went to his office. I asked him, straight out.'

'And what did he say?'

'Exactly what I thought he would. That the experiments I conduct don't necessarily have a use now, but they may do in the future.'

'And you're not happy with that explanation?'

Simon shrugged. 'I've been here three years, Anna. I know how this place works. Our research is among the most advanced in the world. We've got the best equipment, the best staff, the best technology. And all that costs money. A lot of money. I'm just not convinced that we'd embark upon expensive, time-consuming research, just in case it's needed sometime in the future.'

A tiny, tight fist of anticipation gripped her stomach – partly because Simon's lips had just brushed against her earlobe, and partly because she felt she was getting somewhere. She baited him. 'But does it matter, Simon, when most of your research is so obviously worthwhile?'

He hesitated. 'Anna, to tell the truth, most of the work I do here can't be explained.'

She took in a sharp breath. The smell of his warm skin was almost as satisfying as the knowledge that, in Simon, Anna had someone she could trust. There was just one more question she had to ask.

'Why are you telling me all this?'

'I can't talk to the other scientists. And none of my other assistants has ever questioned anything I've shown them. But you did, Anna.'

'So what do we do now?'

Simon visibly tensed. Pulling back, he squinted slightly, his mouth open in concentration as he strained to hear.

'What is it?' Anna gasped.

'Someone's coming.' He looked at Anna, grim determination in his eyes. 'It could be Peter. He sometimes comes to discuss work with me.'

Anna glanced at her watch. 'At this time of night?'

'Time doesn't matter to him. He's woken me up at three in the morning before, to discuss an idea.' Simon grabbed Anna's shoulders. 'Kiss me.'

Anna raised an eyebrow. 'Now?'

'Why else would I have you in my room? He won't be suspicious if he walks in on us. Kiss me.'

His voice was faint and urgent, but Anna didn't need any encouragement. She slipped her hand back around his neck, tilted her head, and pressed her lips to his.

Behind her, she heard the door opening. Without paus-

107

ing in his kissing, Simon's eyes turned to see who it was. Quietly, the door was pulled shut again. Whoever it was walked off down the corridor, their shoes making faint squeaks on the lino. Simon closed his eyes and flickered his tongue inside Anna's mouth.

They carried on kissing for ages, nibbling and caressing each other's lips. Their slippery tongues danced together, tentatively at first. Then Simon's began to thrash inside Anna's mouth. His fingers gripped her face. Struggling for air, Anna had to reluctantly ease herself out of his clutches.

She looked round at the door, then back at Simon. She smiled. 'You can stop now,' she whispered breathlessly. 'Whoever it was has gone.'

'It was Peter.' Breathing hard, Simon put his hand on Anna's knee. 'But I don't want to stop.'

Anna looked down, watching his hand slide up her thigh. She didn't want to stop, either. She wanted to tear off his T-shirt and squash her soft breasts against his hard chest. She wanted to rest her head in his lap and taste his desire on her tongue.

'What do you think of Peter?' he asked.

She looked up. 'He's incredibly attractive,' she said wistfully, teasing Simon.

'What do you think about the answer he gave me? Do you reckon he's using me?'

Anna shrugged, although deep inside she knew the answer. Galloway was using all his staff, lulling them with a fantastic lifestyle so they wouldn't bother to question their work. 'If he is, then you're not the only one that's being used.'

Uncertainty twitched across his brow. 'I'm not?'

'Dr Galloway's been using me to relieve his frustrations.'

Simon tilted his head questioningly.

'Apparently Joan's very jealous of the female staff Peter works with. He ... er ...' There was no delicate way to put it. 'He isn't getting any. At least, that's what he insinuated. And that would explain his behaviour with me.'

Simon's eyes held a curious expression: a mixture of concern and excitement. 'What sort of behaviour?'

Anna smiled coyly. 'He asks me to ... do things for him.'

'You're not talking about the filing, I take it.'

Anna shook her head.

'Tell me,' Simon whispered. 'What's he asked you to do?'

Anna told him. She told him about the way Peter had asked her to bend over the desk, so he could watch as he fondled her arse, and how he'd asked her to type with her dress unbuttoned. She told him about how she'd sucked on Peter's cock while Joan had been in the office. And she told him how Peter had come back from lunch one day and complained that he was still hungry.

'He said he hadn't had time for dessert. I asked whether he wanted me to go to the kitchen and get him something. He said he wanted to eat me.' The wicked pleasure of the memory was intensified by the shock on Simon's face. 'He asked me to sit on his desk and spread my legs. He took off my panties and he ...' She finished the sentence by raising her eyebrows suggestively.

'He's disgusting,' Simon hissed, his upper lip curling with revulsion. 'Anna, I hate the thought of him doing those things to you.'

She was touched by his concern. 'I can look after myself,' she said, putting her hand to his cheek. 'I've got the situation under control.'

Simon didn't seem convinced. 'The bastard,' he seethed. 'It's revolting. He must be twenty years older than you.'

She shivered slightly; his anger was like an aphrodisiac. 'Are you a little bit jealous?'

'A little bit? I'd like to kill him. You know how much I

like you, Anna.' As if to prove how much, his hand hovered over the edge of her stocking, on to the very top of her thigh. 'I want you to myself.' He began to softly stroke the pale purity of her inner thighs. Anna opened her legs slightly, allowing him to trace delicate patterns on her skin. 'Your skin's so soft,' he sighed, his eyelids drooping. His fingertips trailed inexorably upward. Involuntarily, Anna twitched as he discovered the dampness of her panties. The faint jerk of her muscles seemed to spark something in Simon. 'You're wet,' he smiled, his voice soft as his fingers. 'I want to make love to you.'

Anna rested her hand on his groin. He had nothing on underneath his tracksuit pants, and his erection jumped under her palm. Envy had made him hard. She squeezed his balls, then stroked the heel of her hand along his prick. For an instant, her mind clouded with guilt as she thought of Mike, back in London, waiting and worrying. But, she told herself, this was all in the line of duty. If Simon was going to be her informant, she needed to get close to him. She wondered whether all her investigations were going to be so enjoyable.

'I want you to fuck me,' she whispered.

Simon stood up. Pulling on Anna's hands, he urged her to his feet. His fingers wouldn't move quickly enough as he unbuttoned her short black dress. As he struggled she made his job harder, slipping her warm hands underneath his T-shirt and sliding her palms over his chest. His breathing grew rushed and shallow with impatience. 'Fuck me,' she whispered, driving him insane. 'Fuck me, Simon. Fuck me.'

He wanted to. He had to. He couldn't stop himself now, despite Peter's words echoing in his mind: 'No fucking,' the doctor had warned. 'You will make love to her.'

He couldn't make love; it would be impossible to be slow and tender. Anna's body was designed for fucking

– frantic, mindless and gratifying. She was so soft, with curves that made his mouth water, and skin so pure he longed to soil it with his dirty thoughts. And then there were her eyes, glittering seductively, their pale green the exact colour of his lust. No, he couldn't make love to her tonight, although he suspected he could easily fall in love with a woman like Anna.

His penis throbbed angrily as she fell to her knees in front of him. Bowing his head, he watched her lips part as she pulled down his sweatpants. She sighed in appreciation of his long, swollen rod. Then she clasped her mouth around the weeping tip and sucked him into ecstasy.

His fingers twitched in her soft, thick hair as her head bobbed. Her tongue was magic, flickering incessantly over the knob of his prick and lapping all along his proud length. Looking down at her, he groaned at the sight of her open dress and her breasts almost spilling out of her low-cut bra. He could see the edges of the dark discs surrounding her nipples, peering over the lace like twin sunsets. His gaze dropped down between her breasts. Stroking her cleavage with his eyes, he lingered over her sublime curves until he had their shapes embedded in his mind. Then he turned to the mirror over his desk, and grinned wickedly.

There was a tiny camera behind the mirror, linked to a television screen in the monitoring room. At this moment, Peter and Joan would be sitting, avidly watching. Simon could almost hear Peter's voice, cursing Simon for disobeying his instructions. There would be a price to pay, later, for his insubordination. The thought made his penis jerk in Anna's mouth.

She sucked greedily at him, swallowing ferociously as he shuddered and came. Easing his spent cock from between her lips, Simon hooked his hands under her arms and pulled her up. Gazing lustfully into her pale eyes, he gratefully touched her mouth. Her lips were

111

glistening and, when he kissed her, he could taste himself on her tongue.

'Anna,' he gasped, carried away on a roaring, foaming tide of need. 'I want you, Anna. I want to fuck you, now.'

She helped him, shrugging her dress off as he distract-edly pushed the material over her shoulders. Like a greedy child with an insatiable sweet tooth, he tore at her wrapper. He wanted it off; he wanted to feel nothing between his skin and hers. Reaching behind her, he deftly unhooked her bra. Pausing briefly to squeeze her beauti-ful, pert breasts, he knelt and pulled down her panties. He ripped at her boots, unzipping them and wrenching them off her feet with such urgency that she had to reach down to steady herself with a hand on his shoulder. Finally, her sheer black hold-ups were torn off and thrown aside.

Anna laughed softly as he stood up again. 'What's the hurry?'

He answered with a voracious suck of her neck. Christ, her skin tasted so good. He bit her, punishing her for being so irresistible. She drew in a sharp breath.

Simon peeled off his own clothes and roughly pushed Anna on to his bed. Her eyes roamed quickly over his nakedness, hesitating when she saw how hard he was again. He smiled at the look of flushed excitement on her face. Anna smiled back. Resting her head on his pillow, she bent her knees up and spread her thighs. One hand dropped into the exquisite darkness between her legs. Sighing languidly, she rubbed a fingertip between her labia, prising open her succulent, crimson slit. Simon could feel his pulse beating in his prick as her finger dipped into her moist pussy.

It was too much to bear. Pulling her hand away, he dipped his head and sucked on her shining finger. The same sweet musk he'd tasted twice already hit his senses like a smack in the face. He fell on her, lowering his hips between her open legs. Grateful, he watched as she reached down and guided him towards her waiting pussy. Then, with a searing thrust, he was inside her.

It was wonderful in there, the pent-up aggression of his prick engulfed in the infinite pleasure of her beautiful pussy. She was soft and hot, tight and wet, and he slid so fluently in and out of her it was as if their bodies were meant to be joined. Her inner muscles clutched at his penis as he pumped into her, pushing himself further and deeper with every stroke. She moaned loudly and, for a moment while he watched her, he almost forgot his own selfish pleasure. Caught beneath him, pinioned by his powerful body, she was going wild. Her throat was arching on the pillow, a deep blush speckling her skin. Her eyelids were fluttering with pleasure and with every thrust of his cock a new sound of surrender flew from her lips. Her breasts were jiggling slightly with the force of his hips, the creamy mounds tipped by brown nipples turned stiff with delight. Her fingers clung to her hair, so black against the white pillow. A heavy lock had fallen across her face. Completely lost, she looked so beautiful that Simon broke his incessant rhythm. Balancing himself on one hand, he brushed her hair away from her eyes.

'You're gorgeous,' he groaned.

She gave him a self-satisfied look that said she knew. 'You're not so bad yourself,' she said. Running her hands up over his arms, she dug her vicious nails into his bulging muscles. Then she brought her knees right up to her chest, and slid her feet up and around his neck. Digging in hard with her heels, she flashed Simon a smile that belonged to the woman of his dreams; a smile as depraved and downright dirty as he was. 'Now stop talking and finish what you started,' she invited.

Returning to his selfish pleasure, he rammed himself hard and fast inside her soaking-wet pussy. Lowering his body, he crouched over her like a slavering animal with his helpless prey. With her legs hooked over his shoulders he seemed to plunge deeper, until he felt his

113

penis nudge at the neck of her womb. She cried out, urging him on. His face twisted into an involuntary grimace as he felt his climax rush from his body into hers. He shuddered violently while she rolled and writhed on the crumpled sheets.

Simon had finished but Anna's hips continued to move. Levering with her legs, she gently thrust her pelvis upward to his cock, reaching for more. She hadn't come, but she would have to wait for her climax. For just one moment, Simon wanted to savour the ecstasy of holding a woman prisoner to his needs. He had been under Peter's cruel control for so long now he'd almost forgotten how good it felt.

Anna came, trembling and whimpering, with only a few rapid flickers of his thumb on her stiff clit. She clung desperately to his arm as her orgasm seeped over her body, as if she might float away on a wave of pleasure if she didn't hold on tight. Keeping her eyes open, she stared gratefully up at Simon as his face loomed over hers. At that moment she was his; her mind, body and soul belonged to him, just as he belonged to Peter.

He prayed that she wasn't involved in industrial espionage. He wanted her to stay on at the Institute. He wanted her to be his for ever. Already, he was looking forward to the day she completed her month's trial. Then she would be initiated into the Institute's special ways, and Simon was planning on being the one to guide her through that particular ordeal. He had to close his eyes for a moment at the thought of her wrists and ankles shackled, her body wide open – open for him. Another erection began to stir.

'What are you thinking?' she asked, running her fingers through his hair.

He opened his eyes. 'I was just thinking, you're the best assistant I've ever had.'

'Oh.' She rolled on to her side and propped her head

up on her hand. 'And I bet you've "had" a lot of your assistants,' she smirked.

Simon nodded. 'Are you jealous?'

'Me?' She wrinkled her nose. 'What would be the point? Your usual assistant will be better soon, and I expect you'll forget all about me.'

'I won't.' Absent-mindedly, Anna stroked her breast with her fingertips, circling her luscious shape and lightly grazing her wide areola with her nails. Simon avidly followed the path of her touch. He loved to see a woman enjoy her own body. 'What were you thinking?' he asked.

'I was wondering about something you said to me this afternoon, about how your assistants are always female and always attractive. Why is that, do you think?'

'I don't know. It's just the way it is – the male scientists get female staff, and the female scientists get male staff. One of the perks of the job, I suppose.'

'But it doesn't make sense.'

Simon's heart sank. No more questions, he begged. 'What doesn't?'

'Well, everyone here is very good-looking. All the doctors are involved in ground-breaking research, right?'

'Right.'

'Wouldn't you find it easier to concentrate if you didn't have a good-looking woman, in a uniform that's too small for her, working in your lab?'

'Definitely.' He put his fingers over hers, flattening her hand on to her breast. 'But it wouldn't be half so much fun. The Institute was set up to carry out scientific research, but there's no reason why we can't enjoy ourselves doing it.'

She didn't seem sure. 'It is strange though, isn't it?'

Shut up, he thought. Peter's listening. 'Is it?'

'Well, you would think that the staff would be encouraged to leave sex until after working hours. But you're not the only one who mixes business with pleasure, are you? When you sent me to deliver those test results this

115

afternoon, there was something going on in practically every lab I passed.'

'So? We have a different work ethic here, Anna. We get all our research done, but we believe in showing our feelings. There's sexual tension in every workplace. Peter's policy is for people to let their sexual tension out into the open, instead of bottling it up. At the end of the day, it makes for a happier staff.'

'Is that what you were doing in the lecture theatre, then – letting your feelings out?'

She slipped her hand out from underneath his. For a moment he toyed with her nipple, pinching it back into stiffness while he thought of what to say. The traditional welcome for new recruits was just the first test in a series; a series which would determine whether they could stay on at the Institute. But Anna wasn't to be told about the selection procedure. Not yet. If she were a spy, she would be asked to leave. If she wasn't, she would find out all about the Institute's selection process when the time was right.

'When I see a beautiful woman, a woman like you, Anna, I can't help myself. I just want to taste her, to feel her come.' His fingertips trickled down over the soft curve of her belly, into the soft curls covering her sex. She opened her legs as he felt the wetness between her labia. 'Most of you come here because you didn't like the world outside. We like to make the new recruits feel welcome, and to show them that this place is different. The limits that society places upon us don't exist here.' He poked a finger inside her. Her gasp was faintly warm on his face. Rolling on to her back again, she bent her knees up slightly and clenched her buttocks, lifting her hips from the bed. A fresh surge of lust welled up inside his chest as he felt her body respond to his touch. 'I wanted you the moment I saw you, Anna. In the outside world I'd have sat there, looking at you, wishing I could push up your skirt and lick your pussy. But what's the

116

point of keeping your desires to yourself?' He rubbed the heel of his hand against her swollen clit, forcing a bolt of pleasure to jump up from beneath his hand, along her spine and out in a quiet whimper. 'That's what the Institute is all about, Anna. Freeing your thoughts. That's what science is all about.'

'Exploring new possibilities?'

He nodded, recognising one of the Institute's mottoes.

Anna turned her head on the pillow and looked up at him. 'And what if the possibilities you're exploring are illegal?'

His finger froze over her clit. 'What ... What are you talking about?'

She gently pushed his hand away, now that it had stopped giving her any pleasure. Sitting up, she hugged her knees, squashing her breasts. 'You told me that most of your work can't be explained – that it doesn't have an obvious reason. And you said something else, something very interesting.'

'I did?'

'That you're so happy here you've pushed any questions you had to the back of your mind.' Her eyes widened and she jutted her head forward, encouraging him to think about what she was suggesting. 'Don't you see? You said yourself, this place is a scientist's dream. No one telling you what to do; the best equipment; a lab to yourself; not to mention sex whenever you want it, with a choice of extremely attractive women. You know which side your bread's buttered, Simon. You know you'll never get facilities and perks like these in any other job.' She grabbed his arm. 'You are being used, Simon. You're being given all these wonderful things on a plate, to keep you so happy that you won't question whatever Galloway asks you to do.'

He felt tension pulling at his mouth. 'The research we're doing may not have a use right now, Anna, but it certainly isn't illegal.'

117

Her eyes were bright. 'The research may not be, but what Galloway does with all that information is a different matter.'

Simon's heart missed a beat. He held his breath. 'And what do you think he'll do?'

She leant towards him. For a moment, he thought she was going to kiss him, but her lips stopped by his ear. 'I think he's going to try and clone a human. Now, that would be illegal, wouldn't it?'

An uncomfortable smile faltered at the edges of his mouth. 'Yes, Anna. It would. What on earth makes you think that Peter's going to try something like that?'

She searched his face as if she was deciding whether to trust him or not. 'I don't know. I could be completely wrong. But it would all add up, wouldn't it? Why else would you be doing research into eye colour?'

Simon attempted a dismissive laugh, but it came out wrong. 'Cloning is illegal, Anna. It would be insane for Peter to attempt it.'

'But not impossible?'

Deflated, he looked at her for a moment: at her flushed cheeks, her beautiful, clever eyes and her sensual mouth. And he cursed Peter's intuition.

Why? Why did she have to be a spy? And why did he have to find out now, when he'd just discovered how good it felt to fuck her?

Gently, he brushed a strand of sweat-dampened hair away from her cheek. 'Why so many questions, Anna?'

Pulling his hand down on to her breast, she moulded his rapidly cooling fingers to her shape. 'You started it, remember? You're the one who said you had things on your mind.'

'I wish I hadn't now.' Simon couldn't help himself; she was too beautiful to resist. His fingers began caressing her flesh and teasing her areola. 'Perhaps it would be better for both of us to put those thoughts away to the back of our minds. Better not to cause trouble.'

'No, Simon.' She sighed as he tugged at her nipple. 'Like you said, it's better to let your feelings out. It's good to share your worries with someone. Tell me everything that's on your mind. Free your thoughts.'

Chapter Six

*S*imon's thoughts were far from free. They were knotted and frayed beyond repair. He was confused, worried about what was going to happen to Anna, and strangely dejected.

He got in the lift and pressed the button. As he was whirred towards the interview room, he studied himself in the lift's smoky, mirrored walls. He looked tired; not surprising, as he and Anna had got very little sleep. But he looked drawn, too, and not his usual self.

How strange, he thought, that after three years at the Institute – three years of casual sex with beautiful, willing women – he should suddenly feel like this. But it was unmistakable. Beneath his loyalty to Peter and his dedication to the Institute, there was a tiny pang of guilt that he had betrayed Anna. He liked her a lot. Apart from her obvious attractions, she was feisty and intelligent; but then, those would be necessary attributes for an industrial mole. How bloody typical, he cursed, that the one woman at the Institute he would really like to spend some time with would be leaving soon – before her induction. He would have to imagine her handcuffed in one of the cells, her beautiful face contorted with

120

agony, because now he wouldn't get the chance to see it for real.

He stepped out of the lift, sullenly scuffing his feet as he approached the interview room. He knocked on the door, quietly, almost hoping that Peter wouldn't hear.

But he did. 'Good morning,' he said, beaming, as he opened the door. He put his arm around Simon's shoulder and guided him towards the desk. 'And how are you this fine day?' He turned to face him. Standing a little too close, as he often did, Peter parted Simon's lab coat. Reaching inside the pristine white material, he cupped a hand to Simon's crotch. 'Got any cock left, after last night? Kept you busy, didn't she?'

Simon nodded. The familiar feelings stirred in his tight stomach as he looked into Peter's hypnotic grey eyes. 'Were you watching the whole time?'

'Oh yes. It was quite a performance. I've got it all on tape, should you ever want to see yourself in action.'

He mustered a smile. 'How thoughtful of you. A souvenir to remember her by.'

A line creased Peter's brow. 'And why would you need a souvenir when you've got the real thing? You can have her whenever you want her.'

Simon hesitated, his words trapped for a moment as Peter's grip clutched at his balls. 'But surely you'll be asking her to leave today?'

'Will I?'

Simon hurriedly filled Peter in on the parts of his conversation with Anna which the microphone wouldn't have picked up. He revealed Anna's suspicions. 'She thinks we're cloning.'

'So?' Peter watched for a reaction as he rubbed his palm over Simon's semi-turgid penis.

'So . . .' Despite his exhaustion, Simon felt himself thickening again. His concentration wavered. 'So you have to get rid of her, before she finds out anything that could really damage us.'

Peter grinned and closed his fingers around Simon's cock. It was a grin Simon recognised immediately; it was fuelled by power. Galloway knew he had Simon under his control, and he obviously thought he had Anna where he wanted her, too. 'Anna's only a danger to us if she leaves the Institute,' he said. 'But she isn't going to leave.'

'What do you mean?'

'I know what makes women like Anna tick. She's just discovering what it's like to surrender control of her mind and body. Remember that, Simon? Remember how that felt?'

He did, vividly. Relinquishing himself to Peter had been the start of an addiction – an incredible, fulfilling addiction that couldn't be kicked. 'But Anna's only doing these things because she has to. As soon as she's got the information she needs, she'll be gone. And then we'll be in serious trouble.'

Peter watched his free hand smooth down Simon's hair. 'You couldn't leave this place now, could you, even if you wanted to?'

'No. You know I couldn't.'

'Well, it'll be the same with Anna. She may think she's the one in control, but I'm far cleverer than she is. I can see what's going on in here.' He tapped on Simon's forehead. 'By the time I've finished with Anna, she'll be begging me to let her stay.'

'You think so?'

'I know so. Anna's being a spy would explain why she's willing to do what we ask her. But it wouldn't explain why she enjoys it so much.'

Simon gasped as his cock unfurled into an erection beneath Peter's insistent hand. 'I hope you're right.'

'I'm always right, Simon. Anna will stay. She belongs here.'

Simon could feel the back of his neck warming as tension smouldered between the two men. Their bodies were only inches apart and the temptation was strong.

Simon longed to grab Peter's cock and mould it into stiffness; to hold his jaw and force their lips together; to feel his tongue on Peter's. But he daren't make such a bold move. He knew his place, and he relished it.

'Now, there are two things I must attend to today. I need to give Anna a little fright.' He fell silent, his eyes stabbing into Simon's.

'And?' Simon prompted. 'You said there were two things.'

'Ah, yes. I also have to deal with you.'

'Me?' Simon whispered, desperate excitement rolling in his guts.

Peter's hand left Simon's cock and snatched at his wrist. Tugging roughly on his arm, he dragged Simon into the next room. There was no selection panel lurking behind the two-way mirror today, but the medical trolley was there, empty and waiting.

Simon allowed himself to be manhandled on to the bed. Peter unbuttoned Simon's lab coat and shirt, and unfastened his trousers. Then he strapped him down, tying his wrists and ankles so tightly into the leather straps that they immediately began to ache. Moving behind him to the head of the trolley, Peter swivelled the bed around and pushed it right up to the glass. Simon had a perfect view into the next-door office.

'You can watch while I attend to Anna.'

'No,' Simon gasped, lifting his head from the pillow. 'Please, Peter.'

Peter's smile was sadistic. 'I told you to make love to Anna, and you blatantly disobeyed me. You fucked her. You were weak, Simon. You gave in to your body.'

Simon let his head fall back on to the pillow. It was pointless arguing.

'I hope this treatment will help you. You have to learn to control your own body, Simon, before you can be trusted with anyone else's.'

'Yes, Doctor.'

As Peter walked off back towards the interview room, Simon looked down his tethered body. Rearing angrily from his trousers, his prick was swollen and red, and thrusting demandingly from his foreskin. Galloway appeared back in the office, and a moment later there was a tap at the door.

'Come in, Anna,' he said, his voice clear as it was relayed to Simon through the microphone.

'You wanted to see me?' she said, closing the door behind her.

Simon tugged at his bindings but he was buckled in so tightly there was no way out; no way of freeing a hand and relieving the tight pressure on his heavy balls. This was going to be almost unbearably wonderful. 'God help me,' he groaned.

Peter tried not to smile as he looked at Anna's dossier, but the feeling of power was making him deliriously happy. Weaning each new recruit on to his methods was always a satisfying process, but there was an extra dimension with Anna. If she was working undercover – and the fact that she had jumped to a conclusion about cloning would suggest that she was – then she was like a soft piece of clay in his hands, waiting to be sculpted. And he could form her into anything he wanted.

'Anna,' he said, looking up. 'You've been here almost two weeks now. How do you feel things are going?'

'Fine, I think. I'm getting on pretty well with Simon.'

'Really? I'm pleased to hear it.' Opening up a drawer, he pulled out his stethoscope and thermometer. He got to his feet and moved around the desk. 'Now, Anna, I need to give you a check-up. If you'll just unbutton your dress for me . . .'

Anna stood up. 'Is there something wrong?'

The hint of nervousness in her eyes was almost enough to make him hard. 'Nothing's wrong. It's standard procedure. I just need to check that you're still in peak condition. Working in the lab, you're exposed to tiny amounts of chemicals. They shouldn't affect you at all, but we'd like to be sure that you're not having an adverse reaction to any of these substances.'

'I see.' She slowly unbuttoned her dress.

Galloway moved towards her, his breathing deepening. Raising his hand, he watched her as he gently opened up her dress.

He moved slowly, bathing in her attention as she followed his every move. Putting the earpieces into his ears, he warmed the silver end of his stethoscope in his hands for a moment. Then he raised it to her chest.

'Deep breath in,' he said, standing a little too close so that his voice dripped on to her skin. Her breasts rose as she did as she was told. 'And out.' He moved the 'scope slightly, easing the disc just underneath the edge of her bra. 'Breathe in again.' He could feel her eyes on his face. 'And out.'

With gentle fingers, he pulled at the bra cup, crumpling the soft satin and lace until it was folded beneath her pert breast. 'Breathe in.' Her pink nipple rose towards him. Sliding the stethoscope down, he covered her areola with the silver disc. Her heart quickened, racing loudly in his ears.

When he dropped the stethoscope from his fingers, her areola had crinkled and darkened, shocked by the cool metal. 'Was that too cold for you?' Peter whispered. 'Let me warm you up again.' Sliding his fingers over her exquisite breast, he rubbed her with his warm palm. Even without the 'scope, he could feel her pulse reverberating.

Keeping his hand on her, he pulled the delicate material away from her other breast. Gently pushing backward and forward with his thumb, he made the pink silkiness at the tip of her breast darken to brown. Squeezing her full curves, teasing her engorged nipples, he allowed himself a sigh of pleasure.

'Peter?' Her voice was faint and hesitant.

He paused in his worship of her flesh. 'What is it, Anna?'

Her lips parted. Unsure, she looked up at him.

'Well?'

'You said this was a medical check-up.'

'It is.'

She swallowed, as if she was trying to pluck up courage. 'Then . . . Why are you touching me like that?'

'Because you want me to.'

Her mouth opened slightly, as if she was about to contradict, but closed again without a word. Anna lowered her eyes, then slowly, slowly raised them again. As Peter watched her, studying her pale green eyes, he saw her expression gradually change from protest, to confusion, to acceptance. She was struggling with herself, and losing the battle.

All his instincts about Anna had been right. She was different; she was a spy; and she was enjoying Peter's domination. It felt so good to be right. As if the sun had just come out, a stroke of warmth caressed the back of Peter's neck. Having her under his control was deeply satisfying; so satisfying he felt his penis stiffening in his trousers.

'I'm right, aren't I? You want me to touch you.'

Almost imperceptibly, she nodded. 'Yes,' she breathed.

Having got his answer, he let go of her. 'I have to take your temperature now. Turn around,' he commanded. 'Kneel on the chair.' She followed his orders, resting her knees on the soft leather seat. 'Now bend forward. Hold on to the back.' He pressed her shoulders down until she leant towards the chair's high back, her bottom pouting towards him. Sliding his hand down her spine, down over her buttocks, he pushed her dress up over her hips. Taking a second for the splendour of her arse to sink in, he traced his fingers over the tautness of one cheek. Then

126

he pulled her panties down over the lacy tops of her cream hold-ups.

Picking the thermometer out of his breast pocket, he lubricated it in his mouth. Rolling his tongue around it, he coated the tip with his saliva. If he had really wanted Anna's temperature, that would have been pointless; but Anna no doubt knew as well as he did that this examination was not for the medical records.

Rubbing the thermometer's bulbous red tip around her anus, he stimulated the tightly pursed muscles with their sensitive nerve-endings. Anna's buttocks twitched in response, and her fingers made the leather creak as she dug her nails into the chair's back. Knowing what was coming, she held on tight and held her breath.

With a swift, wicked thrust, Peter inserted the glass rod between her open cheeks. It was bigger than the average thermometer: as thick as his finger and long as his hand. Pushing in and out of her pink anus, he heard her whimper and watched her tiny hole grasp to stop the invasion. The backs of Anna's thighs quivered with pleasure. Reaching forward, Peter put his other hand to her chin and turned her face until he could see it. Her mouth was open in abandon, but her eyes were tightly shut as if she was trying to block out what was happening.

'You want this,' he reminded her, urging her to give up the fight with herself. 'There's no need to be ashamed. You're a dirty girl, Anna. Accept it.'

He pushed the rod deeper inside her and she squealed in anguish. Turning her head away, she pressed her face into the chair.

'It feels good, doesn't it?'

She replied with a languid arch of her lower back. Spreading her knees wider apart on the seat, she made her buttocks more open for him. What a wanton, Peter laughed to himself: a confident, clever girl who was so willing to show her dirty, depraved inner self that it only

127

took a nudge and she was over the edge, writhing and moaning and exposing her true needs. That was what he loved, more than almost anything else in the world – to see a woman stripped of pretence and unable to stop herself. And Anna couldn't have stopped herself now even if she'd wanted to. She was probably making excuses for her behaviour inside her mind, telling herself that she had to do these naughty things for the sake of her espionage. But deep down she knew, as Peter did, that she had lost control. Her mind and body were his.

Leaving the thermometer sticking out of her arse, Peter stepped backward and sat on the edge of the desk. He looked at her for a minute: her hips undulating with pleasure, her tiny anus plundered, her pussy open and slick between folds of plump flesh and curls of black hair. She was his prisoner, waiting for his next move. Like a torturer, he had complete control over her. Her pleasure, and the pain that came with it, were in his hands.

He plucked the instrument from her arse and her body sighed with disappointment. She wouldn't be disappointed for long, he thought. 'Stand up and face me, Anna.'

She turned around, rather pointlessly pushing her dress back down. Peter stopped her as she bent over to pull up her panties.

'Take those off.' She did. 'Put one foot up on here.' Peter patted the desk next to his hip. Anna raised her thigh and placed one foot where he directed. Standing just a few inches away from him, she watched, softly panting, as his eyes took her in all over again. Her dress was gaping, her stiff-tipped breasts tumbling from her bra, her sex lips open; open for him. Her mind was open for him, too, and he could look inside her head and see exactly what she wanted. She wanted him to touch her, to sink his fingers inside her slit and then replace his hand with his hard, throbbing cock. But she wouldn't get what she wanted; that was his power.

He pulled the cream plastic rod from his hip pocket. Holding it up in front of her face, he told her he needed to take a sample of her sexual juices. Then he turned the base until it began to hum.

'Put this inside your vagina,' he purred. 'Make it nice and wet for me.'

She gulped, but didn't question him. Frightened and thrilled at the same time, she took the vibrator with trembling fingers. Holding his gaze, she lowered her hand.

'Do exactly as I tell you,' Peter said.

She paused, awaiting her instructions while the gentle buzzing hovered between her thighs.

'Stroke your pussy lips.'

Peter looked down as she slowly brought the stem to her open labia. As she touched the toy's smooth tip to her sex he could smell her, faint but noticeable in the air; she smelt sweet and musky. Rubbing the vibrator's head up and down against her sensitive inner flesh made her sigh loudly, and Peter granted her an encouraging nod, as if she was an excellent pupil.

'Now put it inside you,' he said. 'Slowly.'

Wrapping his hand round her ankle, he braced himself as the ridged length slowly disappeared into the secret of her pussy. Inch by inch, she swallowed the toy until only its base was left visible; a pale, rigid contrast to the dark softness of her cunt.

'Good girl.' He paused to steady his tremulous voice. 'Now, move it in and out.'

As she slid the vibrator in and out of her hungry pussy, Peter's hand slid up her shin on to her thigh. Her muscles were tense with her leg lifted so high on the desk; his muscles were tense, too. He wanted to snatch the vibrator out of her hand, throw it away, grab her hips and fill her with his prick. But he wouldn't because, unlike Simon, he had learnt self-control. This game was not about his pleasure. It was about asserting himself over Anna, and making her feel helpless.

She certainly looked helpless. Once again, she was caught in the sticky web of her own lust. With neither the power nor the desire to escape, she had no choice but to let this happen.

She moaned as she stroked the inner walls of her sex with the vibrator. Her eyelids lowered for a moment and she almost lost her balance. Grabbing her free hand, Galloway placed it on his shoulder so that she could hold herself steady. Her fingers dug fiercely into his skin, but he enjoyed the pain. He savoured the turmoil raging in her body; a lethal mixture of shame and abandon.

'Look,' he said, nodding downward to her busy hand. 'Look at the way that vibrator slides so easily into your wet pussy.'

She bowed her head and looked, her breath catching at the sight. Every time she withdrew her hand her swollen, crimson labia dragged against the cream plastic, leaving it shining with her honey. Every time she pushed inside herself, her inner thighs trembled. Transfixed, she watched as her own hand, finding some impetus from her subconscious, began to pump more rapidly.

'That's it, Anna. Give yourself what you want.' He put his hand to the back of her head, keeping her head bowed, making her watch. 'Fuck yourself, hard. Faster, Anna. Harder. Watch yourself come.'

She was frantic, desperate for release. Her nails bit into Peter's shoulder while her other hand accelerated urgently. She bit down on her lower lip, keeping her moans inside, building them up for the final cry of relief. She was almost there.

In fright, she gasped as the door opened behind her. Peter snatched at her ankle as she tried to pull it off the desk, and with his other hand he gripped her wrist, forcing her to keep the buzzing rod inside her. 'Stay still,'

130

he soothed. He looked over Anna's shoulder at the doorway. 'Come in, Frank. You haven't met Anna yet, have you?'

She stared at Peter with wide eyes, begging him to let her go. He just smiled. 'Anna, this is Frank. Frank – Anna, our latest recruit.'

Frank came and leant against the desk, perching himself just beside Anna's raised foot. Studying Anna's face as all three stood in silence, Peter was amused by her reactions. Humiliation flickered across her green eyes, but it was amazing how quickly she forgot that she was standing there, legs wide apart, breasts and pussy wantonly on show, a humming sex toy buried between her sex lips. As she noticed how beautiful Frank was, her humiliation was overcome by curiosity and arousal. Her gaze fell rapidly down his body and back up again, taking him in.

Peter couldn't blame her; Frank was stunning. The twenty-two-year-old was his pride and joy – a living, breathing person created from the passion of two other people. When Frank had been born, it had been the happiest moment of Peter and Joan's marriage. Every time he looked at him, Peter felt a surge of satisfaction and wonder.

Frank was six foot four. He had golden hair cut short. Thick and messy, it stuck up at all angles, which infuriated his precise mother but charmed the pants off the girls, as it gave him an innocence which was at odds with the power of his body. He was very well built, with hard muscles all over, long arms and legs and a wide chest and shoulders. His skin was sun-kissed, as if he spent most of his time outdoors. Deep-blue eyes sparkled from his chiselled face. He had high cheekbones, a strong jaw and a long, Roman nose. He was, as Joan never tired of saying, perfection.

Anna obviously thought so too. The look of horror she'd had when the door had opened had transformed into a look of shy admiration. A slight smile crept on to her lips.

'Hello,' she said at last.

'Hello,' Frank said, staring at her breasts. Her hard, dark nipples stared back.

'Anna's been here two weeks now,' Peter told Frank. 'She's getting on very well. We're all very pleased with her progress.'

Frank murmured his approval as his eyes dropped to her bush.

'She's been working with Simon all this week,' Peter added.

'Can she work with me next week?'

Peter smiled, touched by Frank's simplistic view of the way the Institute worked. He patted his shoulder. 'We'll see.'

'She's so pretty,' Frank said plaintively. 'I want her to work with me.'

'I told you, we'll see.'

Frank turned to Dr Galloway, sighing petulantly. 'Why can't I ever have what I want?'

Peter tried to reason with him before he made a scene. 'There are other scientists working here, Frank, and they all need assistants. I can't take Anna away from Simon just because you suddenly decide you want her.'

Chastened, Frank looked down at his feet.

'Now, Anna was just about to come before you interrupted us. Would you like to see her come?'

'Yes,' he gasped, his eyes bright and eager again as he looked up.

'Anna, please continue where you left off.'

He let go of her wrist at last, and slowly she began to plunge the vibrator in and out again. Her pleasure had swelled now, and was close to flooding her body; not only did she have the shameful helplessness of her situation to deal with but, as well as Peter avidly watching, she now had Frank there, too. Galloway could tell, as her eyes fluttered nervously from one man to the other, that it was torment for her. He wondered how Simon was coping next door.

Gradually, her hand worked up to the speed she'd reached before. Soon, she was thrusting quickly and deeply and moaning with every stroke. Beside Peter, Frank's breathing became loud and slow. Peter couldn't take much more himself.

'You're ready, Anna. You need to come.' Snatching the vibrator, he flung her fingers away. With a deft twist of the base, he turned the hum into an urgent, angry roar. Spreading the fingers of one hand over her pussy, he flattened her soft curls and exposed the angry red nub of her clitoris. Her open labia wept as they were deprived of the pulsating phallus, but Peter knew exactly where her need lay now. He knew precisely where to put the screaming rod in order to make her scream with ecstasy. Resting its length between her gaping lips, he pressed the smooth end hard against her clit.

Immediately, a tremor shook her body. Reaching for help, she clutched at Peter's shoulder with one hand, and at Frank's with the other. Her mouth twisted with the agony of it, and Peter could see that it was so good she wanted it to end. Her fingers twitched spasmodically; her neck rolled and she cried out in protest. He knew just how hard it was for a woman to handle the full strength of the vibrator as it sent pulsing waves deep into her clit. But he also knew that only by enduring the first shock of pleasure could she climb on to the next plane. So he told her to 'Keep still, don't fight it', and he tortured her with ecstasy.

He pushed the rod into her tender skin. Rolling it slightly from side to side under his palm, he put intolerable pressure on her clit. Tears welled up in her eyes as he rocked the hard tip over the engorged lump of nerve-endings, making her swell even more. And then she was coming, shuddering violently like a wild animal caught in a trap. Whimpering imploringly, she clung on to the two men as a foaming, sticky tide of relief roared over her quaking limbs.

Exhausted, unaware of anything apart from her slowly subsiding climax, Anna sat slumped in the comfort of the leather chair. Frank and Peter talked quietly for a moment, but she didn't even try to listen. Her mind was too overloaded with pleasure for her to take in anything else.

'You liked him, didn't you?'

'Huh?' Blinking, she tried to rouse herself.

'Frank. All the women like him.'

Looking round, Anna was surprised to find that she and Peter were alone again. Still in shock at what had just happened, she hadn't heard Frank leave. 'Mmmm,' she murmured in reply, although she'd already forgotten what the question was.

'He's a good-looking young man, isn't he?'

Oh yes, Frank. 'He's stunning,' she sighed. Her pussy clenched at the thought of him: those eyes, burning lustfully into her flesh; that body, poised casually as she brought herself off; that face, so wonderfully masculine. 'I think he's the most perfect man I've ever seen.'

Peter nodded, seeming pleased at her answer. 'You're right. Perfection – that's exactly what he is.'

Anna stirred at the vague memory of something Simon had said: 'Perfection, that's what we're aiming for.' The echo was eerie, as if Simon had been repeating the party line. 'Has Frank been here long?'

'Since the beginning. Frank's been working with me for years now. You could say he's dedicated his life to . . .' Galloway appeared to be searching for the right word. 'Progress.'

'Is there any chance . . . Will I be working with him?'

'It's unlikely, I'm afraid. I would love to put you with

Frank, but he works on highly specialised research projects. His assistants need highly specialised expertise.'

'Oh.' She couldn't help feeling a tiny bit disappointed. Simon – like every man at the Institute – was very attractive, and she was more than happy to be working in his lab. But Frank was a class above any man she'd ever met. He was almost disturbingly flawless. If he had chosen to be a model rather than a scientist, he could have earned a fortune. There was something intriguing about such a beautiful man. She wasn't sure whether she wanted to sleep with him or just stand and stare; just to see him naked, to touch his sculpted flesh, might be enough. That's what he was, she thought – a living sculpture; an artist's painstaking vision of male perfection, made real.

He chuckled at her obvious disappointment. 'Sorry, Anna, but Frank's studies are so complex that only a handful of our staff actually understand them. He's our best . . . scientist.'

Peter's hesitancy was puzzling; he was always so sure of himself. Frank's almost childish annoyance before was strange, too. But perhaps he was so completely immersed in his work that he'd lost track of normal behaviour. 'He seems very young to be the best.'

'He's exceptionally gifted.' Self-satisfaction widened Peter's mouth. 'He's my son.'

Anna tried not to look as surprised as she felt, but it was hard to believe that Frank and Peter were related. Unless . . . 'From a previous marriage?' It was Peter's turn to look surprised. 'Oh, I'm sorry. I shouldn't have asked, it's none of my business. It's just that –'

'Frank looks nothing like either me or Joan. It's all right, Anna. Lots of people have said that to me.'

His smile was sinister – or was Anna just jumping to conclusions? The trouble was, it all added up. The pieces slotted into place with alarming ease: genetic engineering, cloning, Mary Shelley, a man named Frank . . .

'We created a monster.'

Anna jumped. She looked at Peter, shocked to think he'd read her mind. But his eyes were glazed and he was staring into the distance. He laughed at some private memory, and met Anna's anxious eyes.

'That's what we said, when Frank was born. He was an absolute terror, always screaming for attention. I don't think we slept for two years.'

Anna struggled to smile along with him. It was hard to imagine Joan and Peter in their spotless white lab coats, bending over their baby's cot and cooing soothingly. It was even harder to imagine that two dark-haired, grey-eyed people of medium height and build could possibly conceive a son like Frank. Was he a genetic experiment, a clone, precisely engineered to faultlessness?

'Joan and I couldn't have children,' Peter said. Sorrow clouded his eyes. 'That's why Frank doesn't look like us. He's . . . adopted.'

'Oh.' Was he lying? It was impossible to tell.

'Anyway, back to business.' Galloway sat up straight, shrugging off his sadness. 'I want to ask you something, Anna.'

'Yes?'

His gaze turned to granite. 'Do you trust me?'

Anna faltered at the challenge in his voice. What was this all about? 'Sorry?'

'Trust.' He made the word sound like a threat. 'We trusted you, Anna. We offered you a place here, at the Institute. Now, I'd like to know whether you trust me.'

Anna wished she knew where this was leading. Uncomfortable, and feeling slightly cold, she closed the gap down the front of her dress, pulling the two sides of material together. 'Of course I trust you, Peter,' she lied.

He nodded sagely. 'I'm glad to hear it. So, if you had any questions about the Institute, say, or the work we do here, you would come to me?'

There was an ominous tone to this. 'What sort of questions?'

Sighing impatiently, he stood up. 'It would be normal for a new staff member to want to know about her new environment. Have you any questions? Is anything worrying you?'

'I don't think so.' She swallowed, trying to find some saliva in her dry mouth. Galloway stalked to the door in the far corner of the room.

He turned and waved at her with a cursory flick of his hand. 'Come here.'

Shakily, she got to her feet. Her fingers fumbled to rebutton her dress. She wasn't sure why, but it seemed a sensible thing to do; to hide herself from his penetrating gaze, to try to protect herself in some way. Galloway had an uncanny knack of seeing what was going through her mind. And he was different from normal – calm, as always, but with a hint of anger which was unnerving. Anna was still confused by the way she had acted before, and now, as well as dealing with her suspicions about Peter's 'son', she had to handle whatever confrontation was coming. Her brain reeled. Sharp fragments of thought seemed to scratch the inside of her head, making it hurt.

What was all this talk of questions and trust? Had someone seen her sneaking out to her car to phone Mike? Had her surveillance equipment been discovered? She hadn't seen Simon yet that day; had Galloway forced him to reveal what he and Anna had talked about last night?

Peter stepped through the doorway and motioned Anna inside. With a palpitating heart, she followed him into the flickering light.

Her jaw dropped at the sight that met her. The room was dark, which made the scene all the more creepy. A continuous desk went round three walls. Above the desk, right up to the ceiling, were rows of television screens.

Mesmerised, Anna stepped closer to the bank of monitors. She could see everything: the front of the Institute; the car park, with her car at the distant corner; the cafés, the pool; every lab and every bedroom. Her blood ran cold at the thought that collecting hard evidence was going to be almost impossible. Then she felt as if her blood stopped altogether, frozen stiff in her veins, as she realised that someone had seen her last night, in Simon's room.

Terrified, she was barely aware of Peter as he stepped up to the console set into the desk. He flicked a switch, and a red light flashed in the corner of one of the screens.

Startled, Anna jumped as two clear voices broke the silence in the room. It took her a moment to realise that the dialogue she was hearing – perfectly clearly – related to what was going on on the monitor. A doctor and his assistant were in their lab, discussing the science programme they'd watched on TV the previous night. Every sound was picked up, from a loud laugh to the faint clink of a test tube being put in a rack. Even their footsteps were audible. Peter flicked another switch, and another red light flashed. In one of the bedrooms, one of the staff sang to herself as she changed the sheets. Anna watched, horrified, realising there was a hidden camera and microphone behind every bedroom mirror.

Peter turned his back on the screen and folded his arms. He was waiting for Anna to speak, but what on earth could she say? Her poor mind was racing as she tried to remember exactly what she and Simon had discussed, and how loudly they'd discussed it. The microphones were highly sensitive, but was it possible they had managed to pick up their whispering?

'I know what you're thinking.'

You couldn't possibly, she thought, trying to summon a smile.

'You're wondering why there is closed-circuit television in every part of the Institute. The answer is simple.

The research we are conducting here is highly sensitive, ground-breaking, even. We have to constantly be on guard against industrial espionage.'

Anna nodded.

'Our research is top secret. It has taken us many years of painstaking work to make any progress in our field. If a mole from another lab managed to get into the building, she could potentially collect enough data to bring her lab up to speed with ours – without the years of hard work. Now, that wouldn't be fair, would it?'

'No,' she said, wondering why he'd described the hypothetical mole as a 'she'.

'So we have cameras everywhere. If there's an intruder in the building, or one of our staff is up to something they shouldn't be, she'll be found out.'

There was that 'she' again; it made Anna flinch.

Peter sat down in a swivel chair and invited Anna into the one next to his. 'I'm explaining this to you, Anna, because I don't want you to think of this –' he swept his hand across the bank of screens '– as an invasion of privacy. The cameras are an unfortunate but necessary precaution. There's always someone out there who wants what you've got without having to work for it. The world of science is no exception. Do you understand what I'm saying?'

He was saying he thought she was a spy; that he'd seen and heard her with Simon. But what Anna couldn't work out was why he was revealing his suspicions. With all these cameras, there was nowhere to hide. Why didn't he just wait and catch her in the act? 'I think so,' she said.

'I'll tell you what I think, shall I?' In the background, the gentle, lilting singing continued, strangely incongruous in the room's tense atmosphere. 'I think there may be something you want to ask me. After I walked in on you and Simon last night, I came back here. I watched you all night. I couldn't take my eyes off you. You two could fuck for Britain.'

Anna laughed nervously.

'But there was more than sex going on, wasn't there?' Anna was silent. Peter shook his head slowly, menacingly, as if he couldn't quite believe it. 'You two were taking great pains to whisper so you wouldn't be heard. What was so secret?' He raised an eyebrow at Anna's hesitation. 'Let me guess ... Simon was telling you he has worries about the research he's doing. Am I right?'

'Well ...'

'It's all right, Anna. Simon said the same thing to me. There's nothing wrong with him questioning what he does here. We all have doubts about our work, from time to time. We wouldn't be human if we didn't.' Diving for Anna, he clutched at her legs. Leaning right forward, he looked deep into her eyes. 'If you have doubts, I want you to know you can come to me. You're part of our team, Anna.'

Sweat erupted from her palms. His words should have been comforting, but they weren't; they were threatening. 'Thank you,' she whispered.

'So?' He held her hands in his, and spoke slowly as if she were a child. 'Do you have any questions about what you've seen here so far – or about what Simon said?'

Go on, she urged herself, ask him. 'Well ... I was a little puzzled by the eye-colour experiment I was typing up yesterday. I mean, why ... What ...?'

Galloway nodded, as if he understood her curiosity. 'I told Simon the same thing – that experiment has no use now. But in the future it may help eye surgeons, or it may be used in forensics ... Who knows? As research scientists, we don't place boundaries on our work. Genes are our area of expertise, and we have to study every gene.' He chuckled softly. There was genuine warmth in his voice. 'I'm glad you asked, Anna. It shows you have intelligence and an enquiring mind. Remember, you can ask me anything – we have no secrets here.'

He was lying. But at least it seemed she was off the

hook – for now, at least. Anna nearly broke down. Allowing herself to breathe again, she silently thanked any god who might be listening for saving her, and promised to be good for the rest of her life.

'I'd like to put that mind of yours to good use. That's why I'm entrusting you with special duties.' He winked. 'Duties ideally suited to someone as inquisitive as you. Will you watch the screens for me? I'm on the roster, but something more important's come up.'

What an opportunity. 'I'd be happy to,' she said.

Peter stood up. Tenderly, he stroked one side of Anna's head, running his fingers over her silky bob. 'Joan's wrong about you.'

'Wrong?' she said, trying to stop her voice from cracking, and hoping she was pulling off the expression of innocence she was aiming for.

'You'd never betray me, Anna. You belong here, at the Institute.' He turned at the door. 'Here.' He threw something at her, and in the dim light she had to rely on her reflexes to catch it. 'In case you get bored,' he explained.

She looked down at the vibrator. When she looked up again, he'd gone.

Anna was alone with her work for the next few hours. At first it was distracting, and a little nauseating, to have so many screens dividing her attention. But gradually she became accustomed to the constant flickering, and found she could switch between images and pick up what was going on. She thought of her flatmate, Suzy, and her infuriating habit of flicking between TV channels. Suzy rarely watched a programme all the way through; she would rather pick up a snippet of a soap, mixed with a fraction of the news and a pinch of a cookery programme. Suzy would have loved this.

And as Anna switched the microphone from one image to the next, she began to enjoy herself. This was better than a soap. It was almost addictive, dipping into real-life scenes for a moment, sharing in their conversations and then moving on. It was like being on a train speeding through suburbia, and catching glimpses of people through their bedroom windows. Not one person was self-conscious – they obviously didn't know they were being watched. Anna had typed up the security rosters when she'd been working for Peter, and she remembered that the same small group of names had cropped up in tight rotation. This job was clearly entrusted only to a few.

Anna congratulated herself that she'd been selected to be one of them. It meant that Peter trusted her – or, more likely, that he had a growing soft spot for her. And that could only help her investigation.

She had thought the game was up earlier, but someone up there was looking out for her. She would have to be careful, as Mike never stopped warning her – especially now that she knew Galloway was constantly on the lookout for infiltrators. But she was building up an incredibly useful relationship with Peter, one which made her privy to secrets like the monitoring room. It seemed that, the more she indulged in his sexual games, the further she was accepted into the Institute. It was as if she was being rewarded for her obedience.

Anna's mind began to drift as she watched the screens. Despite the progress she'd made, the Institute's secrets were still heavily shrouded in mystery. There were hundreds of unanswered questions, and Frank's appearance had raised a hundred more. Was it possible that he was a clone, or was she taking things a bit too far? If he really was adopted, then that explained his looking so different from his 'parents'. Anna resolved to try to make contact with Frank again. She couldn't remember ever seeing him downstairs in the leisure centre – she couldn't possibly have missed him – but he must use the facilities some time. She needed to find out about the specialised research he was conducting.

There were Simon, Joan and Peter to play off against each other. There was evidence to compile – although that would be incredibly difficult, with the ubiquitous cameras to contend with. And almost as intriguing as the Institute's research was its liberal policy where recreational sex was concerned. That was another aspect that needed investigating, especially since Anna suspected it was somehow significant. She couldn't quite believe that staff happiness was the simple reason Galloway allowed everyone to behave as they did.

As if to illustrate her thought, a doctor in one of the labs moved behind his assistant and began touching her up. Anna turned on the sound and heard the woman sighing contentedly. Watching the man's fingers rub the woman's buttocks, then slide down her thighs and back up under her dress, Anna felt a surge of desire deep inside her pussy. Whatever the reasons for the Institute's sex-laden atmosphere, it was a bizarre working environment. But she couldn't pretend she wasn't enjoying it.

Her stomach lurched as she thought of Galloway. She shouldn't like him: he was the enemy, her subject, and quite obviously involved in something strange. In fact, she didn't like him; her feelings about the doctor were far more complex. There was something about him she found disturbingly attractive. It was as if he had a magnet where others had a heart and, try as she might to resist, in the end there was no option but to yield to the force which pulled her towards him. It was a first, she realised, for her to feel overpowered by a man. Perhaps that was what she enjoyed when she was with him – the way he made her feel; the way he reached into the darkest, most unfathomable depths of her soul and plucked out her thoughts before she could make sense of them herself.

A camera picked him up as he strode down a corridor, and contradictions fought amongst themselves in Anna's mind. An image flashed behind her eyes of her lying down on a medical bed, submitting to Galloway and allowing him to do whatever he chose with her body. But there was another image, too – an equally gratifying one – of Anna discovering what he was up to, bringing him down, and wiping that confident look from his face. It would feel so good to turn the tables on him, and to regain the position of control.

As she was thinking all this, Peter disappeared from one screen and reappeared on another. Inside Joan's office, he walked up to her desk and sat down in the chair opposite her. Anna eagerly turned on the microphone, but not a sound came out. She flicked the switch back and forth, hoping it was a temporary fault, but there was nothing.

Frustrated, she leant forward and peered at the silent screen. The only way of telling what was going on was by interpreting their body language. Joan sat, tight-lipped and prim, continuing with her paperwork. Her husband, on the other hand, seemed to be laughing to himself. Opening his lab coat, he spread his knees and unzipped his flies. Through the gap in his trousers, he unfurled his long, proud cock. His hardness shocked Anna.

It seemed to shock Joan too, because she glanced up quickly and then bowed her head determinedly, poring over the papers on her desk. Peter said something, resting his hands on the chair's wide arms. Joan ignored him. Peter slammed his fist down on the armrest with such force that, despite the silence, Anna jumped. Joan jumped too, looking up worriedly. Slowly, she stood up and moved around the desk to her husband.

Anna felt her pulse begin to race again, as if she was the one getting to her knees in front of Galloway, as if she was the one taking the swollen plum of his penis in her mouth. She wet her lips with her tongue. She held her breath as Joan's head lowered into Peter's lap.

It was a strange scene, and the strangeness of it made Anna's pussy wet with desire. Joan reached for Peter's cock, but he angrily pushed her hands away. He seemed to shout at her, and following his order she held her hands behind her back. She looked so different from usual. Her cold confidence was gone and she was like his slave, prostrating herself at his feet and doing as she was told. The thought of that woman being dominated by her husband gave Anna a sharp, inexplicable thrill.

Peter held Joan's auburn head down as he shuddered into her mouth. Without a moment's pause, and without the slightest hint of affection for his wife, he pushed at her shoulders and sent her falling backward. Standing up, he grabbed her wrist and pulled her to her feet. He was rough with her as he turned her round and planted her hands on the desk. Bent over, with her back to him, Joan's face was aimed right at the camera. Her expression was thrilling to see: thin lips open in wordless terror, eyes squinting as she braced herself. And yet she wasn't afraid at all. There was no struggle as Peter pushed her dress up over her hips and spread her legs. Joan – cool, clinical, self-assured Joan – wanted this desperately. Anna knew just how that felt.

With a hand between her shoulders, Peter pushed Joan further over the desk until her cheek was pressed on to the wood. Standing behind his wife, he ripped her knickers down and spent a moment looking at her arse, rubbing his hands together. Then, looking directly into the camera, he held Joan's waist with one hand and raised the other high in the air.

Joan's body jerked across the desk as Peter whipped his hand on to her naked behind. Anna winced in sympathy as she watched Joan's shoulders and neck twitch with the shock. As Peter spanked her, taking his time and talking to her between strokes, Joan closed her eyes tightly. Anna could almost share her pain, and the strange, intense pleasure that went with it.

Peter used all his force to chastise his wife. A wicked leer upturned the corners of his mouth as he salivated over the sight of her helplessness. He paused between slaps, bending slightly to inspect her buttocks and her sex. Anna wondered whether Joan was as wet as Anna had been, that morning, with the thermometer poking out of her arse; as wet as she was now.

Before the thought had even reached Anna's mind, her fingers were moving towards her damp pussy. Delving beneath her dress, she found her panties soaked with longing. Sitting right back in her chair, she opened her legs, undoing the last two buttons on the skirt to give herself more room. Looking down, she watched as she pulled at her white knickers with one hand. Holding the flimsy material aside, she ran a finger along her labia.

Her lungs seemed to fill with desire as she discovered how wet she was. Her labia opened with ease, heavily lubricated by her arousal. Stroking up and down, Anna felt how smooth the skin of her lips was; how smooth, and warm, and swollen. Beneath her lush triangle of curls, her pussy lips were plump and dark with longing. She had to have something inside her, now.

Reaching for the vibrator, she glanced up at the screen. Joan's small hands were in tight fists, screwed up on the desk. Behind her, Peter was holding her hips and watching as he slid his erection inside her. As he eased into his wife's pussy, Anna turned on the vibrator and eased it into her hungry sex.

Twisting the base, she made it hum. It echoed inside her, reverberating deep in the walls of her vagina. She didn't know where to look: at the screen, where Peter was slowly fucking his wife, or down where her hand was slowly fucking herself.

Deciding on the monitor, Anna sat transfixed. Joan's face was no longer in torment. She was racked with another torment now: the feeling of too much pleasure. Peter was pushing into her with long, deliberate strokes. Anna knew how that position would let him in deep. She knew just how Joan would be feeling.

She matched Peter's thrusting. When he slid his prick into Joan, Anna slid the vibrator inside herself; when he withdrew, she did, bringing the rod's buzzing tip practically all the way out, until only an inch hummed between her lips. Then Peter would plunge again, and Anna would follow, pushing the thick shaft deep into her lust. As Peter lost his steady rhythm and started pumping frantically into Joan, Anna was overcome with need. Watching Joan's head lift from the desk, Anna jerked the phallus in and out of her wet hole. Her inner thighs twitched with desperation. She needed more.

Anna hooked her knees over the chair's arms. Sliding the vibrator into the depths of her pussy, she left it buried between her soft folds of flesh while she tore open the rest of her dress's straining buttons. Her fingers were shaking, along with the rest of her body, as she scooped her heavy breasts out of her bra. Rubbing her tender areolae, she teased the tips of her breasts into stiffness, then cruelly pinched her poking nipples. She made her spine arch with the pain, but she pinched again, harder still. She was craving sensation. Her need was immense.

A thrill flashed across her empty mind at the thought of her position. Thighs as wide apart as they could go, she must have looked like a dirty, depraved animal. And that's what she was, at that moment, all thought of shame pushed aside in her thirst for cock. Any cock would do – even a fake plastic one – as long as it filled her. Reaching between her legs, she turned the vibrator up to full volume. It screamed in reply, assaulting her nerve-endings with the strength of its throbbing. Moaning uncontrollably, Anna filled her vagina with the sound, pumping frenziedly until she could take no more.

She hadn't realised that Peter had left the screen but, as she pulled out the rod and pressed it against her aching clit, she became vaguely aware of someone entering the room behind her. He resumed his seat beside Anna as she began to shake with the intolerable pleasure.

Calmly, as if he was simply observing her at work, he watched as wave after wave of ecstasy washed her body. Through half-closed eyes, Anna could just make out his smile.

He caught the vibrator as her fingers let it drop. Holding her eyes with his unswerving gaze, he pushed the still-buzzing phallus into his mouth. Anna heard a grunt of pleasure in the back of his throat as the taste of her juices seeped on to his tongue. Licking his sex-flavoured lollipop, he leant closer to Anna. She gasped as he slipped two fingers between her labia, stroking the ridged walls of her pussy. He slid another finger in, then another, stretching her. Then, before the fire of her climax had even begun to cool, he rubbed his thumb across her clit and brought her, moaning, back to insanity.

It seemed strangely quiet when the vibrator was finally silenced. Drained of energy, Anna watched like a child as Peter fastened her dress for the second time that day. She smiled sleepily at him as he sat back in his seat.

'Anna, were you watching, before, when I . . .' He nodded to the screen where Joan was now sitting back behind her desk.

'Yes,' Anna said. 'I'm sorry. I couldn't help it.'

He raised a hand to stop her. 'Don't apologise. I wanted you to see it.' His velvet voice lowered provocatively. 'It made me hard, to think that you were watching.' He looked into her eyes for a moment. 'I'd appreciate it if you kept what you saw to yourself.'

'Of course –'

'Only my wife would be mortified if word got round that she enjoyed being treated like that. And she does enjoy it,' he added quickly, as if Anna might have doubts.

'I could tell she did,' she said.

'It's Joan's little secret. We all have our secrets, don't we, Anna?'

What are yours? she wondered. Did Peter have a

foible; a weakness which could be manipulated? It was hard to envisage him ever being out of control.

'We all want something we won't admit to.' Peter's eyes bored into her soul. 'What do you want, Anna?'

'I . . . I don't know,' she faltered, not sure how she was supposed to answer.

'You don't, do you? But I do.' Raising his hand, he stroked her flushed cheek. 'I know exactly what you want. And I'm going to help you get it.'

She didn't know what he was talking about, but she almost didn't care. Mesmerised by the softness of his touch, the richness of his voice and the unwavering strength of his gaze, all she wanted at that moment was to stay there and wrap herself in his attention.

'You may remember me telling you that the Institute is all about opening your mind, exploring new possibilities.'

'Yes,' she whispered. Her voice was faint, as if he'd stroked it away.

'I can open your mind for you. Whatever it is you want, it's in there, hiding in the darkest recesses. I want to help you let it out, Anna; to help you free yourself.'

That sounded a bit too much like New Age guru-speak for Anna's liking. She was reminded of what Mike had told her, and an image of Galloway force-feeding her mind-altering drugs crept into her slumbering brain and woke her up. Suddenly roused from her post-orgasmic stupor, she remembered why she was there and silently promised herself she wouldn't fall for Galloway. She had to stay focused; to keep telling herself that Galloway was dangerous. He was sexy, too, and enigmatic, but she couldn't be drawn into his mind games. She had to play along, but at all times she must remember that this – the flirting, the domination – was just a game. And, to be the winner, she would need to keep her wits about her.

'What do you say, Anna? Would you like me to help you explore what's going on in here?' His fingertips brushed her forehead. 'And here?' His other hand slid beneath her skirt.

'Yes,' she gasped, but despite his searching fingers her mind was clear. Yes, he could touch her. He could play whatever games he wanted. But she would always be in control. Always. And if she told herself that often enough, she might even begin to believe it.

Chapter Seven

*F*rank couldn't sleep. Sighing heavily, he laced his fingers behind his neck and stared up at the ceiling above his bed. He tried to relax; to empty his mind as Peter had taught him to do when insomnia struck. He tried to focus on his breathing, but it was impossible tonight, more so than most nights. His mind was full of Anna.

He hadn't felt this bad for weeks. But seeing Anna in his father's office had brought back all those confusing feelings again. There was an aching void of loneliness, like a chill buried deep inside his body, and no matter how tightly he pulled his covers around him it wouldn't thaw. There was fear; only a slight tinge, but enough to keep him awake. Above all, there was longing.

He closed his eyes and retrieved the picture of Anna he'd stored in his mind. She had looked so beautiful before, when he'd walked in on her medical check-up. Beneath her gaping dress, her body had been so pale and soft. Tender – that was the word to describe her, he thought. Pressed beneath his hard frame, she would feel so tender, yielding, and incredibly soft.

The thought of her softness made him hard. A dagger

of guilt twisted in his stomach as he felt his penis thicken and rise beneath the sheets. 'No,' he whispered, urging his body to stop playing these tricks on him. Why did his cock always do that when his mind knew it was wrong?

It wasn't fair, but he couldn't have Anna. He had to quash his burgeoning desire to discover what it was like inside her. He would never feel the hardness of his prick inside the softness of her.

Frustrated, he rolled on to his front and punched the pillow with his fist. His penis ached as he rocked his hips into the mattress, pretending it was Anna. But rubbing himself on the sheet wasn't enough to relieve his need. His balls were heavy and hard, and his brain was hurting. He had to go and see her, to touch her breasts and that secret, hidden place between her legs.

His head pounded as he got out of bed, and he waited for it to stop before going to the door. He peered out to see if anyone was looking, but there was no one there. Still, that never seemed to matter. Whatever he did, his father always seemed to find out about it. His father was even cleverer than he was. He ventured into the corridor. It was quiet, the only sound the slap of his bare feet on the cold lino.

Pausing by the lift, Frank checked the noticeboard. There was a list of staff members and their room numbers, and he looked for Anna's. Seventy-two. One floor up. Ignoring the lift, he went to the stairs.

His penis, fully erect now, bobbed from side to side as he took the stairs two at a time. He wondered what Anna would think of him. Would she gasp, and smile, and tell him he was huge, like the other women did? Like them, she would probably want to touch him, to pull him into that heavenly place between her legs. But he wouldn't let her. He would be strong, this time.

He wondered, as he had done a thousand times before, why it was so wrong to feel such pleasure. Every time he was inside a woman he felt his yearning loneliness melt away. He felt at home with his prick inside a woman's pussy; the movements felt right, as if his body had been made for that purpose. The pain that constantly ached in his soul was soothed by female flesh. And those sounds a woman made – even the ones who almost screamed – they were enchanting. Frank always slept well after nights like those.

And yet it was wrong. He knew that for sure. Striding down the passage towards Anna's door, he shook his head slightly in bewilderment. That pleasure, so glorious, dark and sticky, was also so bad that, once a woman had experienced it, she had to be punished severely.

Carefully, so as not to wake her, he opened the door and padded inside. Leaving the door ajar, so that a triangle of light fell across her face, he knelt at her side. He swore to himself that Anna would not be punished. As much as he wanted to feel what it was like inside her, he wanted to spare her the agony his other lovers had suffered. He would just look at her, maybe touch her – but nothing else.

Her breathing was slow and steady; she'd found the sleep that was so elusive to Frank. She looked incredibly peaceful. Her head was turned to one side, facing him, and her arms were thrown casually across the covers. Her lips were slightly apart. He wished he could see her beautiful green eyes, but they were shut, her long eyelashes dark against the paleness of her face. Lifting his hand, he delicately brushed her face with his fingertips, tracing down her cheekbone on to her lips.

Blinking, her eyes opened. For a moment, as she hovered between sleep and consciousness, she just lay there staring at him. Then, with a jolt that made the headboard bang against the wall, she sat up.

'Frank?' she said.

'Hello, Anna.'

She seemed nervous. She looked over her shoulder at the open door, then leant out of bed and closed it. Frank felt sad as her features merged into the darkness, but then she switched on her bedside lamp, and he could see her even clearer than before. He smiled.

'What are you doing here?' she whispered.

'I wanted to see you.'

She put a hand to her forehead. 'God, you gave me such a fright. I was fast asleep.'

'Sorry.' Reaching up, he moved her hair where it had fallen over one eye. 'I didn't mean to scare you.' His fingers carried on exploring her face. Her skin felt cool and smooth. He ran his touch across her forehead, down her nose, then all around her open mouth.

Watching him, she sighed as she recovered from her shock. 'Do you always sneak up on women when they're sleeping?'

'Yes.' He loved the way her lips moved beneath his fingers as she spoke.

One of her eyebrows arched questioningly. 'Can I ask why?'

What a strange question. 'By the time I finish work, everyone's asleep.'

Her eyebrows moved again, creasing a line across her brow. 'Is that why I've never seen you downstairs – because you work long hours?'

He nodded. 'Mother and Father say it's good for me to work, because my mind is more capable than anyone else's and it needs stimulating. The job I do is the most important one in the whole Institute.'

Anna nodded slowly. 'Yes, your father told me that.'

'Everyone else sleeps, a lot, but I hardly ever do. My brain won't stop. I couldn't sleep tonight. I was thinking about you. I wanted to touch your skin.'

He cradled one side of her face in his hand. Inexplicably, he liked the way his hand looked so big against the delicacy of her face. It made him feel protective and strong; it made him want to keep her safe in his arms.

She seemed to like his hand, too. She rested her fingers

on top of his, tilting her head and closing her eyes for a moment. 'That's a coincidence. I was thinking about you before I went to sleep.'

'You were?'

'Yes.' Her eyes smiled. 'I'm glad you came.'

'Why were you thinking about me?'

It was her turn to seem confused at a question. 'Why? Because ... you're gorgeous. Because ...' She paused, taking in a breath. 'When we met in your father's office I wanted you.'

He swallowed hard; she was just like the other women. Didn't she know it was wrong? 'When you say you want me, do you mean ... this?' He knelt up to show her his cock.

She gasped. With a faint wisp of sound, her mouth opened, and it stayed open as she stared at him. 'Oh God,' she whispered. After an age, her eyes slowly returned to his face, after a slow detour up over his stomach and chest. 'I was wondering whether you were big all over. Some of these heavily muscled guys, they're ...' She nodded downward. 'But you ... you're ...'

He stroked her hair. 'I can't put it inside you.'

Her eyebrows shot up. 'You can't?'

He shook his head sadly. 'It's bad, Anna. I would love to put it inside you, but you would be hurt, later.'

'Oh, I don't think so,' she breathed, squeezing his hand. 'It'll be all right, as long as we take it slowly. You'll have to be gentle with me.'

Her fingers slipped out of his as she shuffled across the bed towards the wall. Frank wondered whether she understood what he was saying. He was about to explain when she dropped the sheet she'd been holding around her body. He saw her breasts, so full and round, and he forgot all about explaining. They couldn't hurt her if he didn't enter her. If he just touched her she'd be all right; he was sure of it.

He climbed into the empty space beside her. Lying down, he propped his head up on one hand. She lay on her back, looking expectantly up at him.

'You're beautiful,' he sighed. Lifting his free hand, he touched her face again. He lightly brushed over her eyelids and lashes, then down her cheek and on to her lips. Her breath was warm on his skin, her tongue even warmer as it darted out and wet his fingertips. Pushing her head up from the pillow, she sucked in two of his fingers up to the first knuckles.

She seemed to be savouring the taste of his fingers, and he would have stayed there longer, letting her roll her tongue around them, were it not for the sight of her breasts urging him onward. Easing his hand away, he trickled his damp touch over her throat, feeling it arch with pleasure as he moved inexorably towards her cleavage.

Her breasts were incredible. Everything about them made him hungry inside: their swooping curves, their full, heavy shapes and the delicious darkness of the wide circles on their tips. Involuntarily, his fingers followed the edge of an areola, trembling slightly at the unbelievable smoothness. Hypnotised, he watched as the soft disc turned from rosy pink to brown, and crinkled into stiffness. Her nipple poked out towards his touch, and as he flicked over it Anna sighed and reached up for him. Putting her hand around his neck, she gently squeezed.

'Oh, Frank, that feels so good.' She pulled his head down. 'Kiss me there.'

Her nipple tasted sweet. Frank sucked on it, closing his eyes for a moment as he realised how good he felt. As she urged his head over to her other breast, he began to feel warm, at last. The cold loneliness was dissolving, washed away by her beauty as it seeped into his own body.

He licked at her breast, feeling the soft mound quiver as he lapped all over it. Anna looked down at him, breathing deeply as she watched him suckle on the darkening peak. Spreading her hand around her curve, she offered it up to him. He fed from her skin. The lovely, faint sounds of her pleasure echoed down his spine and made the hairs stand up on the back of his neck.

She bent her knees and lifted her hips from the bed, reminding Frank of the secret place he hadn't tasted yet. Kissing his way down, he worshipped the invisible, downy hairs on her stomach. He darted his tongue into her belly button. Reluctantly removing his lips from her skin, he sat up, changing his position so that he was kneeling on all fours, facing her feet. As his mouth dipped to her pussy, her heady scent filtered into his brain. For a moment, he felt just the same as when Peter gave him those injections to make him sleep: slightly dizzy, heavy-headed and deeply contented. Then Anna whimpered beneath him, and he woke up and buried his face between her thighs.

Leaning diagonally over her hips, he delved inside her with his long tongue. Her pussy lips were open and wet, and the musk was intoxicating down there. His wide lips crushed against hers as he unfurled his tongue into her tight, hot hole. She levered her pelvis up from the bed, lifting herself into his face as she'd done with her breast. She cried out, quietly, telling him that it was so good and begging him not to stop. He didn't want to stop. He wanted to stay there for ever, kissing and tonguing her honey-soaked pussy and making her squirm with delight.

Wriggling across the bed, she moved until she was lying directly beneath him. Her face must have been just under his straining penis, because he felt her mouth close around the swollen tip. Shocked by the feeling, he paused while her lips moved down his rod. Sucking greedily on him, she grunted with effort, and Frank remembered what he was doing.

Their bodies merged into one. Conscious thought

blurred into a beautiful, jumbled mess of shared sensations. Her small hands were on his heavy balls, gently moulding and squeezing. His tongue was exploring deep inside her, while hers darted around the end of his penis, teasing him and wetting his skin. His face was wet with her, his lungs full of her scent as he inhaled deeply. Her soft curls tickled his chin.

Suddenly, her inner thighs jerked and her mouth slipped from his cock. 'There,' she pleaded. 'Just there, that feels amazing, oh . . . please . . .'

He knew what she was asking for; other women had shown him that tiny, innocuous hump of flesh and told him what to do with it. Sucking hard, he pulled on her scarlet clit with lips eager to please her. The shudders running through her body gave him pleasure too, as he absorbed the aftershocks of her tremor of ecstasy. Waves of warmth rippled over his skin as he pushed her towards her climax. Anna's thighs enclosed his head, tensing hard against his neck as if she wanted to trap him there. Frank nibbled on her tiny, engorged bud, alternating his tentative biting with generous laps of his tongue all along the inner edges of her open labia, and fluid swirls around her clit. Her hands reached between his legs and smoothed over his buttocks, pulling his hips down. She started work on him, sucking and licking as frantically as he was. But before Frank had reached his climax her mouth froze. Her pelvis juddered. He felt the muscles of her inner thighs go into spasm as they clutched at his neck.

As he rolled on to his back, they both sighed loudly, letting out the breath they'd been holding in. Frank watched his fingers for a while as they idly stroked her open thighs and slipped in the wetness spilling from her pussy. Then he looked up her body, and his heart seemed to clench tightly in his chest. She looked so lovely, her cheeks flushed pink and her trembling fingers playing with her breasts. How he longed to be inside her.

'Frank,' she whispered. 'Oh, Frank, I want you, now.'
Heaving herself out of her cloud of pleasure, she crawled
on all fours towards him. 'You're so good,' she said
breathlessly. 'I want to make you feel good.' Straddling
his hips, she bowed her head. Placing her hands on either
side of his waist, she began to lower her open pussy.

'Don't.' He grabbed her, holding her tight. His huge
hands almost fitted around her slender waist. 'Anna, we
mustn't.'

Her eyes flashed with frustration. 'Why not? Why can't
we?'

'You'll be hurt.'

'Frank, I know you're big, but –'

'If I put myself inside you here,' he explained, his
finger poking into her sex, 'they'll see.'

Her eyes flicked to the mirror. 'Who will see, Frank?'

He didn't know who, exactly. But he had to make her
understand. 'They'll see. And then they'll take you away
from me and punish you. They'll hurt you, Anna.' He
shook her gently, emphasising the importance of his
warning. 'You've got to believe me. I'm telling the truth.'

'I'm sure you are,' she said, concerned. 'But I don't
understand. Why would I be punished?'

'Frank.'

Startled, he looked up as the door opened. His mother
and father were standing there, with strange looks on
their faces.

'Frank,' Joan repeated sternly. 'I think it's time you
stopped bothering Anna. Unlike you, she needs her sleep.'

Frank relinquished his grip on Anna and she sat down,
covering up her body. He eased his aching limbs from
the bed. Standing, he felt his legs shaking. He also felt
the ice of his mother's eyes burning into him, and he
guiltily covered his erection. 'Mother ... I was only
kissing her down there – I didn't put my penis inside. I
wasn't doing anything wrong, was I?'

She gave him a pained smile. 'No, Frank. But it's very

late. You've a lot of work to get through tomorrow, and so has Anna.'

His father stepped further into the room. With a hand on Frank's shoulder, he urged him towards the door. 'Come on, son. Your mother will take care of you.' He turned to Anna. 'I'm sorry. He's under a lot of stress. His work really takes it out of him.'

Anna didn't say anything. Her anxious gaze moved from Peter, to Joan, to Frank, and she gave him a sweet smile. 'Goodnight, Frank.'

'Goodnight, Anna.'

His parents gave each other that look as they marched him down the corridor. He knew that look so well, and yet he still didn't know what it meant.

'You won't punish Anna, will you?' he asked them.

'No, son.' Peter guided him into the lift. 'Like your mother said, you two have done nothing wrong. But you must let Anna sleep.'

'I couldn't sleep,' he moaned. 'I can never sleep.'

Peter and Joan shared another look. It was as if they were deciding something, silently, because his mother nodded.

'We'll help you, darling. Don't worry.'

The lift arrived on his floor. They went to his room, and he got back into bed. Joan straightened the rumpled sheets over his tense body. 'You like Anna, don't you?'

'Yes. She's beautiful.'

She smoothed down his hair. 'Not as beautiful as you, darling. You're perfect.'

Peter crouched down by the bed. Straightening Frank's arm, he tapped several times on the inside of his elbow. Then he pulled a syringe from his lab-coat pocket. There was a pinprick. Frank watched as the plunger pushed the viscous liquid down the needle and into his brain. Sleep oozed over him.

'You can rest now.'

The voice was faint and distorted. He thought of Anna's green eyes.

Chapter 8

'*S*imon!' Anna beamed as he came in, then remembered the cameras and tried to look nonchalant.

He returned her smile. 'Sorry I wasn't around yesterday. I got . . . tied up.'

'I wasn't here either. I was working for Peter,' she said, trying to show him with a flash of her eyes that all was not well. She got up from her desk and went to his side. 'I started typing up your notes, but there was a bit where I couldn't read your handwriting. Could you just take a look at it?' She handed him a dossier.

'Which bit?'

She pointed to the small handwritten note she'd inserted in the file. 'You were right to make us whisper,' she'd written. 'There are microphones and cameras everywhere.'

Simon glanced up at her, his eyebrows raised in surprise. 'My handwriting isn't that bad, Anna.' He read out a section of the notes. 'Is that clear, now?'

'Yes, thank you.' She took the dossier back. Slipping a hand around Simon's neck, she kissed him on the cheek, by his ear. 'Something weird happened last night,' she whispered, in a voice so faint she wasn't sure he would hear it.

But Simon got the message. A smile eased across his mouth as he put his hands around Anna's waist. He kissed her on the lips, his mouth full of the passion of their night together. His tongue slithered on to hers, and then his lips moved down, over her chin and on to her throat. His fingers held the back of her head and tangled in her hair as he smothered her neck with kisses.

'I met Frank,' she breathed, bowing her head so that her hair swung forward and hid her from the camera. She aimed her hushed words at his ear. 'Do you know him?'

He nibbled on her earlobe. 'He's Peter and Joan's son.'

Anna pulled his head up to face hers. Resting her lips on his, she whispered into his mouth. 'He came to my room last night. He was acting very strangely.'

'How do you mean?'

Unable to resist his open mouth, she thrust her tongue inside and stole another kiss. 'He refused to fuck me,' she breathed, when she'd finished sucking on his lips.

Simon looked bemused. 'Anna, we've a lot of work to catch up on,' he said, raising his voice back to its normal level. 'We'll have to carry on with this later, in my room.'

She smiled, knowing that Simon would be looking forward to 'later' as much as she was. He wasn't quite as flawless as Frank, but he made a very attractive confidant.

'So, what did he do to you?'

A quiver of wicked excitement jumped from her belly to her sex. They were lying on the bed, facing each other, with their heads propped up on their hands. Anticipation glittered in Simon's brown eyes. Remembering how he'd enjoyed her stories of what Galloway had done to her, Anna smirked. And hoping that Galloway was watching and listening in the monitoring room, she spoke too softly for him to hear. 'I woke up and he was in my room,' she whispered. 'He was naked.'

'What's he like?'

Was that a hint of jealousy she detected in his face? 'Oh, he's gorgeous,' she crooned. 'He's got the most perfect body. He's huge . . . all over.'

Simon pinched her nipple so hard the pain made her gasp. 'Do you prefer him to me?'

She thought for a moment, teasing him. 'Well . . . he's the most beautiful man I've ever seen. But there's something not quite right about him. I mean – I was a bit disappointed. He wouldn't . . ."put it inside me", as he phrased it.'

It was Simon's turn to tease. 'Perhaps he didn't fancy you.'

'Oh, I think he did. He spent ages touching me, licking me –'

'Where?' Simon's voice rasped urgently.

'Here.' She trailed her fingertips over her forehead, nose and mouth, following the path Frank had taken down her body. Her hand trickled down her throat and spread over the curve of her breast. Simon grunted and rested his fingers over hers as she squeezed her pliant flesh. 'Here,' she continued, easing her palm out from under his. Caressing a line down over her stomach, she moved over her pubic hair and cupped her mound. She could feel herself throbbing with anticipation. 'And here,' she breathed.

Simon's touch trailed behind hers. Gently pushing her hand away, he closed his fingers over her mound. Anna lifted her knee to give him room, wrapping her top leg over his.

'He touched you here?' Simon asked, licking his lips salaciously.

'With his mouth.' Her body tensed as Simon rubbed a finger along her sex, prising open her labia. 'He put his tongue inside me.'

Simon slid a finger into her warm pussy.

'He made me come.'

163

Another finger entered her. Slowly, as he held her gaze in the seductive warmth of his, he began to pump his hand in and out of her. Tension gave way to simmering pleasure, and Anna let out a sigh that seemed to come from somewhere deep inside.

'Did you moan?' Simon whispered.

'Yes.'

'Did you beg him not to stop?'

'Mmm.' Her answer was smothered by the heel of his hand and the hot friction it was causing on her clit.

'Were you very wet? Did you wet his face?'

'Mmm . . . oh.' Delirious at the mixture of memory and reality, she flopped on to her back. She flung her arms up, holding on to her soft hair with trembling fingers. Her thighs flopped down on to the bed, open flat; open for him.

'Did you want his cock inside you?' A third finger joined the two already exploring her slippery sex. His face loomed over hers. He bit her lower lip. 'Did you want his cock, Anna? Did you want that huge cock inside you? Did you beg him to fuck you hard?'

Anna moaned pitifully as he thrust his hand up into her pussy, banging against her clit.

'Hello, Anna.'

Simon froze; Anna jumped with fright. 'Jesus Christ, Frank,' she gasped, clutching her heart. 'Why do you always sneak up on people like that?'

Simon's fingers slipped out of her as he rolled away from her, following Anna's startled gaze. 'Frank!' he said brightly. 'We were just talking about you.' He glanced back at Anna, giving her a reassuring wink. 'Don't just stand there, come in. And close the door behind you – there's a draught.'

Hesitantly, his eyes already drifting over Anna's nakedness, Frank shut the door and stepped inside. 'She's beautiful.'

Simon sat up. 'Yes, she is.'

Frank continued to stare at her body. Anna looked at him, wondering why he always walked around naked, and drooling over the size of his erection. Simon looked from one to the other and patted the bed. 'Sit down, Frank.'

Very carefully, as if Anna might run away at any moment and deprive him of the view, Frank perched on the edge of the mattress beside her knee. 'Do you think she's beautiful?' he asked Simon, addressing Anna's breast.

Simon caught her eye. 'She's gorgeous,' he agreed, smiling naughtily. 'She likes you, too. She was telling me how nice it felt when you were touching her. Why don't you touch her again?'

Frank raised a huge, heavy hand. Anna held her breath as he tenderly circled the sensitive tip of her breast. His fingers were so long, his arms so muscular, his skin so deliciously tanned, it was like being fondled by a fantasy. She itched to feel his strong body pressing down on hers.

'I like to touch her down there,' Simon said, combing his fingers in her pubic hair.

Frank's eyes dropped. 'It's so soft, down there.'

'Soft and wet,' Simon added. 'Feel how wet she is. Put your finger inside her.'

Simon smoothed her hair as she whimpered. As Frank's long finger edged its way between her labia, Simon's finger reached into her open mouth. He stroked her tongue, and Anna could taste her musk on his skin. Frank stroked the inner walls of her pussy, and more of her scent filtered into the air. In silence apart from her sighs, both men worshipped her prone body. Anna looked from one to the other, and felt her brain melting with the thrill of it all. Her mind struggled with the sums: four hands, two tongues, two pricks, one woman.

It added up to insanity. It was almost too much to bear, just having them both touching her. As well as their attention, she could almost feel the hidden eye of the camera peering at her. The thought of someone watching in the monitoring room, eyes fixed to the screen and penis thickening between his legs, added another pressure on to her already overloaded senses. Anything more and she might faint.

But Simon didn't know – or didn't care – that she was on the edge of madness. Sliding his hands beneath her shoulders, he sat her up. He pushed her forward until she was on all fours, diagonally across the bed. Her head was hanging over Frank's lap, and a potent mix of fear and deep, dark longing brewed inside her as she saw his penis grow harder still. As his thick rod bobbed up towards his taut stomach, a drop of moisture oozed from the tiny, blind eye. Anna had had lots of men, but never had she seen such a long, thick muscle. It had to be nine or ten inches. Her mouth and pussy flooded with the juice of anticipation.

Behind her, Simon held on to her hips. The bed bounced as he shuffled closer to her. Anna felt his penis nudge at her open sex.

'What are you doing to her?' Frank asked.

Anna looked up at him. The worry in his voice was echoed in his deep-blue eyes.

'I'm going to fuck her.' Simon laughed. 'What do you think I'm doing?'

'Don't.' Frank's hand closed around Anna's wrist. He looked imploringly into her eyes, then over her head at Simon. 'You can't do that. Don't you know it's wrong?'

Simon plunged his prick inside her. Groaning as he filled her, Anna arched her spine at the feeling. 'Does that look wrong to you?' Simon asked.

Frank shook his head forlornly, silently pleading with Anna.

'It's all right,' she gasped. 'I promise you, it isn't wrong. It's . . .' She lost the will to speak as the pure essence of pleasure was pumped into her veins. Simon took deep, deliberate strokes, rubbing the tight walls of her vagina with his cock. Anna felt so full she couldn't imagine what it would feel like to have Frank inside her, stretching her soft pussy with his hardness.

Bending her elbows, she dipped her head into his lap. As Simon grunted out a steady rhythm, she licked the swollen plum of Frank's cock. His saltiness hit her taste-buds and sparked a hunger in her belly. Sliding her lips around his meat, she lowered her mouth until she felt him at the back of her throat. With only half his length inside her, her jaw was already aching with his width. She sucked hard on him, trying to ease his tension away with her lips and tongue. She licked up and down, from the weeping tip to the root. His penis seemed to be straining to get away from his heavy, hairless balls. Anna nuzzled him there, and she heard him whimper above her. The sound seemed incongruous coming from such a massive man.

She heard Simon too. He was getting noisier, and his pace had lost its measured beat and was turning frantic. His fingers cut into her hips as he levered himself deeper and harder into her yearning flesh. Shuddering, he released his climax.

Barely giving her time to catch her breath, he was withdrawing from her pussy and manhandling her again. Pulling at her shoulders and pushing her rump, he turned her round until her sticky sex was facing Frank's bewildered face. Anna could feel warm juices trickling down her inner thighs. She could feel a pulse beating in her clit as she thought again of how big Frank was. But she wanted, and needed, to have him inside her. She braced herself, watching as Simon folded his legs under-neath her face. His penis was shining wet. At the back of her neck, his hand gently pushed her downwards; he wanted her mouth, now.

'Fuck her,' he suggested to Frank.

'I told you . . . it's wrong.'

167

Anna looked over her shoulder at him. 'Frank ... please ...'

Simon shook his outstretched hand at Frank. 'She wants you, can't you see that? Look at her beautiful pussy. Look at her fantastic arse ... Don't you want her?'

Frank seemed to waver. A fingertip explored the valley between her spread cheeks, running over her anus and down to her slick, hairy lips. 'I do want her,' he said under his breath.

'So?' Simon was almost screaming with frustration.

Frank's eyes cleared as he came to a decision. Anna collapsed with need as he stood up and walked to the door. 'I mustn't do it,' he mumbled. 'They'll take her away. They'll hurt her.'

'Who will?' Anna begged for an answer. She turned to Simon, who looked strangely shifty. 'What's he talking about?'

'No idea,' he said.

Anna jumped from the bed. Her legs almost gave way. Snatching at Frank's thick wrist, she steadied herself. 'Frank, you've got to explain what you're talking about.'

He looked uncertainly at Simon.

'Simon's my friend. Just tell me what you mean. Who will take me away? Why?'

'I don't know who,' he said, looking earnestly into her eyes. 'I don't know why. But every time I do that –' he nodded towards the bed '– the woman I do it with has to suffer afterwards.'

Anna reached up to stroke his furrowed brow. He looked so upset, his eyes so full of sorrow, that she felt a pang of maternal protectiveness towards him. 'Calm down, Frank,' she soothed. 'No one's going to hurt me.'

'They hurt all the others.' He closed his eyes tightly as if the memory was painful. 'I put my penis inside the other women and they took them away to the other place. They held them prisoner and tortured them.' His eyelids slowly opened again. 'I don't want you to be punished, like they were. I like you.' He put his hand on his chest, where his heart lay. 'I like you, in here. I don't want to see you in pain. You're safe, as long as I don't put my penis in you.'

In the long silence that followed, a sense of foreboding oozed over Anna. Simon seemed uncomfortable with what Frank had said; stranger still, he neither questioned nor denied it. What and where was the 'other place' Frank mentioned? What was the reason for the torture and punishments he spoke of? And why did Frank talk in such a strange, stilted way?

The faint creak of the door opening broke the silence. Peter's clothes – his clinical lab coat, his pristine slate-grey suit beneath – were quite a shock among all that sweaty nakedness.

'Anna,' he leered, holding out his hand. 'Please come with me.'

'You're not going to –'

'No one's going to hurt her,' Peter snapped at Frank. 'Like I keep telling you, you've done nothing wrong. Now go to bed.'

'He's been under a lot of stress.' Peter grimaced. 'I do apologise if he's been acting a little . . . oddly.'

Anna smiled nervously at him, and then at Joan. Joan ignored her smile and looked disdainfully at Anna's bare body, pursing her lips contemptuously as if Anna was a fallen woman. Perched uncomfortably on a hard wooden chair in front of the long table, Anna shivered with cold and embarrassment. The last time she'd seen this room was on the day of her interview. Then, a whole row of scientists had studied her from behind the table. The situation was no less tense with only Peter and Joan sitting there.

'Frank is involved in our most advanced study yet. Unfortunately, I think the stress is getting to him.'

Anna nodded. 'He did say he couldn't sleep.'

169

'His mind is so brilliant, so active. Many geniuses find it difficult to sleep.'

It was hard to believe Frank was a genius, although perhaps that would explain the way he spoke. Anna had met hyper-intelligent people before, and they did tend to be a little odd. It came from spending their lives shut away within their infinitely superior intellects; they lost the ability to deal with the average person, and to speak on their level.

'Frank doesn't realise it, but he gets very tired from so little rest. He's even been known to hallucinate from lack of sleep.' Peter tapped his fingers together thoughtfully. 'Did he seem confused at all to you?'

'Well, he was talking about a place where women are taken to be punished.'

Peter didn't flinch. 'How did that come up?'

'He . . .' She paused, wondering how Joan would react. 'He wouldn't fuck me. I asked him why not, and he told me it was wrong – that I'd be taken to some sort of prison cell and tortured for it.'

Peter glanced at his wife, smiling fondly as if his child had said something enchanting. 'Like I said, Frank is prone to flights of fancy when he's exhausted.'

'So what he told me is all made up?'

Peter's eyes glittered secretively. 'Anna, no one at the Institute is forced into anything they don't want to do.'

That seemed a rather obtuse way to answer. 'So I wouldn't be punished if I slept with your son?'

'Oh, Anna.' He chuckled patronisingly. 'You're a clever girl. You should have worked out by now that sexual activity is positively encouraged here. You can go to bed with whoever you want.'

'Whoever will have you,' Joan muttered bitterly.

'And this "other place" – it doesn't exist except in Frank's imagination?'

Peter eyed her for a moment, weighing her up. 'Some

170

of our staff get to visit that place, but only if they want to.'

Anna was intrigued. 'Can I see it?'

'You will see it, one day.' He stood up and strode into the centre of the room, to Anna's chair. 'But not yet. I don't think you're ready.'

Anna's mind was in a whirl. She only vaguely noticed as Peter gently pulled her up from her seat and walked her towards the medical trolley.

'Pop yourself up here for us, Anna. We need to take a quick look at you.'

She wondered whether this was going to be the same sort of check-up she'd enjoyed the other day. She soon had her answer. Standing at the foot of the bed, Peter reached under the trolley and produced a pair of black leather straps, one at each corner. He fastened each ankle, then moved to her head and buckled her wrists so her body was spread-eagled in an X.

Joan's low heels tapped across the floor. Her cold face showed nothing as she looked at Anna harnessed to the bed, and it was impossible to tell what she was thinking. Emotionless, she seemed to be waiting.

'Take her temperature,' Peter said, and Joan sprung into action. Plucking a thermometer from her coat pocket – a thermometer as big as the one Peter had poked into Anna's arse – Joan leant over Anna's hip. Without any hesitation, she inserted the glass rod into Anna's sex.

The memory of Simon's prick was still embedded in her flesh, and the thermometer was thin and cold in comparison. It made Anna gasp. Husband and wife both peered at her, their faces close to her open pussy, and their clinical attention made Anna gasp again. Like every other encounter she'd had in the Institute, this was unbelievable. She was restrained, powerless to escape and totally at their mercy; and it felt incredible. Just like the anticipation of Frank's cock, it was frightening and exhilarating at the same time.

171

'Did you want Frank?'

It took Anna a moment to realise Joan was talking to her. 'Huh? Sorry?'

Joan tutted impatiently, pulling the thermometer out and inspecting the reading. 'Did you want Frank?' she snapped. 'You said he wouldn't fuck you – did you want him to?'

Anna looked to Peter for help. 'Tell the truth,' he urged.

'He's very handsome,' Anna said, wincing as Joan fingered her labia. Her hands were quick and business-like, and unbearably stimulating.

'Were you worried about how big he was? Have you ever taken a lover that big?'

'No. I was a bit worried, but . . .'

'But like all women, you were greedy. You wanted that huge prick inside you.'

Anna caught her breath as Joan teased her clit, pinching the nerve-endings into burning arousal.

'Are you thinking about him now? Your labia are swollen. Your clitoris is engorged and you're streaming with lubrication.'

Anna swallowed hard. It was impossible to say exactly what she was thinking about. She couldn't distinguish one lucid thought amongst the scrambled mess of her brain. Peter's avid attention, Joan's deft touch and her tone of voice, Frank's prick, Simon's prick, humiliation, submission – disparate desires and emotions all merged into one bizarre realisation. Whatever Joan and Peter were going to do to her, she wanted it.

Joan crouched down, disappearing from view while she fumbled under the trolley. When she straightened up she was wielding something black and menacing, and there was undisguised and sadistic pleasure on her face. 'I'm going to show you, young lady, what it feels like to take such a big cock. Peter,' she barked. Peter moved behind his wife. Wrapping his hands around her waist,

172

he lifted her compact body so she could kneel on the bed between Anna's ankles. Shuffling forward on her knees, Joan lowered the huge black dildo. 'You young women are all the same – think you can take it. Let's just see whether you can take this.'

Straining her neck, Anna looked down her fettered body. Hovering between her open thighs, Joan's tiny hands brought the glossy black phallus closer. Peter reached over and held Anna's pussy lips open. All three watched, transfixed, as the distended tip of the huge rubber rod eased inside her sex.

Joan pushed it in slowly, easing it into Anna's pussy inch by inch. It was painful pleasure, the way her inner muscles were being gradually stretched. It was unendurable agony and inconceivable ecstasy. Anna thanked God it wasn't a real penis: a man wouldn't have been so slow. A man would have rammed himself into her vagina and sent her rigid with shock.

It was still a shock to feel full up to her eyeballs. And it was another shock when Joan stood up and picked her way over Anna's body until she stood over her face, a foot either side of her neck. Beneath her lab coat, Anna could see the dark auburn triangle of her pubic hair.

'You're not the only slut who walks about without panties on,' Joan cackled, mocking Anna's surprise. Kneeling again, she hitched up her white coat and lowered her pussy to Anna's face. Anna barely had time to gulp a lungful of air before her mouth was smothered with Joan's sex.

Trapped, she had no choice but to do what Frank had done to her. But as she unfurled her tongue into the succulent folds of Joan's flesh, she found, to her amazement, that the sensation was quite wonderful. Apart from the intoxicating smell and the delicious taste of sex, the yielding softness of Joan's pussy made Anna's mouth water. She'd never been so close to a woman, and now she could see why so many of her lovers liked to spend hours with their faces buried between her thighs. She loved the complex beauty of the creases and folds, the way Joan's labia swelled as Anna opened them with her tongue; and she loved the slipperiness coating the satin skin just inside Joan's pouting lips. Apart from the physical pleasure, there was mental pleasure at the soft, animal-like sounds Joan was making above her. In that instant, Anna understood how it must feel to be a man, prising ecstasy from a woman's body and making her cry out using just his lips and tongue. It gave her a sense of power. She longed to do the other things men do. Her wrists chafed against their bindings as she tried to free herself. She wanted to slide her hands over Joan's buttocks, to finger her tightly closed anus, to tweak the hard tips of her breasts.

But Joan's body was being lifted away. Peter carried her around to the foot of the bed and sat her on the edge. He pushed her down until her back was flat on the bed, her torso fitting neatly between Anna's open legs. Peter's greedy eyes alternated between his two women. His hands slid around Joan's thighs and he propped her legs up against his chest. Joan's slender ankles flexed by his ears as he pushed up her lab coat. Anna could see his prick looming towards his wife's wet pussy, and then it was slowly disappearing inside her. Standing still, he rubbed his hands up and down Joan's thin legs and smiled menacingly up at Anna. 'Turn her on,' he said.

Joan reached up above her head to where the dildo lay buried in Anna's hole. Anna thought she heard her laugh cruelly as she grabbed the rod in one hand and twisted its base with the other. From that instant, all Anna could hear was an angry, throbbing drone which shook the tightly stretched walls of her pussy and reverberated in her soul. Helpless, her eyes closed as the noise took over. It was mind-blowing; already completely full, there was no room inside her for the merciless buzzing. It was more than she could take.

Her pitiful crying seemed to give impetus to Peter's warped mind. He began to thrust into his wife. Joan's sighs of pleasure mingled with his grunts of effort. Caught in their own rocking desire, they ignored Anna's pleading.

Marooned on the bed, assaulted by her own senses, Anna gave up the struggle. Her whole body sighed as she surrendered. The vibrator's throaty buzz screamed its way into her head, the intolerable noise flushing out a half-formed, impossible idea – that what Peter had said to her in the monitoring room was right. She belonged at the Institute.

Chapter Nine

*A*nna swam slow, measured lengths of the lukewarm pool. Her body was heavy with the memory of last night; every muscle seemed to have been strained. But as she eased herself through the water her limbs began to loosen and her mind to clear.

She had to forget about the four lovers she'd been with yesterday. As much as she wanted to wallow in the memory of Joan and Peter, Simon and Frank, she had more pressing thoughts to turn to. This was her first complete day off, and she had to make some progress with her investigation. How she was going to manage that with the cameras watching, she had no idea – so she had to concentrate on finding a way around that obstacle.

Mike, as usual, had begged her to be careful when she'd rung him earlier. He'd been worried as she hadn't phoned for a couple of days. He'd have been even more worried, she thought, if she had told him the intimate details of the previous two nights at the Institute. Instead, she'd given him an edited version, concentrating on Frank and her suspicion that he could be a clone. But Mike had assured her that that was impossible; he'd spoken in depth to leading genetic engineers, and every one had told him that human cloning was still a long way off. The technology wasn't in place yet and, besides, there were strict laws to ensure the procedure would never be allowed. It seemed to be the one area all Mike's contacts from the scientific community agreed on. Cloning cells and vegetables, and even animals, could have some benefits; and engineering genes to eradicate hereditary diseases was an aim they all shared. But trying to replicate a human was like playing God, and it raised too many ethical dilemmas. 'Once you start along that road, there's no way of stopping,' an eminent professor had said to Mike. 'Pretty soon, you'd have parents wanting to design their unborn babies. You'd have ambitious mothers breeding children for their intelligence or their athletic prowess. It would be madness, and it would create a class divide far worse than the one we've got now. We'd end up with a genetically engineered super-race – stronger, cleverer and altogether superior to the rest of us. Hitler had the same idea. No one will ever be allowed to carry on where he left off.'

Anna shivered in the water, despite the soothing temperature of the pool. It seemed her theory about the Institute's work was wrong. She hoped so. But if it was, then what was the real reason for all those experiments which couldn't be explained? And why was the Institute named after Mary Shelley?

She climbed out of the pool and went to get showered. As the strong jets of heat pummelled her skin, she tried to work methodically through what she'd discovered so far. But the facts she had stored in her brain only threw up more questions. There had to be a link between the way Peter and Joan treated her and the Institute's secrets. Perhaps the answer lay in that 'other place' – the place Peter had told her she would see when she was ready. As far as Anna was concerned, she was ready now.

She dried herself. Leaving her hair damp, she got dressed again in her tracksuit and trainers and made her way to the entrance hall. The front door clicked open in recognition of her security bracelet and she stepped outside.

She jogged down to the perimeter fence and then followed its wide circle around the building. Looking up at the huge white monstrosity, she mapped out what went where. The ground floor was taken care of, as were the next three floors which housed the labs, offices and bedrooms. She had walked around those levels and knew they hid nothing. But the top floor of the Institute was a different matter. Anna had seen the office Peter had used for her interview, as well as the adjoining rooms: the one she'd been in last night on one side and the monitoring room on the other. But what else was up there, lurking behind the blank, windowless walls? Whatever it was, she hadn't seen it during her stint at the monitors. It had to be the only part of the building that wasn't covered by closed-circuit TV.

She jogged around the building once more, deciding on her plan of action. If she explored, she would be seen in the monitoring room. She hadn't been shown the top floor of the Institute during her guided tour; but then again, she'd never been told it was out of bounds. If someone caught her snooping about she could always say she was looking for Peter or Simon or Frank. It was a chance she'd have to take, because she needed something to crack open this story with. She needed hard evidence.

Hoping she would find some, and wanting to be prepared for it, she ran around the back of the building to the car park. Hovering, she waited while the distant camera slowly swooped away from her before sprinting to Mike's car. Hidden from view, she crouched down beside the passenger door and felt underneath the car. Fixed on to the undercarriage was a small plastic casing. She undid the catch, slid the little box to one side and prised out the tiny camcorder hidden inside. It was small enough to fit in the palm of her hand, and she kept it there while she ran back round to the front of the building, slipping it into her pocket as she went back inside.

There were a few people milling about in the hallway, although not as many as Anna would have expected. This was a day off for all of the staff, and yet Anna had barely seen anyone since breakfast. The pool had been empty. The staff normally congregated in the hall to chat and discuss which of the leisure facilities to use, but today there were only three people standing by the noticeboard. The place seemed deserted, and if Anna hadn't known better she'd have assumed everyone had gone out. But as Peter had said on Anna's first day, none of the staff went outside much. As far as Anna could see, only a handful ever got any fresh air at all. Like her, a few jogged or walked round the fence, and they would wave at her as she'd casually return from her telephone calls with Mike. It was strange to be in the Lake District and never venture out of the research centre. What kept them here, these young, attractive people? What made them so contented? And where were they all today?

Anna walked past the waiting lift and went up the back staircase. She was out of breath again by the time she reached the top floor, and she peered through the window in the top of the door while she recovered, checking to see who was around. There was no one. She put her hand in her pocket and wrapped her fingers tightly round her camera. She stepped through the door.

It was pointless creeping, so she strode purposefully down the passageway, past the interview room. As she reached the corner of the building, she was surprised to find that the corridor running at right angles to this one was partitioned off. It was separated by another doorway and, unlike all the other doors in the Institute, this one was black. It looked forbidding, but when Anna tested it she found it was open. It was irresistible.

The corridor beyond was black, too. Walls, ceiling, floor; the only lights filtering through the darkness were thin slivers of yellow coming from beneath the doors lining the right-hand wall. Anna stepped up to the first one. Pressing her ear to the door, she felt her blood chill at the sounds she heard on the other side. Feeling something move slightly against her ear, she peered through the gloom. Seeing with her fingers, she made out a letterbox-shaped flap at eye level. With her heart in her throat, she lifted the flap.

What she saw inside that room forced the breath out of her in a rush which was deafening in the thick silence of the passageway. For a nerve-shattering instant, she thought that Frank was right: there was torture being inflicted at the Institute, and these were the torture chambers. But as she stood, transfixed, she realised that the people inside were not in pain at all. What she was witnessing was torture of a different kind.

Anna recognised the woman. She was tall, with dark chocolate skin, a lean body and high, slight breasts. She worked in the lab next to Simon's, and she beamed at Anna whenever they passed each other. But today her wide smile was set in a grimace. Her teeth were clenched, her eyes closed, her eyebrows dipping together. Her face and body were taut with agony; the agony of too much pleasure.

She was strapped into a device which hung from the ceiling. Her slender wrists were held above her head, fixed into cuffs attached to heavy chains. A complex leather cage held her torso suspended, pushing up her breasts where the dark-red leather bands crisscrossed her body. More bands wound around her open thighs, and chains attached to these sections held her upper legs parallel to the floor while her lower legs dangled free. It was a type of swing, and the man standing between her spread thighs was using it as such. While he stood still, he pushed and pulled on the chains, moving her body towards and away from him. Every time he swung her close, her pussy enveloped his cock; when the backward swing took her away again, their bodies were parted. It was a complicated way to fuck, but as Anna watched she understood the pleasure. Not only was the woman helpless, a prisoner in her leather harness, but as the momentum gathered force their bodies were slammed together more and more fiercely. The girl groaned through gritted teeth as her partner's cock was plunged deeper and harder inside her with every swing. Anna couldn't keep her eyes off the place where the two of them joined, where his angrily rearing prick slid remorselessly in and out of her scarlet folds of flesh. Anna's pussy yearned to feel what that woman felt. Her knickers grew wet as her hunger spread down from her belly and across her hips.

With a jolt, she remembered why she was there. She needed evidence, and here was the perfect opportunity to capture one part of the Institute's secret activities. Fumbling with her tiny video recorder, she flicked the switch and held it up to the hatch. She filmed for a moment, then put it on pause, moving on to the next doorway.

Through every hatch there was another scene of torturous ecstasy. Here, being played out, were desires Anna had only dreamt about, and even then only in her subconscious. Perhaps her subconscious had been trying to tell her something. Perhaps the manipulative games she played with men had become boring, and her mind was craving darker distractions. Whatever the reason, the bizarre images flitting across her eyes were sending sparks of longing flashing over her skin.

Trying to concentrate on her work, she attempted to distance herself from what she was seeing and to push her own thoughts away. But it was impossible. As she watched the men using the harnessed women, she could barely keep her tiny camera steady. If this was the place Peter had promised to show her, she wanted to experience it now. But she knew she was kidding herself when she silently promised that her curiosity was only for the sake of her investigation. Deep inside, in the twisted, black core of her soul, she knew beyond doubt that her curiosity was rooted in her own selfish pleasure. Her panties were seeping with warmth, and that had nothing to do with her excitement at finding her way into the Institute's covert activities.

She reached the final door, her fingers trembling as she raised the hatch. A whimper curled from her lips at what she saw. Pressing the camera's lens right up to the opening, she dropped her other hand. Easing her palm beneath the waistband of her tracksuit pants, she slipped her fingers into the heat of her knickers.

So far, it seemed, Anna had only been given a hint of Joan's hidden sexuality. Here, the woman's most depraved desires were on open display. Blindfolded, she was dressed in a black PVC leotard with holes for her breasts and pussy. She was lying on her back, on a black leather stretcher in the centre of the small, dark room. Trussed like an animal, both her hands and ankles were cuffed together. Ropes hoisted her arms and legs straight up to the ceiling. Her buttocks were on the edge of the bed, the PVC stretched tight and shiny over her rump. A man dressed from head to toe in rubber was standing at the foot of the bed, thrusting into her sex. Only his cock and balls were visible, protruding from his catsuit as if they were the only parts of his body that mattered. At Joan's head, kneeling over her as she had done to Anna, a similarly dressed man was pumping his rigid cock into Joan's mouth. Joan was being used, and by the sound of it she was having the time of her life.

One of the men was coming, grunting so loudly that Anna never heard a sound behind her. The next thing she knew, the camera had been ripped out of her fingers and a hand had been clasped to her mouth.

'Don't say a word,' Peter whispered. 'They're lost in

their own fantasy world. You'll ruin it if they hear you talking.' His breath was hot on her ear. 'I'm going to take my hand away now. You're not to speak until I say so, do you understand?'

Anna nodded. Peter's hand eased its grip on her face and fell down to her waist. Turning her round, he guided her away from the hatch and towards the end of the corridor. Anna's pulse raced out of control as he showed her through a door into another passageway.

'They can't hear us in here,' he said. His eyes burnt hot and cold. 'Now, would you care to tell me what you're doing? And don't lie,' he added, as Anna opened her mouth. 'I'll know if you're lying.'

This corridor was painted black too, but there were small lights overhead. Peter was standing directly underneath one, and it cast dramatic shadows on his face. God, she prayed, if you exist, please help me out of this one.

'I . . . I wanted to find the place you told me about last night.' She looked imploringly up at Peter, begging him to be lenient. She was telling the truth, after all; if not the whole truth, then half, at least. 'I'm sorry. Maybe I shouldn't have come, but . . . I was curious.'

'No, you shouldn't have come. I told you, you would see this place when the time was right. You're not ready yet.'

'I'm sorry,' she whispered, scared of the menace in his voice.

'What's this?' he asked, brandishing the camera.

'I . . . I brought it with me when I came to the Institute . . . I . . .'

How could she explain it? Terrified, convinced that her cover must have been blown, she watched as Galloway studied the little silver box. He fiddled with the tiny buttons, stared into the lens, then seemed to realise what it was. Holding the viewfinder to his eye, he pointed the camcorder at Anna. When he lowered his hand, there was a nasty, crooked smile on his lips.

'Well, Anna. Either you're a spy, sent from another lab to get information –' he took a step towards her '– or, you're a well-equipped, voyeuristic little pervert.' Anna gasped as he shoved his hand inside her pants. His middle finger slid easily up into her wet pussy. 'And judging by the state of your knickers, I'd say you're a pervert. Am I right?'

Anna was speechless. She couldn't believe she'd got away with it, again. Peter seemed to want to believe she'd brought the camera with her because she was a voyeur. Fixed to Galloway by his probing finger and his searching eyes, she could do nothing but wait for him to speak again.

'You're even kinkier than I first thought, Anna. I admire your enterprising spirit, bringing your camcorder along to fuel your warped imagination. You were specifically told not to bring anything with you when you came here. And yet you deliberately flouted the rules. Your desire to watch must be very strong.' He took his finger out of her pants and rubbed the tip across her lower lip. 'Perhaps you are ready for this. What do you think?'

She didn't know. Part of her wanted to surrender herself to whatever cruelty Galloway had in mind. Part of her felt afraid. This was his territory she'd stumbled into, and what he did with her now was his decision. Whatever she said wasn't going to influence him.

'You've integrated well here, Anna. But are you prepared for the next step? Are you strong enough to find out what we're hiding in this Institute – what you're hiding, in your mind?' He kissed her forehead with fatherly tenderness. 'Are you prepared to give yourself to us?'

His hushed voice sent a shudder down her spine. Anna didn't feel prepared for anything, and yet she knew there was no turning back. She had to carry on, not only for the investigation, for Mike and the programme, and journalistic acclaim, but because she wanted to. 'I'm ready,' she said. 'Peter, please. I'm strong. Let me take the next step.'

He seemed to be mulling it over, his eyes narrowing slightly as he stared down into her face. Then, all of a sudden, his decision was made. He strode off to the end of the short passage. 'Get dressed in those clothes. When you're ready, come through here.' He left her alone, closing the door behind him.

In a daze, unsure of what she'd just agreed to, she moved to the wall Peter had waved at. There was a row of pegs running along it. Hanging from each one was a black outfit of some kind, hard to make out in the dim light. With trembling fingers, Anna got one set of clothes down and moved under a light to look at it. There were seamed fishnet stockings and suspenders, a satin basque and a short, straight skirt with a slit up the back. Anna kicked off her trainers and got rid of her tracksuit and underwear. Leaving her pussy bare – as she presumed she was supposed to – she unrolled the stockings and fastened them. They only came halfway up her thighs, several inches beneath the tiny skirt. Seeing the suspenders pulling on the nylons was distinctly tarty; but then, as she put on the basque, she realised that was the point. The satin corset was tight-fitting, and underwired for support beneath her heavy breasts. But there was nothing to cover her breasts, and they perched provocatively over the scooped edge of the material. Stepping into the unfeasibly high, shiny black stilettos waiting under the empty peg, she felt like a dirty wanton displaying her wares. And she liked it: she liked the way her calves tightened; the way her breasts were pushed up, on show; and the way her naked buttocks would be seen up the split in her skirt. As she opened the door to the next room, her barely covered pussy began to throb in anticipation of the effect she would have on whoever was inside.

She had expected to make an entrance, but not one

185

head turned as she walked in. So this was where everyone was, she thought, looking at the rows and rows of seats. It was a lecture theatre of sorts, with everyone sitting in their lab coats as they had done on her first day. But this time, the audience wasn't looking at her. It was no surprise that her entrance hadn't caused a stir; the audience had something far more shocking to look at.

This room was long and thin, stretching the length of the corridor Anna had just walked down. The sex chambers all backed on to this room. She realised now why the small cells each had huge mirrors filling their entire back walls. These mirrors were made of one-way glass, giving the audience a secret view into every chamber. They could see into every room at once; it was like a cinema, with seven small screens instead of one big one. But these weren't films; they were real scenarios being acted out by real people. And the audience was more deeply involved than at any movie Anna had ever been to.

A blonde girl, dressed identically to Anna, took her hand. They climbed the shallow stairs running along the wall, up to the back of the room. There was a long bar up there, and as the woman fiddled around behind it Anna stared down at the seats stretching out in front of her. The audience was completely silent; mesmerised, as she had been, by the sex shows being performed behind the glass.

'Take this.'

Anna spun round. The blonde had prepared a silver tray, with five tall glasses.

'Walk up and down the aisles,' she said to Anna. 'Someone'll stop you when they want one.'

'What is that stuff?' Anna whispered. It looked like real lemonade, slightly fizzy and cloudy.

'Don't touch it.' The woman stopped Anna's hand as

she reached for a glass. 'You're not allowed to drink while you're working.'

She waved Anna away. Concentrating hard as she got used to her impossibly high heels, Anna set off down the far aisle. It was hard tottering in the stilettos and trying not to spill the drinks, and when a hand tugged at her skirt she almost overbalanced and dropped the lot.

'I want one.'

Anna turned and handed the man a drink. He kept hold of the hem of her skirt, watching her as he drained the glass. Handing it back to Anna, he licked his lips with satisfaction. But he didn't let go of her, and Anna wondered whether he was still thirsty. 'Do you want another one?'

He smiled salaciously. Instead of answering, he put both hands to her thighs and pushed up her short skirt. He stared at her naked pussy for a while, muttering to himself and breathing deeply. Then he seemed to have his fill, and he straightened her skirt down again. His attention turned back to the front of the room and Anna moved on, bemused.

A few paces further on she was stopped again. This time the man beckoned her to lean closer to him. As her upper body bowed towards his head, he motioned her lower and lower. She wasn't sure what he wanted until his head darted forward to one of her dangling breasts. Opening his mouth wide, he took as much of her soft flesh in his mouth as he could, sucking hard on her skin. Anna felt the backs of her thighs quivering as he grazed her with his teeth. Then, like the first man, he'd had enough. He took a drink from the tray, and waved her on.

Her third customer put his hand up the back of her skirt, fondling her buttocks as she stood beside him. The fourth took a swig from his glass, and then licked her nipple with a tongue so cold and wet from the drink that it gave her goosebumps. The fifth was a woman. She asked Anna to kneel down by her seat, and she French-kissed her and played with her breasts, squeezing her mounds and pinching her nipples.

This is incredible, Anna thought, as she went back to the bar to refill her tray. She was being viewed as an object. No waitress ever got treated with this little respect, she was sure. Her customers were using her body as if she were a dish of bar snacks, picking out the bits they liked and nibbling greedily on them for a moment. It was selfish and impersonal; she could have been anyone; any pair of breasts would do. And yet she was glad it was her breasts they reached out for in the gloom. She wanted it to be her arse they leered at through the slash in her skirt.

'You haven't done this before, have you?' the woman asked as she arranged more glasses on Anna's tray. 'Enjoying yourself?'

'Yes,' Anna said. Knowing she meant it, a bolt of reality shot through her. She got an image of herself back in the flat with Suzy, the pair of them giggling and planning who they would seduce on their next night out. Another image followed, of her at work; of the feeling of satisfaction she got when she'd had a good day, and Mike had given her a backhanded compliment. Those seemed such simple pleasures now – now that she'd tasted pleasure far more complex. In her head, she took a step back and looked at herself. Was this the real Anna? Would any of her friends recognise the confident, cockily independent woman they knew? They wouldn't believe their eyes if they could see her dressed as a strip-club waitress, parading around topless and knickerless. But allowing herself to behave like this was the most thrilling thing Anna had ever done. Had her life outside dulled in comparison to this? Without a doubt. Had the old Anna gone missing, frightened away by the new version?

Her sexuality had flipped. Where she had wanted domination over her lovers, she now found herself craving submission. Total control had been hers; now, she wanted to hand that control to someone else.

Whatever the reasons for her transformation, they were hidden somewhere deep inside her mind; probably the same dark place these desires were coming from. It was impossible to analyse and, as another audience member slipped his hand up her skirt, she gave up trying. Just enjoy it, her body told her.

A man sitting in the centre of a row held up his hand for a drink. Putting down her tray, Anna took a glass and squeezed down between people's knees and the row of seats in front. There was just enough room for her if she shuffled along sideways. Moving slowly, the men she passed took the opportunity to stroke the backs of her legs or pat her behind. When she reached the man who'd called her, he took the glass and put it down on the floor. Without a word, he grabbed Anna's hips and turned her round to face the front of the room again, so she had her back to him. Then he pushed firmly in the centre of her back, making her bend over. Anna's breasts brushed the head of the man in front, and as she held on to the back of his seat he turned his head and began to suckle on a wide nipple. Behind her, she could feel the other man's breath on her sex, and she could feel her sex lips swelling at the thought of his face, so close to her. She imagined what he could see: her buttocks peeping naughtily through the split, her pussy, dark and glistening. The image made her shudder with debauched delight.

His hands spread over her buttocks and opened her cheeks wider apart. He muttered something to the person sitting next to him, and then Anna felt his tongue against the skin between her anus and pussy. Her spine jerked with shock as cold liquid was trickled down her crack. The man lapped frantically, trying to catch every spilt drop from her skin. Anna shook her head slightly at the thought of being used as a drinking vessel. The feeling of his thirsty tongue on her behind was insane and intense. More of his drink was poured over her and the man licked in expansive strokes from her throbbing clit to her wincing anus. Anna gasped as the man in front of her bit her nipple, and the man behind swirled his sticky tongue around her tiny arsehole. Pressing at her opening, he made her flinch as he tried to gain entry to her most intimate place. Anna could feel her muscles flexing, trying to expel the intruder, but he kept on trying until her body accepted defeat. Anna had to close her eyes as her tight hole opened for his strong tongue. It was an amazing, unnatural feeling to have his mouth probing her forbidden hole. Broken shards of pleasure leapt from her sensitive anus and sparkled behind her dark eyelids.

Her hands were shaking by the time he had finished with her, and she shuffled back out to the aisle. She barely had the strength to carry her tray any more; her body was on a different plane now, and all she wanted was to lie down and let the silent audience members use her. Desperate for release, she purposely squeezed her way down another row. The men and women touched her, slipping their hands beneath her skirt and squeezing her breasts. But they wouldn't give her what she wanted. She was a servant; a plaything for their fleeting amusement. It was driving her wild.

After refilling her tray once more, she reached the front of the room. Her heart leapt as she noticed Peter sitting in the aisle seat. Surely he would let her have what she so desperately needed. But he practically ignored her as she offered him a glass. His eyes were fixed on his wife in the room directly in front of his seat. He took a drink and waved Anna on. 'Kneel down,' he snapped. 'You'll spoil the view.' She knelt. 'All fours,' he barked.

So she was forced to crawl across the front row, pushing the tray of drinks along the floor in front of her. It was incredibly degrading, her breasts dangling heavily and wobbling as she shuffled on her hands and knees, her buttocks and pussy visible through the wide-open split. But the most degrading part was that no one was looking at her. Their eyes were fixed on the action taking place above her; things so perverse that a sexy, barely dressed woman on all fours wasn't even a distraction.

'Anna?'

She looked up. 'Simon,' she breathed thankfully. Surely he would want her.

He held his hand out for a drink. Anna sat back on her heels while he gulped it down. Wiping the back of his wide mouth, he greedily admired her outfit. 'Touch yourself for me,' he said.

Sitting right in front of him, Anna opened her knees. Her skirt was so short it rode right up, giving Simon a glimpse into the darkness beneath. Anna dropped her hand between her legs and rubbed a finger along her labia. Her sex lips were swollen and they opened easily as she pressed her fingertip between the moist folds. The juice was overflowing from her pussy. Anna stroked upward, covering the hard knob of her clitoris with the sweet musk. Her pelvis arched as she circled the bundle of raw nerve-endings. In her state of desperation it was almost too much, and she moved her hand back down again and slipped a finger inside her tight hole. Looking up, she watched Simon's eyes as he drank in the sight of her, her finger dipping in and out of her moist pussy. Simon wouldn't be able to resist. He would want his cock where her hand was; he would make her come.

But just like the others, he lost interest and waved her on her way. Almost sobbing with frustration, Anna crawled unsteadily to the end of the row and back again, emptying her tray. This was too much, she thought. She had to have something inside her, now. Perhaps there was an empty bottle behind the bar. She'd go up there and bring herself off.

She stood up to find Peter waiting for her in the aisle. 'You see, Anna,' he smirked, 'you're not the only one who likes to watch.' He swept his hand across the room. 'They're so busy watching they've barely got time to look at you.'

Anna raised a pitiful smile. For the first time since she'd come in, she had the chance to share the audience's view. In the room nearest to her, Joan was now curled into a ball on the leather cot, with her hands cuffed behind her back. Her bottom was poked up in the air, and one of her lovers was pumping into her from behind. The two men had swapped places, and the man who'd been fucking her before was now lying beneath her, holding her head over his cock.

'It's driving you mad, isn't it?' Peter laughed quietly, teasing her. 'All these people watching, and you have to work. Well, you can have a rest now, Anna. You've earnt it.'

Thank God, Anna thought, hoping as he took her hand that the torment was over. But he pulled her to the very front of the room. Calling Simon up from the audience, he left Anna standing there while he and Simon went to opposite walls. In the dim light, Anna couldn't really see what they were fumbling with, but as two cuffs lowered from the ceiling she realised it was some sort of pulley system. When the cuffs had reached her head, Peter returned to her side.

He turned her round to face the glass-walled cells. 'Now you can enjoy doing what you like best,' he said, fixing her hand into a fur-lined cuff. 'You can be a voyeur.' He cuffed her other hand, and went to resume his seat.

This was far worse than being felt up by the audience; at least then she'd had contact with other flesh. Now, imprisoned only feet away from the sex show, she couldn't even touch herself. Frustrated to the point of screaming, Anna tugged on the cuffs holding her hands out at head level. But that was no use: the pulley system lifted her heels off the floor as she pulled on the ropes.

She was trapped in her own lust, tortured by the images in front of her.

And those images were getting headier. In several of the rooms, physical games had turned into games of control and submission. These lovers had taken their exploration to such levels that fucking was no longer a thrill. There were whips being used on bare buttocks, clamps gripping hard nipples, and gags silencing protests. One man was wearing a mask which covered his entire face, apart from holes for the nostrils and a zip opening for his mouth. His partner was grinding her pussy on to his mouth, and tugging on the contraption that was separating his cock from his balls. Women and men wielded dildos of every size and shape, forcing their victims to screw up their faces and pull in vain on their restraints. They were playing with each other's minds as well as their spent bodies. It was compelling to watch, and made even more eerie by the silence; the audience could see every detail, but could hear nothing.

Anna could hear her heart pounding. Already driven wild by her provocative waitressing job, this was pushing her rapidly towards madness. Her pussy wept with juice and her clit throbbed insistently. The tiny nub of flesh felt as big as a fist and hard with the pent-up desire that was controlling her body.

She moaned, not realising how loud the sound was until Peter appeared in front of her. 'Had enough?' he soothed, stroking her hot cheek. 'Well, we haven't. We like watching you, Anna.' He summoned someone from the audience, and Simon joined them again. 'Poor little Anna, I don't think she can take any more,' Peter sneered. 'She needs something to . . . fill her hunger.'

Simon obviously knew what this meant. Without a word, he walked out of sight. He returned and handed something to Peter, who moved behind Anna and unzipped her skimpy skirt. Pulling it down, he lifted her ankles and helped her step out of it. Anna looked down as something hard and cold brushed against her calf.

Peter was fitting her with some sort of contraption. As he pulled it over her stockings and suspenders, Anna watched with mounting dread. It was a soft leather G-string of sorts, but with a long, narrow hole in the crotch to allow access to her pussy. That wasn't the worrying bit; it was the cold, greasy knob nudging into her cleft that was sending her pulse into overdrive. In front of her, Simon bent to help. With a hand behind each knee, he lifted her legs up, bending them towards her chest and holding them up above the floor. Anna knew what was coming, but that didn't make it any easier to take. When the oily dildo was pushed inside her anus, she let out an involuntary cry of anguish. Just having a man's tongue in there before had been divine insanity. Now, a thick plug filled her arsehole. The end seemed to be rubbing at the base of her brain. Spasms twitched in her buttocks. She fought with Simon to let her legs go. She wanted to kick out, to flail against the feeling.

Simon held on. Wrapping his arms around her, he pressed her folded legs between their chests and absorbed her panic. As the spasms subsided, a deep warmth radiated from her arsehole. Fiddling behind her back, Peter tightened the adjustable straps of the leather thong, buckling her in so that the plug was held firmly inside her. That was one part of her body taken care of, she thought, as waves of pleasure rippled over her skin. Now for her pussy. Would it be Simon or Peter?

It seemed it was going to be neither. Peter moved around to Anna's side, calling someone else out from the audience. A stocky man with dark hair arrived, together with the blonde waitress. Simon and the man positioned themselves on either side of her hips, and each took a thigh. Cradling her upper legs, they opened her in readiness. She was now in a man-made version of the swing she'd seen before, except with hands holding her thighs instead of leather and chains. Anna wondered why Peter wasn't getting ready to fuck her, but he seemed disinterested. Leaning against one of the glass panels, he was tinkering with something; her camera. Wide-eyed, Anna watched as the blonde dropped her mini-skirt and put on her own leather thong. The difference was, this one had a smooth, curved dildo rearing from the triangle that covered her pubic hair.

The phallus was long, but it was rubber; Anna craved real flesh and hot skin sliding against hers. 'Peter,' she whimpered. 'Won't you fuck me, please . . .?'

'I can't,' he said. 'I've had a drink.'

Anna squirmed with frustration, making the ropes swing as she pulled on them. 'Let Simon, then. Or someone else. I need a man,' she whined.

Peter shook his head. 'Impossible, I'm afraid. Everyone here has had a drink apart from Louise. Don't worry, that thing she's wearing will satisfy you, I promise.'

Anna met Louise's eyes. 'What's so special about that drink?' she asked, as the woman and her fake penis loomed nearer.

'It heightens the senses,' Louise explained, slipping her hands around Anna's hips. 'It sends you into a state of virtual reality. Whatever you look at, you experience it as if it's happening to you. That's why we drink it in here. That's why they can only touch you for a little while. They want to, but it's too much for the brain to take. It's like sensory overload. If you tried to screw someone while you were under the influence, you'd pass out with the pleasure.'

'What's the point of taking it then?'

Peter came up behind Louise and rested his hand on her waist, watching over her shoulder as the dildo nudged at Anna's pouting sex lips. 'Louise just told you why we take it. We don't come into this room to screw, Anna. We come here to watch, and to open our minds.'

He put the camcorder to his eye, and slowly raised his head. 'And now, we're going to open your mind.'

Anna threw her head back as Louise plunged inside her. Peter was right; it did satisfy her. With a dildo in each hole, ecstasy throbbed in the pit of her stomach and made her eyelids flutter. Just like in the scene she'd observed through the hatch, Louise stood still, allowing the men to swing Anna back and forth. Her fettered hands gripped the ropes suspending her from the ceiling. Looking up, she saw the pulleys swinging as she was eased on and off the phallus. Her breasts swelled and her hard nipples ached for pain. Four people – Louise, Anna and her two attendant men – were united in their aim and steady in their rhythm.

Peter moved to his own rhythm, his body dipping and leaning as he swooped in close with the camera. Anna looked back into the beady eye of the lens as it inspected her. He filmed every inch of her harnessed body, taking a lingering close-up of her vulva as it was plundered again and again with the rubber rod. He honed in on her quivering breasts and went behind her, probably focusing on the way her pale arse cheeks were separated by the black leather thong. Then, having made his visual exploration of her body, he concentrated on her face, watching her expression change as her orgasm built.

'Keep it on her eyes,' he instructed, passing the silver box to Louise. 'I want to be able to see the moment her mind opens.'

Anna turned her head, straining to look over her shoulder as he circled her. But he pushed her face back towards the camera, and she was left to guess what he was up to as he unfastened the thong. She was surprised, and disappointed, when the short plug was pulled out of her anus. A moment later, while busy fingers worked something warm and oily into her puckered rim, she realised the anal dildo had been there only to stretch her; to prepare her for a real invasion.

Everyone was motionless. The two men flanking Anna held her still. Their heads were bowed, their eyes fixed to the point behind her back, where a much bigger dildo than the first prodded for entry. 'No,' she groaned, her voice crushed by the feeling of her most sensitive skin being stretched. 'Let me go,' she gasped, but they knew as well as she did that she didn't mean it. She wanted every hole filled, and every sense bombarded.

She got what she wanted. As the rubber cock was buried into her grasping anus, the real assault began. Up until now, Simon and his accomplice had been swinging her slowly, and Louise's dildo had only been entering her halfway. Now they kept her still in the vice of their fingers. One of Louise's hands held the camera, while the other grabbed on to Anna's hip to steady herself. Knowing what Anna needed, Louise thrust her hips ferociously, slamming the phallus in up to its root. Now Anna got the full effect. Attached to the base of the dildo was a disc covered with tiny, rigid rubber fingers. Every time Louise slammed between Anna's legs, the fingers pressed against her burning clit. The sensation was different with every thrust. Sometimes the little protrusions rubbed her, and the friction would sear her tender skin. Occasionally, one of the minute pointing fingers poked deep into some magical, white-hot place, and sent her whole body twitching.

Behind her, Peter was creating more unbearable friction. His slow strokes quickly gave way to a frantic pace which was making Anna's eyes roll. To add to the torment, Simon and his friend had decided to join in. Still keeping their hands tightly wrapped around her thighs, they had dipped their heads. Each had an engorged nipple in their mouth. One pulled on an areola with his teeth; the other sucked as if he was trying to prise the sweat from her pores. Pleasure and pain, ecstasy and despair formed an unending loop around her body, until it was impossible to distinguish one from the other.

Full to bursting point, with every sense being mercilessly attacked, Anna felt her eyes welling up. She didn't need to be drugged, she thought, to experience the ultimate sensory overload. She looked through her tears at the depraved scenes still going on in front of her, and she could feel everything she saw: the crack of a whip singeing into soft flesh; the tortured delight of a woman pinned down and used; the humiliation of the man begging for mercy from his mistress. Anna could feel everything they felt – the pain, the shame, the twisted longing. She shared it all. She was at one with them, her mind and body joined to theirs in unholy communion. She wasn't Anna any more. Her soul had been drained and refilled with something sticky and tainted.

Her anguished cries filled the quiet room as she came. This orgasm wasn't like anything she'd known before. It had no source, no beginning or end, but pulsated from a million different places. Somewhere deep inside her bowels, her body screamed.

Anna's shoulders were aching painfully. But then, so was every other part of her body. She'd kicked off the five-inch heels ages ago, but still the balls of her feet were throbbing persistently. Getting rid of her shoes might have alleviated the stress on her feet, but it had increased the strain on the rest of her muscles. Peter and Simon had fastened the pulleys before they'd left, and they'd given Anna no room to manoeuvre. Stepping down from her stilettos had meant her back being stretched as if she were on a rack, with her shoulders nearly wrenching out of their sockets. She was strung up like an animal waiting for slaughter, and with about as much concern for her health.

Now this really was torture, she thought. Too much pleasure might be hard to cope with, but it was a hell of a lot easier than too much pain. Peter had smirked sadistically as he'd turned at the door. 'I'm going to leave you alone for a while,' he'd sneered. 'I want to be sure you're keeping out of mischief while I go and talk to my wife. We need to discuss what's to be done with you, now you've discovered our little secret. I'm sure you've a lot to think about, too.' He seemed to find himself very amusing, leaving his laughter trailing behind him like a puff of smoke.

Anna hadn't laughed then, and she was close to crying now. It must be half an hour, she estimated, since the sex shows had finally finished and the audience had trooped out. Five minutes in suspension would have been more than enough; thirty was agony.

So she nearly wept with happiness when Frank appeared. 'Thank God you're here,' she said, as he cautiously poked his head through the door. 'You've got to get me out of this thing.' He took a step inside, and anxiously scanned the rows of empty seats. 'There's no one else here,' Anna said. 'Please, Frank, it's hurting . . .'

He unfastened the pulley nearest to him, then strode across the room to the other one. Summoning the little strength she had left, Anna pulled on the ropes. Her hands were shaking as Frank uncuffed her. Free at last, she rolled her neck and shoulders, sighing heavily with relief.

'Oh, thank you,' she breathed. 'I don't know how much longer I could have stayed like that.' She took a step towards him, but her legs gave way. He caught her in his arms, effortlessly picking her up and cradling her deflated body against his wide chest.

'Where are your clothes?' he asked.

Weakly, Anna waved towards the door he'd come in through. Frank carried her into the small anteroom and gently put her down on the floor. Leaning back against the wall, Anna felt her body gradually resuming its normal shape. Frank knelt at her side, holding her wrists and tenderly rubbing away the indentations the cuffs had left in her skin.

'I told you they'd punish you,' he said sadly. 'I did try to warn you.'

Anna watched him, his azure-blue eyes full of earnest naïveté. Frank had obviously not been initiated into the particular delights of this part of the Institute. His innocence was almost childlike – how could she explain? 'You may not understand this, Frank, but –'

'You're the one who doesn't understand.' His hands flew to her face. Cupping her jaw in his long fingers, he held her still as if this was the only way to make her listen. 'They'll hurt you, Anna. They'll imprison you and torture you.'

She smiled sweetly, trying to calm his melodramatic concern. 'No one's going to hurt me, I promise you.'

Exasperated, his hands dropped to her shoulders and he very gently shook her. 'Anna, you've got to listen to me. They are going to hurt you. I just heard them talking about it.'

'Who?'

'My mother and father.'

Anna began to absorb the worry in his voice. He did seem very upset. 'What were they saying?'

'That they have to keep you here, at any cost.'

Anna sat up a little straighter. 'You heard them say that?'

Frank nodded. 'I was going to see my father. His door was open. I heard your name, so I stood outside and listened. They said you were ideal research material. They . . .' He hesitated, panic flickering across his face. 'Anna, they said that once they'd got what they wanted from you they were going to lock you in one of those cells, and keep you there until you begged for mercy.'

Anna was puzzled. She couldn't help thinking maybe Frank had got the wrong end of the stick again. 'And what is it they want from me?'

'They didn't say. But you're in danger, Anna. You've got to get out of here, now.'

Anna still wasn't convinced. Frank didn't realise that the Institute's staff went willingly into those cells. The mysterious thing that his parents wanted from Anna was most likely something sexual. She stroked his forehead, easing away the creases in his perfect skin. 'Don't worry. I'm sure I'm not in any danger.'

'But you are.' Standing up, he paced up and down the short room. 'I've seen them do it to other women. They string them up in those cells and leave them there, just like they left you this afternoon. The women . . .' He pressed his hands over his ears. 'They scream to be let out. The noise is awful . . .' Alone with his memory, he stood for a moment with his eyes glazed and his fingers clamped to his head. Waking up, he dived back to the floor and took Anna's hands in his. 'It's the truth, Anna. It's happened to every woman I ever liked. I have feelings for you, in here.' He lifted her hand up to his chest and slid it beneath the opening of his lab coat. Anna could feel his heartbeat, strong and slow. 'I don't want the same thing to happen to you. You've got to leave, before it's too late. How can I make you believe me? How can I prove that you're in danger if you stay here?'

Anna looked up at him. He was an amazing man: so beautiful, so sincere, and so completely different from all the others in the Institute. There she was, slumped against the wall in only a topless basque and stockings. But Frank, totally absorbed in his concern for her safety, had barely given her nakedness a glance. Perhaps he deserved to be taken a little more seriously.

'There is a way you could prove it,' she said.

Frank stood guard outside while Anna crept into the deserted monitoring room. She knew that all the security footage was kept on tape, and that it would be a simple matter to rewind the appropriate video. Selecting the machine marked with the relevant screen number, she watched as the images flickered backward on the

201

monitor. Finding the section with Peter and Joan together, she pressed play.

Everything Frank had said was right. Her blood turned to ice as she listened to Peter and Joan discussing how they would keep her locked away – once they had made their 'extraction'. A vague theory began to swirl around Anna's mind like fog. She couldn't see the answer clearly, but she suspected that the Institute's research and its staff's sexual tendencies were inextricably linked. It was obvious from the way the Galloways were talking that she had been recruited for a reason. They were planning to use her – or a part of her – for some sort of experiment. And they were scheduling it for tomorrow.

Anna put her hand to her mouth as she thought. Her fingers were quivering uncontrollably. She was so close to uncovering the story it would be devastating to leave now. And yet it was clear that she was in danger. And Mike had made her promise to run rather than put herself at risk for the sake of the programme.

She screwed up her eyes. Her head was hurting. A battle was raging in her brain. Go, her common sense was urging. Get out now, while you still can. But her professional zeal was making a very persuasive argument too, seducing her with the promise of acclaim and promotion. A gold award for best current affairs programme was winking temptingly behind her eyes.

And there was something else, something she hardly dared admit to herself; another reason she wanted to stay. She thought of Peter, Joan and Simon, and her stomach lurched. She thought of being tied up, pinned down, shamed and humiliated in front of a slavering audience, and she swallowed hard. It was ridiculous, and incredible, but her sexual hunger had been aroused by the taste of something she'd never tried before. Now, she wanted more.

But what she wanted didn't matter. Exploring perversions that had been hidden for years may be thrilling, she thought, but staying alive is more important. Opening her eyes, she took one last look around her as her mind cleared. Who knows what Galloway had planned for her? She didn't intend to find out.

Once her mind was made up, Anna was desperate to go. But she forced herself to wait until after dark before sneaking outside. She went for one last jog around the fence, checking to see if anyone else was around. Pausing by the front gate as if she were out of breath, she waved her security bracelet across the sensor. The gate clicked open, and Anna pushed it further in preparation for her escape. She didn't want any delays once she got inside the car.

The engine hadn't been started for ages, but Mike's Golf fired first time. Knowing the cameras would pick her up, she thought there was no point in keeping her headlights off or in making a slow crawl towards the exit. She had slammed into fourth gear by the time she sped through the gate.

Her hands gripped the steering wheel tightly as she followed the driveway out on to the country lane beyond it. It was pitch black outside, and she should have kept her eyes on the road, but she couldn't help glancing in the rear-view mirror every other second. Sure that someone would be sent to chase her, she peered into the darkness she was leaving behind, searching for headlights. None appeared.

Five minutes later, she still hadn't seen another car, either behind or in front of hers. She wouldn't let herself believe that she was home and dry, and yet it seemed that way. She was driving quickly, but a fast car could have caught up with her by now. Perhaps, like before, there was no one manning the monitoring room. In which case, it could be hours until they discovered she was missing. She'd be well on her way to London by then.

She slowed down. Keeping one hand on the wheel and one eye on the road, she reached across to flip open the glove compartment. She pulled out the keypad of her carphone and dialled Mike's number. As his answerphone message came through the speakers, she glanced at the clock. Nine – Mike rarely left the office before then. She'd probably only just missed him. She tried his home number, but he wasn't there either. And no luck with his mobile, which diverted her to an answering service. He was probably on the tube home and unable to get a signal.

'Mike, it's Anna. Don't worry, I'm fine. I've a lot to tell you. I'll call you again later.'

She picked up speed again, swooping around bends and drifting over to the middle of the road on tight corners. There were no lights on the road, but there weren't any cars either, and she made good progress. Another couple of miles and she'd be on the dual carriageway, heading towards the M6. They'd never catch her now.

Adrenalin rushed through her veins as she realised she'd outwitted them. OK, she hadn't uncovered the truth behind the Institute's façade; but she'd thwarted their plans to experiment on her, and she knew enough to send in the police. She wondered whether Galloway would look so smug when he was languishing in prison.

Anna recognised the little church as she raced past it. It was the last landmark before the main road. She gave the rear-view mirror one final glance.

She froze as she looked back at the road. There was a man stumbling out of the shadows towards her. Reality went into slow motion as she waited for the impact.

Anna took her foot off the accelerator and started to press the brake. She didn't see his face. Her headlights lit his knees as he ran straight for the car. In a split second, her mind weighed up the options: crash into him, slam on the brakes, swerve to the right, swerve to the left.

Not enough time to brake, she thought. Stone wall to the right. Think there's a field on the left. Why is he running straight towards me?

She wrenched the steering wheel hard to the left, squeezing the brake. There was a deep ditch between the road and the field. As the ground gave way and the car tipped violently, Anna thought she was going to die.

Chapter Ten

She was in heaven. A pure white light was beaming on to her face, bathing her skin in its cleansing glow. Her body was cushioned on a cloud, and covered in finest gossamer. In the distance, angels sang a chorus of welcome. Her own angel stroked her hair and whispered words of love and peace.

Anna opened her eyes. She had to close them again; the light was too bright. Gradually, she tried again, squinting to relieve the pain as it flashed behind her eyeballs. How strange, she thought, that there was pain in heaven.

'Is it too bright for you? Here, I'll close the curtains a bit.'

The light diffused, turning from white to a pale yellow. Anna watched the dark figure approaching.

He sat down on the chair by the side of the bed. 'How are you feeling? Better now you've had a good night's rest?'

Anna turned her head to look at him, but her neck was gripped with a sharp spasm and she could only move an inch. She sucked in her breath at the shock. 'What happened?'

'Don't you remember? You were in a nasty accident.' With gentle fingers, he stroked her hair. 'I found you and brought you here. I called the doctor.'

Anna tried to remember, but her brain felt too heavy to think. 'Dr Galloway?' she mumbled.

The man smiled. 'You're still confused, aren't you? The doctor who came to see you gave you a sedative to help you sleep. That's why you feel a bit woozy.' He leant forward, supporting Anna's shoulders as she tried to sit up. 'The doctor said you were very lucky. Only cuts and bruises and mild whiplash. You'll be fine in a couple of days.'

Anna didn't feel fine. Her mind was full of syrup, which was slowing down her thoughts and making her slur her words. 'A couple of days? I can't ... I have to get back.'

The man chuckled. 'You won't be going anywhere for a while, Anna. Your car's a bit of a mess, I'm afraid.'

Turning her whole upper body so she didn't have to move her neck, she looked at him. There was something wrong with what he'd just said. She waited patiently for her befuddled brain to catch up with itself. 'How did you know my name?'

'It was on your bracelet.'

Anna held her wrist up to her face so she could see it. There was a bruise on the back of her hand. Her memory stirred. 'What happened to that man? I was swerving to avoid him.'

'There was a man? You can't have hit him, Anna. You were the only one there when I found you in the ditch.' He stood up. Plumping her pillows, he eased Anna back against their softness. 'Will you be all right for a minute? I have to go and check on the choir practice.'

Anna nodded, forgetting her neck was immovable. 'What's your name?'

'I'm Father Lawrence.' He smiled benignly, and placed

a tray across her lap. 'I've made you some breakfast. You'll feel better when you've eaten something.'

'Thank you,' she said, touched by his kindness. He glided out of the room, and she looked down at the orange juice, grapefruit and toast. Whatever the doctor had given her had left her with more than a thick head. She clasped her hand to her mouth as nausea bubbled up from her stomach.

For the rest of the day, she did little more than sit in bed and wallow in the bath. The sedative took its time wearing off, as did the whiplash, although a long soak in hot water helped. The vicar brought her meals and chatted for a while, but he was busy with church business and for most of the time Anna was alone. She was glad of the solitude, because she needed time to think.

She had no car and no money. Her credit card was hidden in the Golf, but according to Father Lawrence that had been towed away. The nearest village was only five miles away, but what good was that without any cash? Besides, that village was the one nearest the Institute. The staff rarely ventured out, but there was always a slight chance of bumping into one of them there, and Anna wasn't prepared to take any chances after the shock of her accident. The most sensible thing to do, she concluded, was to phone Mike from the vicarage and tell him what had happened. He could come and pick her up, or send his friend who lived not far away.

Anna groaned, holding on to her neck as she got out of bed. She was feeling a lot better, but still her muscles were sore – although how much of that was from the crash, and how much from being suspended from the ceiling at the Institute, she wasn't certain. She shuddered at the memory. At the time, it had all seemed so deliciously depraved. Looking back from the peaceful cocoon of the vicarage, it seemed like the Institute was a den of perversion and madness, a refuge for those who wanted to explore their kinks instead of trying to straighten them out. She was lucky to have escaped before she was drawn any further into Galloway's sick mind games.

She eased on the bathrobe the priest had given her, and left her room for the first time. Padding across the wooden-floored passageway, she followed the sound of the radio into the living room. How quaint, she thought, as she pushed at the door. It was a timeless scene: the vicar sitting by the fire with a glass of red wine and only a radio programme for company. Anna couldn't imagine life without television. But then, she couldn't imagine life without sex, or parties, or the rush of living in a culture-saturated city. Father Lawrence had obviously decided that he needed none of those things for a satisfying life.

'Anna!' he said, beaming as he noticed her standing there. 'You're looking much better. Come in. Sit by the fire with me.'

Anna joined him. She sat in a perfect fireside chair: deep red, wide-armed, and with a seat big enough for her to curl her legs up. Accepting the glass of wine Father Lawrence handed her, she smiled up at him.

'You've been very kind. I can't thank you enough. Is there anything I could do for you when I get back to London – make a donation, or something?'

'That's really not necessary, Anna. It's my job to be a Good Samaritan.'

They sat in silence for a while. Father Lawrence stared into the fire and listened to the radio. Anna gazed at him. He was much older than she, but still handsome, especially for a man of the cloth. What a waste, she thought. His lean body was draped casually in the chair, with that eye-catching ease that some men have. His short, dark-brown hair was being overtaken by grey, and he had a strikingly angular face. His eyes were quite stunning, a piercing grey which reminded her of Peter. In fact, he reminded her of Peter in other ways too. His voice was rich, and just as compelling as the doctor's.

She imagined Lawrence's female parishioners swooning as he spoke down to them from the pulpit. Now that was kinky, she thought – to be taught about sin by man who'd never sinned. She imagined a congregation full of wet-knickered housewives all eager to lead him astray.

She wondered whether he'd taken a furtive look at her body as he and the doctor had undressed her and put her to bed. It would only be natural if he had done, whereas vowing chastity was the most unnatural course a man could take. Priests, she had always suspected, were raving perverts who'd taken to God because they were running away from their sexual urges – and their guilt. Father Lawrence must have desires, like any man. Why deny them? She would certainly like to introduce him to the sins of the flesh.

She looked at his hands, and wondered whether his fingers had ached to touch her while she had been under the safe blanket of sedation. Had he longed to explore the curves of her sleeping body? Had he lain awake, his cock painfully hard, thinking of the pleasure waiting for him in the next room?

Anna gave herself a mental slap across the face. What the hell was wrong with her? Father Lawrence was kind and gentle – the personification of Christian values. He'd probably never had a dirty thought in his life. His fingers had never yearned to be anywhere they shouldn't. He was serene, and content in his solitude. Not everyone's a complete sex maniac like you, she told herself.

The radio play finished and Father Lawrence looked up at her and smiled. Anna flinched at the sweet sincerity on his face. If only he knew what she'd just been thinking. If only he knew what an utterly filthy mind she had – he would probably have left her in her mangled car.

He reached over to turn off the radio. 'So, Anna,' he said, settling back into his seat. 'You were on your way to London last night?'

She nodded.

'And what draws you to that wicked city?' His eyes twinkled; his tongue was in his cheek.

'I live there.'

'Were you up here for a holiday, then?'

'Not exactly. I was working, at the research centre. It's about seven miles up the road. Do you know it?'

'The big white building? I didn't realise it was a research centre. What were you researching?'

That was a tough one. Anna still wasn't sure what the real purpose of the Institute was: genetic studies, or sexual experiments. 'Well, I was only a lab assistant,' she said. 'I wasn't really told a lot about the technical side of things.'

'You obviously didn't enjoy your job.'

She thought of the time she'd spent there, of the incredible debauchery she'd willingly tasted. Her eyes glazed. 'I did, actually. I enjoyed every minute.'

'Then why were you running away?'

Startled by his tone, she glanced up. 'What makes you think I was?'

His eyes were full of concern. 'Anna, the man who came to tow your car away said you must have been driving very fast. You left twenty metres of skidmarks on the road.'

She didn't want to go into this with him. There was no point. 'I always drive quickly,' she explained.

Father Lawrence got up from his seat and walked across the fireplace to Anna. Kneeling in front of her, he gently took her glass. 'Anna,' he said softly, taking her hands in his, 'you don't have to hide your worries from me. I'm used to people coming to me with their problems.'

Anna suspected that no one had ever come to him with quite such a problem before. She couldn't imagine a parishioner telling him that yesterday she'd been strung up like an animal and fucked with dildos, and that today they'd been planning to donate her body to medical science. 'I'm fine,' she assured him. 'I missed London, that's all. I decided to go home.'

'There's fear in your eyes,' he said. 'Anna, if you're in trouble, or if you've done something wrong, I can help you.'

'I haven't done anything wrong. But you could help me with something.'

'Anything.'

'Could I use your phone?'

'Anything but that, I'm afraid,' he chuckled. 'My phone's out of order at the moment. You'll remember the gales we had a few nights ago? Well, a tree fell across the line. One of my parishioners called the engineer, but I'm afraid I'm not top priority, out here in the wilds.'

'Oh,' she said, keeping her swearing inside. 'Could you give me a lift to a call box, then?'

'If there was a public phone box anywhere near, and I had a car, I would gladly do that.'

Anna couldn't help herself. She didn't want to look ungrateful, but she sighed with frustration.

'If you like, I could ask my congregation after Communion tomorrow. I'm sure one of them would take you home and let you use their phone.'

'That would be wonderful. Thank you.'

'That's settled then. You'll stay here tonight. Anything else I can do?'

'I don't think so.'

He smiled knowingly. 'But I think there is something. Perhaps you're just too frightened to tell me about it.' His eyes pierced into hers. He was looking into her soul. 'I can see you've got a troubled mind, Anna. It may help to share your fears with me.'

'But I'm not afraid,' she insisted.

He studied her. His attention was as warm as the fire; it felt good on her skin. 'You know, Anna, we're all afraid of something. We're all running away from our demons.'

As he caressed the backs of her wrists with his thumbs, Anna could feel herself melting. It was a strange situation, to be so close to a man who wanted to share her feelings but couldn't share her body. She longed to know what demons lurked behind his eyes. 'What are *you* running away from?' she asked.

He bowed his head, watching his hands in her lap. His smile faded. 'I had feelings for a woman once,' he said. 'Feelings which frightened me, because I couldn't control them.' His eyes narrowed as he searched for the right words. 'This woman . . . she made me feel powerless. She seemed to know what I wanted, before I knew it myself. She understood me better than I did. It's terrifying when someone holds a mirror up and you discover who you really are.'

He met her eyes again, and Anna understood. She gasped – those feelings he was talking about were the same ones she'd been struggling with ever since she'd first met Dr Galloway. 'I know exactly what you mean,' she whispered.

'Yes, I knew you did. I recognise myself in you. You're about the same age I was, when I decided to escape my feelings and enter the priesthood. I remember what I was going through, then. Let me help, Anna. Unburden yourself.'

She would have liked to. She was dying to tell someone about the things she'd seen and done at the Institute, and how her experiences had confused her. But she daren't mention anything until Mike, *Undercover*'s lawyers and the police had been briefed. 'I . . . I can't talk about it. I know you're only trying to help, but . . .'

'You can talk about it to me. You can tell me anything, and it'll go no further, I promise.'

She was very tempted. It would be welcome therapy to confide in this man, and to hear his softly spoken words of comfort. 'I couldn't . . . The things I've done . . . You'd be shocked.'

'Anna, the things I've heard in that confessional ... Believe me, I'm not easily shocked any more.'

Anna was sure he wouldn't have heard a confession quite like hers.

'Come on,' he said, gently tugging at her hands as she wavered. 'I can sense you have something you want to tell me.'

She hesitated, but only for a moment. She couldn't pinpoint what it was, exactly – his voice, his eyes, or the wine perhaps, blurring her senses – but something made her give in. She *would* confess, she decided, following as he led her through the vestry and into the church. She would tell him what was on her mind, and with any luck he might be able to clarify her thoughts. And maybe – although she could hardly bring herself to admit that such a dirty thought could enter her mind in a church – Father Lawrence would find her stories arousing. Somehow, she had the urge to excite this calm, peaceful man.

Shivering as the stone floor radiated coldness up through the soles of her feet, she clutched her bathrobe tighter around her. She looked around the tiny, ancient church as Father Lawrence lit a candle. The only other light was from the moon, pouring through the stained-glass window above the altar and casting a dramatic, cross-shaped shadow on the slabbed floor. In the dimness, the religious icons peered down with faces either racked with agony or blank with piety. No wonder people were afraid of God, she thought. His house was so unwelcoming.

Father Lawrence motioned her over to a small, ornately carved wooden cubicle with two adjacent doors. Opening one, he invited Anna to step inside and passed the candle in to her. She heard him opening and closing the other door as she settled on to the short wooden bench. Separating the two halves of the cubicle was a burgundy velvet curtain.

His voice was velvet too, as he spoke from behind the

thick drapes. 'You're safe to tell me anything you want in here, Anna. Whatever you say, I'm forbidden from repeating it to anyone. Only God can hear us.'

Anna winced. It wasn't a non-existent god she was worried about; it was Father Lawrence. 'I don't know where to start.'

'Well, why don't you tell me what it was you were running away from?'

She thought for a moment. 'Well, there was a man at the Institute . . . He frightened me.'

'Doctor Galloway?' he asked.

'Do you know him?'

'No, but you mentioned him when you came round, this morning. Were you frightened of him, Anna?' The priest didn't sound convinced. 'Or of how you felt when you were with him?'

Christ, he was perceptive. 'Maybe it was how I felt that worried me.'

'And how did you feel?'

She took a deep breath, trying to quell the strength of the memories which were making her pussy clench. 'I felt powerless,' she whispered. 'Out of control. When I was with him, I did things . . .' She scrunched up her eyes. 'Things I wouldn't normally do.'

'Go on, Anna. Tell me about some of those things.'

Flinching, stuttering and sweating, Anna sketched a picture of Dr Galloway. Omitting the intimate details, she told Father Lawrence of how she'd been asked to do certain things, and how she'd enjoyed them. Gradually, her embarrassment faded and the words began to flow, lubricated by the heady wine she'd drunk before. She admitted that Galloway had made her feel dirty and depraved, and that she'd loved it. The further he'd pushed her, the more she had craved. She had had to stop herself; to get away, before things went too far. Father Lawrence made encouraging comments when she faltered, his voice a soothing antidote to the torrid

215

thoughts she'd stirred up. When she'd finished, she almost felt relieved that someone else knew what she'd been up to, even if he did only know the vague outline. It was therapeutic to bring her feelings out, and to hear herself talk about them – especially since Anna could tell that Father Lawrence understood.

'So it's the strength of your desires that scares you,' he said, summing up, 'and the way this doctor seems to toy with your emotions.'

'Exactly,' she sighed.

'I remember how that felt when I went through it. You've discovered a new side to your personality, Anna. It's natural to be unnerved by it.'

'Perhaps. But is it natural to want more? I went to the Institute to work, to do a specific job. But there were times when I forgot all about my job, and all I wanted was to . . .' Give myself to Galloway. She swallowed the words before they reached her tongue.

'You wanted to give in to your feelings for this man.'

'Yes,' she breathed. Astounded, she watched as the vicar's fingers appeared through a slit in the dividing curtain. They were sitting closer than she'd realised, and he rested his hand on her knee.

'But you were finding it harder and harder to fight those feelings.'

'Yes.'

'We all find it difficult, Anna. We all have urges we'd like to surrender to.'

Anna looked down. The disembodied hand eased her bathrobe open so it could rest on her bare skin. It was clear where Father Lawrence's urges lay, and that he couldn't fight them any longer after what Anna had just told him. Mesmerised, she watched as he gently stroked her lower thigh. This was far more shocking than anything she'd done at the Institute. A bare knee in a confessional, and a priest admitting he had urges – didn't this qualify for eternal damnation?

'Father?' she gasped, as his touch eased an inch beneath the white towelling.

'Tell me why you left that man. What happened yesterday to make you drive away so quickly?'

She gripped the edge of her seat as his hand slid further upward. 'I heard him saying that he planned to keep me prisoner in the Institute, in a part of the building where . . .' How to phrase it? 'Where people let their forbidden feelings out.'

'And you didn't want to stay in that place?'

'No, I did want to stay.'

There was a long silence. 'And yet you ran away?'

'I didn't want to. I had to.' Her hushed voice trembled at the importance of her admission.

'Tell me about your forbidden feelings.'

She barely hesitated. She was caught up in the thrill of confessing, and aroused by the fact that the priest's fingers were edging inexorably higher. 'I was so used to being in control I thought that was what I wanted. But now I know that being out of control is so much better . . .' She closed her eyes as the priest's fingertip reached her inner thigh. The potent image of Galloway watching her as she masturbated for him reached the forefront of her mind at the same time. The volatile mix of touch and memory ignited familiar flames in her belly. She parted her legs. 'I don't want to dominate my men any more,' she said, breathless as he accepted her invitation and touched her most intimate flesh. 'I want to be completely dominated.'

'And that's what frightens you – the thought of relinquishing control of your mind and body to someone else.'

She nodded slowly to herself. She knew then that if Frank hadn't warned her away she would have stayed. And if Galloway had asked her to surrender herself to him for ever, she would have agreed.

217

'So why deny yourself what you want? Why leave, just when you discovered all this about yourself?'

'There were other things going on ... I was worried about what would happen to me if I stayed. They were going to use me for –'

She stopped, struck dumb by the sight of a long, thick penis peering blindly through another slit in the curtain.

'Jesus,' she gasped. She clapped her hand to her mouth as she realised she'd just blasphemed, then thought that, under the circumstances, taking the Lord's name in vain was probably not such a big deal. 'Father? What are you doing?' she asked, rather pointlessly.

'Anna, it's obvious from what you've told me that you're a lost cause. You're addicted to sexual submission. Now you must submit to the Lord our God. Get down on your knees.'

Anna obeyed his booming voice. If she hadn't known better, she might have thought it was the supreme being himself bellowing down at her. Father Lawrence, it seemed, had power games of his own to play. She almost laughed as she wondered how many women had repented their sins in the confession box. Quite a few, it seemed: one of his dedicated flock had carefully reinforced the slits in the curtain with neat stitching.

'Pray with me,' he said, his voice quivering with zeal. 'Let's pray together for your salvation.'

She'd never heard it called praying before, she thought, as she sucked on the swollen knob of his cock. She hoped God was watching.

The stone floor was cold and hard on her knees, but her body was hot. Father Lawrence had obviously lost his morals a while ago, and he grunted with unashamed delight as she licked and sucked him. Anna's sex burnt with the wickedness of it. Father Lawrence made Peter Galloway seem positively conservative. A few weeks ago, having a priest expose himself to her would have shocked her rigid. Now, she accepted it. Everyone, it seemed, had their own secret agenda. Lurid fantasies festered just beneath the skin, and you only had to lightly scratch the surface and they would ooze out.

The priest groaned loudly and jerked his penis out of her mouth, dribbling his warm come over her lips and throat. Both his hands were through the curtain now, and he roughly pulled her up on her feet. His fingers tore blindly at her robe, pushing it off her. He turned her around. 'Bend over,' he barked. 'Prostrate yourself in front of the Lord. Let him look into your soul.'

Anna had always wondered exactly where her soul was. Now she knew.

He slipped two fingers between her fleshy labia. He mumbled the Hail Mary again and again as he stroked the ridged walls of her sex. He delved deeper, reaching into her succulent moistness; reaching for her soul, perhaps. 'You're wet with sin. Let Him hear your cry for mercy,' he wailed, grabbing on to her hips. 'Repent, you fallen woman!'

She repented, shouting out God's name as His servant rammed his length inside her. She held on to the bench with all her might, steadying herself against his ferocious thrusting. He was remorseless, pumping into her honey-soaked pussy as if his energy was fuelled by a higher power. 'Whore,' he cursed, sliding in and out, in and out. 'You slut, you filthy wanton.'

'Yes,' she moaned, as he rammed in up to the hilt. 'Oh yes,' as his heavy balls banged between her legs. A giggle simmered in her stomach at the idea that the Institute's nearest neighbour was a priest with a custom-built confessional. Father Lawrence's religion was about as corrupt as Galloway's science. Was there something in the water up here?

Her smile turned to a grimace as he withdrew. Her sex clasped desperately at the emptiness, wanting him back. But he was dribbling over her again, spurting his juices into her crack. Anna felt her tightly pursed anus oozing with the fluid as it spilt. She heard his breathing, deep and eerily steady, as his fingers worked the stickiness into her puckered rim. He dipped inside her pussy, gathering the juices spilling from her slit and spreading them upward into her cleft. He took a long time over his task, diligently lubricating her and poking his fingertip into her bottom. Anna felt another erection brush against her inner thigh, then he held her tight and pushed his way inside her arse.

'Oh God, oh help me please,' she begged. It was too much, too soon after yesterday's plundering of her body. Thankfully it was too much for him, as well. The tightness of her most secret hole must have shocked him, because he moaned with ecstasy and slowed his strokes right down. Relishing the sensation of stretching her arsehole, he slid in and out with calm steadiness. The frenzied pace of before was gone. It was as if he wanted to savour every second; every forbidden inch of her inner flesh. His gradual, inexorable progress in and out of her quivering buttocks was delicious torment for Anna, and it brought tears to her eyes – but it was a bearable agony. The nerves inside her anus had been rubbed raw by yesterday's ordeal, and she couldn't have coped with another onslaught like that one.

But Father Lawrence had savoured her enough. Anna's lips pulled back over her teeth as he thrust forcefully into her helpless body. The pleasure was so close to pain it was enough to turn a sane person into a quivering, gibbering wreck. It was like having a fist buried deep inside her pelvis, right in the core of her where she couldn't reach it. She could do nothing but let out strangulated cries as the fist rubbed over her raw and bloody innards, searing her flesh. The friction sparked a fire which flickered just under her brain. It was impossible to endure. Anna closed her eyes, shut off her mind and succumbed to the darkness.

* * *

Curled up on the hard floor, Anna began to shiver as the heat of a million orgasms rapidly subsided. Sitting up, she pulled her crumpled bathrobe back on and let the thick towelling soak up her trembling. Gingerly, she rolled her neck. The ferocious sex had left her body in a state of deep relaxation, but it hadn't done much for her whiplash.

She didn't have the energy to move. Hugging her knees, she sat in the dark confessional with only the flickering candlelight for company. Father Lawrence had left her – gone to pray for his own forgiveness, perhaps. Anna shook her head, wondering whether anyone would ever believe what she'd just done. She couldn't get her head round it. She wasn't that surprised to come across a kinky priest – after all, anyone who took a vow of chastity had to be a little suspect. It was like a child promising his mother that he wouldn't eat sweets; as soon as her back was turned he'd be gorging himself. The surprising part in all of this was that Father Lawrence had taken a risk in assuming that Anna would comply. She had, of course, but her willingness didn't shock her any more. 'You're addicted to sexual submission,' the priest had said. It was true. The thrill of seducing a man had never felt as good as this – the feeling of giving her body for a man to use. The men she'd dominated seemed dull and boring now compared to these men, with their rampant desires and warped, wicked minds. Father Lawrence had sensed her sharp need, just like Galloway had done. The two men shared more than the piercing grey of their eyes and the smooth syrup of their voices.

Anna slowly heaved herself to her feet and stepped out of the booth. Lighting the way with the candle, she headed back towards the vestry and the vicarage. Hearing voices, she stopped and strained to listen. There were people outside, in the churchyard – men, talking and laughing. She moved towards the sound. Putting the candlestick down, she stepped up on to a pew and peered out of the stained-glass window.

She caught her breath. Her heart did a double beat as it dawned on her. It was so obvious – why hadn't she thought of it? Father Lawrence and Dr Galloway were more than similar. They were brothers.

As she eavesdropped on their conversation, everything that had been puzzling her fitted into place. The man who'd stumbled out of the night towards her car had been the vicar, intercepting her escape. It was the good cop, bad cop routine – Anna had run from Peter's evil clutches, straight into the arms of a priest. And who wouldn't trust a priest? That explained the vicar's story about his lack of phone and car. Father Lawrence's job was to keep Anna there, and to try to persuade her to go back to the Institute. Anna listened with horror as they sniggered over her willingness in the confession box. She'd fallen right into their trap. It was petrifying to think that they knew her better than she did.

Peter thanked his brother and walked out of sight. A car started up and the sound of its engine moved off into the distance. Anna sat down on the pew and tried valiantly to gather her thoughts.

Chapter Eleven

She looked out of the window at the distant mountains as the Institute's gate opened for the car. Father Lawrence had claimed it was a minor miracle when Joan happened to call in at the church, only ten minutes after Anna had told him she wanted to return to the Institute. So much for your phone being out of order, she thought, you lying, conniving, perverted bastard. She'd had enough of being manipulated. She'd been a fool to be taken in by the thrill of all their games. But she wouldn't fall for it again. She was back at the Institute for one reason only – to complete her investigation.

Joan kept up a stony silence as she marched Anna up to her room. She watched with folded arms and pursed lips as Anna showered. Roughly, she dressed her in her tight, white uniform again, scratching with her nails as she fastened Anna's suspenders. Scratch me as hard as you want, Anna thought. I'll get back at you. I'm in control now.

She was marched into Peter's interview room and made to stand in front of the desk. After ten minutes alone, as she stared into the mirror and wondered who was staring back from the other side, Peter came in and took his seat in front of her.

He sighed. 'Well, Anna. What are we to do with you?'

She looked blankly at him, steeling herself against the lure of his eyes. Last night, lying awake in bed, she'd resolved to be strong. She had to be single-minded now. He could dominate her body, if that's what it took for her to get closer to the truth, but her mind was out of bounds to him.

'Why did you do it, Anna? Why did you run away?'

She hung her head. 'I'm sorry, Peter, but I was afraid.'

'Of what?' His voice was hard, unforgiving.

She closed her eyes, feigning embarrassment. 'Of myself. The things I've discovered here have changed me, for ever. It's almost as if I'm not in control of myself any more.'

'Why have you come back?'

Slowly, she lifted her gaze and met his. She gave him a look she knew he would love: innocence, tainted at the edges with wickedness. 'Father Lawrence made me realise that it was useless to fight my desires. I'm not going to fight any more. I give in. What you do here – what you've done to me – I like it. I want it.' She took a deep breath, prolonging the moment. 'I need it.'

Galloway nodded wisely. 'I know you do, Anna. I knew from the minute I saw you that your sexuality was crying out for a firm hand to guide it. You did the right thing, coming back.' His slight smile quickly disintegrated. 'But you've presented me with a problem. You've left us once, and the general consensus is that you should be expelled. We conduct sensitive studies here, Anna, and we do things in our spare time which would be not be understood in the world outside. The longer you stay here, the more you will discover about our work . . . and our play. We don't want you to go, but we'd rather you left now than in another month's time, when you change your mind again.'

'But I've made up my mind. I won't want to leave again.'

'I don't think you understand. All of our staff are completely dedicated to what we do here. They've agreed to live their lives within the confines of this establishment. There are big rewards for their sacrifices, but we must have that level of commitment from everybody. Our activities here have to remain strictly secret. If you decide you want to stay, that means you stay – for good.'

'I told you, I want to stay.' He seemed unmoved by the pleading note in her voice. 'Please, Peter. I don't want to go back – I can't go back, now.'

He tutted uncertainly. 'I'm going to have a hard job, convincing the rest of the board that you should be given a second chance. Quite frankly, you're a risk. Our research and facilities are expensive. Training every new recruit is an investment in our future. We can't afford risks.'

'Peter, please ... what can I do to prove my commitment? I'll do anything.'

His gaze dropped as she eased up the hem of her dress. 'Showing me your panties is not going to prove anything,' he snapped. He took her hand and led her into the monitoring room. Shoving her into the seat, he whipped the belt from his trousers. Wrapping the leather around her wrists, he buckled them tightly together in front of her. He went to the cupboard and retrieved a video cassette. Sliding it into a video recorder, he pressed play. Anna watched as she appeared on the screen, dressed obscenely in her revealing waitress outfit.

'I suggest you watch this carefully, Anna. Watch your face as you come. If those are the sort of feelings that frighten you, then you're clearly not strong enough to stay here.' He bent close to her, brushing her ear with his mouth. 'It takes a brave person to surrender. Are you brave enough to surrender to me?'

Anna looked round as he walked out. 'Where are you going?'

'To discuss your future here,' he said over his shoulder. 'It might be an idea for you to give it some thought as well. When I come back, I'll have thought of some way you can prove your allegiance to me, and the Institute.'

Turning round, Anna was startled by the image on the monitor. As an extreme close-up showed the curved dildo being swallowed up by her open pussy lips, she groaned and tried to free her hands.

'So what do we do with her?' Dr Jeffries asked.

Peter stared at the credit card, as if it would give him the answer. He looked at the other things he'd found secreted in Anna's car: the dictaphone, the camera, the mobile phone keypad and its microphone. It had taken them a while to find that, hidden in the speakers.

In a way, he was pleased. It proved that his intuition was still infallible. Anna was a spy, sent from another lab to uncover the secrets they'd gone to such pains to hide. She knew a lot already, but not enough. The cloning theory she'd shared with Simon would be scoffed at, should she tell it to any other scientist. It would be just about safe to expel her now, with only vague suspicions and no hard evidence.

But Peter didn't want to expel her; neither did Joan, or Simon, or anyone who had seen her swinging from those cuffs in the observation room. Anna was the most willing subject they had ever recruited. But she was also more intelligent than most, and more likely to have ethical questions about the donation they would ask her to make. And she was a mole.

Peter took a deep breath, narrowing his eyes and looking up at the ceiling as he weighed it up. He knew Anna was wavering, caught between her task as an infiltrator and the pleasures she'd been subjected to. The Institute was a dream come true for a girl like her: a place where she could fully explore the darker side of her psyche. She did like it here, but did she really want to forsake the outside world? Had her hungry sexuality won out over her professional pride? Could he really allow himself to believe she had surrendered?

'She'll stay,' he decided.

There was sucking in of breath, tutting and other sounds of disapproval all around the table. 'I think you're making a mistake, Peter,' Sullivan said. 'She's too risky. How can we be sure she won't run away again?'

'She won't. I'm sure of it.'

Jeffries shook his head. 'I hope you know what you're doing.'

'I do,' Peter snapped, unable to keep the indignation out of his voice. 'Have I ever been wrong before? Was I wrong about her being a spy? Anna wants to stay. What do you think, darling?'

Joan gave him a reassuring smile. 'If you're happy, then I am. You know I don't want to get rid of her.'

Peter nodded. 'At least I can rely on my wife to trust my judgement.'

'We trust you,' Dr Jeffries said. 'It's Anna we're not sure about.'

'In that case, I suggest you all make your way to the observation room.'

'Why?' Joan asked eagerly.

'Because I'd like you all to witness Anna's transformation from new recruit into full staff member. It's time for Anna to make her decision. I'm going to persuade her that staying is the only option. Give me an hour with her, and I promise she'll never set foot out of that door again.'

'And what about the extraction?'

Galloway looked at Sullivan and smiled. 'You'll have your piece of Anna by lunchtime.'

* * *

Anna was almost sobbing with frustration when he returned. Grabbing the tightly wound belt, he pulled her to her feet. He delved between her legs, making her jump with the suddenness of the movement. Her panties were sodden.

Peter dragged her through his office and into the room beyond. He lifted her up on to the medical trolley and told her to lie down. Ignoring her questions, he wheeled the trolley out into the corridor and through the black doorway. He smiled proudly at the professionalism of his staff as he steered the bed into the first cell. They were all there waiting, just as he had instructed. Anna's eyes widened as she looked around at the faceless men. It was an imposing sight: rows of leather-clad guards lining two of the walls. They were motionless, standing to attention with silent poise worthy of the Grenadier Guards. But Galloway's troops wore more provocative uniforms than the Queen's. Their faces were covered with black hoods, only their eyes, nostrils and mouths vaguely visible through the holes. Their torsos were bare, their wide, muscular chests glistening with oil just as he'd asked. They wore black leather trousers, tight around the hips so their erections would be seen pushing against the soft calfskin. A couple already had distinct bulges in their pants. To complete the effect, they had heavy-soled leather boots on their feet. Peter suspected the Queen would look a lot happier if she swapped her guard of honour for his.

He parked the bed in the centre of the room and put on the brake. Clicking his fingers, he summoned two of the guards to undress her. They eagerly complied, taking every opportunity to touch her as they unbuttoned her dress and rolled down her stockings. Unsure of what to do or where to look, Anna gazed up at Peter as one man squeezed her breasts, while the other moved behind her and unhooked her bra. This is it, Anna, he thought. You've got a mind of steel if you don't succumb to this.

He was aroused by her self-consciousness as she hugged her knees to her chest and looked around at the men. It was impossible to tell whether they were ogling her from behind their hoods, and Anna clearly found their stillness unnerving. Peter was glad; he wanted her to feel a little shame and fear. It would heighten the experience if she did.

Right on cue, Suraya came in with her equipment. She was a dark-skinned beauty of Indian descent, and her deliciously dusky skin was sullied by the tawdriness of her outfit – a red satin version of the one Anna had worn yesterday. Peter winked at Suraya as she placed the basin of water on the bed. She'd come to the Institute to escape an arranged marriage, and had ended up being dominated in far more exotic ways than a husband would have offered her. But it had been her choice to stay, just as it would be Anna's.

Anna grew even more uncomfortable as she watched Suraya prepare. Her eyes flickered worriedly to Peter. He just smiled as Suraya pushed her back on to the bed. She bent Anna's legs and spread them wide apart. Hoisting her agile body up on to the end of the trolley, Suraya crouched between Anna's knees.

Now, Peter didn't know where to look. He was spoilt for choice. He slowly paced around the bed, relishing every view and every angle. There was Anna, lying on the bed with her legs apart, watching with wide eyes as Suraya began to shave her. There was Suraya, her small breasts pouting over the top of her gaudy satin basque, her dark pussy hair peeking out from her skirt, which had ridden right up as it was designed to. But best of all – so good it made his erection thicken – was the way the women were looking at each other. Suraya's dark-brown eyes were fixed with concentration on Anna's mound, following her fingers as she swept the blade across the delicate folds of skin. Anna's eyes were taking furtive glances at her attendant's delicate breasts with their dark, soft nipples, at the view beneath her skirt and at Suraya's long fingers, deft and arousing on her intimate flesh. Anna was falling – he could tell by the quiver in her open lips, and the tremor that rippled across her pelvis as Suraya opened out her delicate creases.

Suraya soon finished. Peter thanked her as she left. 'What do you think, Anna?' he asked.

Speechless, she looked down her body at her naked mound. There was shock in her eyes, but he could tell the sight thrilled her as much as it did him. Standing at her side, he took her hand and draped her fingers over her bare pussy. His fingers entwined with hers as they both discovered the incredible smoothness that had been hidden beneath her thick bush. Peter loved to see a woman's sex exposed. Her desire was obvious now. There was no soft hair to hide her scarlet clit as it rose angrily, or to shield her wonderfully fleshy lips from view. It was all he could do to stop himself diving down there and eating her until she came.

He took a step away, removing himself from temptation. He clicked his fingers at a pair of men, and they approached the bed and undid the two small bottles Suraya had left. Pouring the aromatic oil into their big hands, they rolled Anna on to her front and smoothed it into her skin. Teasing her with their greasy fingers, they rubbed the perfume all over her body. Anna groaned as her neck and shoulders were massaged, and whimpered as two searching hands spread her buttocks and another poured oil into her crack. Flipping her over on to her back, they anointed her breasts, belly and mound, working gently as they fingered her most tender parts. Her body jerked out of its stupor as an oily thumb brushed over her clit. The tiny hump was red with desire, and she had to grip on to the sides of the bed as the epicentre of her pleasure was circled and tweaked.

Her pure skin shone with oil. Her pussy lips shone with dew. She was ready. Time for her ordeal to begin.

'Present her,' Galloway said. Her masseurs positioned themselves on either side of the bed and picked her up. They put her arms around their shoulders, and cradled her around the back of her waist and underneath her thighs. Lifting her up from the bed, they waited while Peter pulled the trolley out from underneath her. He pushed it out of the way. Leaving it across the doorway, he walked back into the middle of the room to watch.

Anna was carried to the first man in line. His eyes glinted from his black shroud as he looked her up and down. 'Mouth,' he said curtly, and Anna's attendants hoisted her pelvis up to his face. They hooked her knees over his broad shoulders and presented him with her open sex. Galloway felt his own mouth watering as the man's pink tongue poked from his hood. Anna's head fell slowly back as he lapped at her. Upside-down, she looked directly at Peter as she sighed.

The men held her still, adjusting their grip as her muscles reacted to the pleasure and she squirmed to get closer to that long, searching tongue. Peter could probably have asked her now, 'Do you want to stay here for ever?' and she would have said yes. But he'd only just started; by the end, she would be screaming, 'Yes! Yes!'

The first man brought her to shaking orgasm with only his tongue. Without a pause, her carriers moved her on to the next in line. 'Cock,' he said, undoing his leather trousers and unfurling his thick penis. Anna was tilted upright into a sitting position, and lowered without ceremony on to the waiting cock. An arch rippled up her pliant spine as she was filled with the rigid meat. Peter saw her shoulders twitch as she tried to free her arms and hold on to her new lover. But the men blocked her, pushing her hands away and pinning her arms down by her side. She wasn't to touch any of them, except where they instructed. This was sex in its crudest, most primitive form: no emotion, no feeling, faceless and nameless. She wouldn't even see the pleasure stretched across their

231

mouths and glinting in their eyes. All she would feel was cock and pussy, tongue and anus.

Her thighs were held open at his waist as she was lowered up and down on his straining rod. He came quickly and without a sound, but Anna's assistants knew when it was time to move her on. And so she progressed down the first row, sometimes having an orgasm, sometimes giving one. The third man wanted to tongue her anus, and her body was turned face down and raised up on to their shoulders. Supporting her shoulders and hips, they offered number three her arse. Her head and legs dangled straight down as he spread her pale cheeks and explored her most secret place.

Number four wanted her breasts. Anna was made to kneel, and the men on either side of her squeezed her breasts together while the third thrust manically between the heavy mounds. The fifth man wanted to fuck her, and she was sat astride his cock. He also wanted to feel her torso against his, and her oily, come-streaked breasts squashed and slid against his smooth chest as she was plunged on to his prick. Number six Peter recognised as Simon, partly because he wanted to lick her out, but mainly because he took so long. He relished his task.

It took an hour for Anna to be ferried around the stiff-cocked ranks. She was manoeuvred in every possible direction and fucked in every orifice. She was tilted and turned, her body undulating with ecstasy within her attendants' strong fingers. By the time it was their turn, the oil covering her skin was mixed with sweat, and come, and juice from her gaping pussy. The pungent smell of sex was heavy in the warm air. Unable and unwilling to do anything else, she allowed the last two men to arrange her limbs the way they wanted. Delirious, she rested her head on one man's shoulder as he pulled her down over his lap. She knelt astride his hips, sheathing his penis inside her, unaware that the second man was kneeling behind her. Wrapping his muscular body around hers, he pressed his chest against her back. Grasping his prick, he brought the weeping head between her open cheeks. Slowly he pressed, waiting for her sphincter muscles to relax and let him in. The men put their arms around each other's shoulders, encasing her in the heat of their bodies. Trapped between them, Anna cried out. Tears streamed down her flushed cheeks and dripped from her open lips. Peter stood in front of her and opened his lab coat to reveal his rearing penis. Through half-closed eyes, she watched as he stepped closer to her. Her moans were smothered as he filled her mouth. Then, every orifice was full with cock. It was all she would smell, and taste, and feel. And if he could have seen inside her mind, he knew he would have found cock there, too – his cock, fucking with her brain. Power surged through his veins as he came on her tongue.

The three men lifted her used body back on to the medical bed. She lay just as they left her: legs sprawled, arms thrown back over her head. Her pussy was still in spasm at the ferocity of her final climax, and thick white juice trickled down her inner thigh. Galloway smiled at the sight of her, spent with too much pleasure. That was how he liked his women: their eyelids heavy, their eyes clouded, their bodies used and their spirits tamed. Anna was broken.

He stroked her damp hair as the men silently filed out. She blinked sleepily, confused like someone coming round from anaesthetic. 'I hope I didn't push you too far,' he said, soothing her with his voice and fingers. 'It usually takes new recruits a while to work up to what you've just done. It can be too much for some people.'

She smiled weakly. 'I always was a quick learner.'

'And what did you learn today?'

'That I want to stay here.' Pulling on her reserves of strength, she reached for Peter's hand. 'Please . . . please let me stay. I swear to you I'll never set foot outside the door again. I don't want to, not any more. I don't want my old life back – I want this life.'

Galloway nodded. 'I think we can safely say you proved that to all of us this afternoon. You belong here, Anna. We want you here, with us.' He wiped a tear away from her cheek. 'But I want you to fully understand what you're committing yourself to.' He caressed her throat. 'The lucky ones who are offered permanent places here – and I'm happy to say you're one of them – can enjoy a fulfilling existence. Life here has no limitations, Anna. One of the reasons I founded this Institute was because I was tired of having limitations put on me.' He tutted, narrowing his eyes at the thought of the world outside, and how it had tried to stop him from reaching his full potential. 'Right from being a student I was told I couldn't do this, mustn't do that. I got frustrated by all the constraints put on my work. After all, who were these people telling me what not to do? – people with closed minds and blinkered views. A closed mind is a dangerous thing, Anna. It stops you from exploring new possibilities.' His touch drifted down to her breast. He gently touched the bite marks on her flesh. 'I wanted to open my mind to everything. I wanted no constraints, either on my work or on what I chose to do outside of work. And yet I found that people even wanted to control my private life – to put labels on me, and to brand me.' He seethed at the memory. He took a couple of slow breaths to calm himself. 'So I set up this place, Anna. Within these walls there are no limits. Our research has broken boundaries. We've opened our minds, and taken genetic studies further than any of our competitors. People told us it couldn't be done – mustn't be done – but we did it anyway.' His voice rose as he got carried away. 'Joan and I decided from the start that we'd only have like-minded people working for us. We would expect the best from them, and in return we'd give them the best working conditions possible and the opportunity to free their minds. If someone had a scientific theory that

234

had been scoffed at outside, we would let them test it here. And if someone had a dark, deeply buried desire, we would help them admit to it. Our policy wouldn't suit everyone. But it does suit people who felt uncomfortable with their desires in the outside world. People like you, Anna.' He paused as he looked again at the beauty of her naked pussy. The sight made his penis ache once more. He tenderly fingered her swollen lips.

'I never realised I had these desires, until I came here,' she whispered.

He gave her a gentle smile. He'd never got quite so much pleasure from breaking in a new recruit. The fact that he'd known all along about her ulterior motives made it all the sweeter now; now that she was his. To make any woman admit to her animal longing was deeply gratifying. But to make a spy forget her real purpose – to lead her willingly astray from her work and down a path towards her own corruption – that was enough to give a man a permanent hard-on.

'It must have been fate that brought you to me, Anna. The first day we met I could see that you needed me. I knew you belonged here.'

'I knew it too,' she said. 'It just took me a while to realise it.'

Her creamy inner thighs were bruised where the staff had slammed their hard bodies into her. Peter brushed his fingertips over the faint blemishes. 'You must stay here now, Anna. There's nothing left for you outside. The heights of pleasure you've reached here aren't allowed in the so-called real world. From now on, you can climb to those heights whenever you want. The Institute is full of men and women eager to help you.'

She sighed wistfully.

'Of course, we do ask for a few things in return. There will be days when you must work, just like everyone else. We do have a research laboratory to run.' He chuckled, trying to diffuse the importance of his next statement. 'And now that you've been accepted on to the permanent staff, we ask you to donate a few cells for our gene bank.'

Her brow creased slightly. 'What sort of cells?'

He picked up her hand and sucked on her fingertip. 'It's a painless procedure. We need a constant supply of cells for our scientists to study. On graduation, we ask each new recruit to donate a tiny piece of skin from the tip of one finger.'

'What do you use it for?'

'Where do you think we find genes to study?' He rolled his tongue around her finger. 'It's a small price to pay, don't you think? A few cells in return for a life of unimaginable pleasure.'

She smiled. 'You can have as many of my cells as you want.'

She watched dreamily as he pulled out a scalpel and test tube from his breast pocket. Taking the guard off the blade, he made a neat incision in the tip of her middle finger. With practised skill, he sliced off a tiny circle of her priceless skin and dropped it into the tube. Holding it up, he looked at the sliver of flesh and wondered how much it would be worth, in months to come.

He gently lowered her hand and eased her finger into her mouth. He'd barely gone below the epidermis, and there was only a pinprick of blood where he had. 'Just suck on that for a moment,' he said. 'Genetic donations are vital to our work here, Anna. In recognition of the contribution you've just made, and to welcome you as a proper staff member, we offer a little reward. For the next week, you're excused from all work. You'll stay in this room and do whatever you want, with whoever you want.' He wished it could be him first, but he had to get the cells labelled and put in the freezer. Turning at the door, Peter took a last lingering look at her beautiful body. 'Who shall I send in first?'

She smiled coyly. 'Can I have Frank?'

Chapter Twelve

*F*rank looked doleful. His deep-blue eyes were over-flowing with sorrow. 'Why did you come back?' He shook his head as he perched on the edge of the bed. 'I told you this would happen. Oh,' he sighed mournfully. 'Look what they've done to you.' His fingers went where his father's had been: over her smooth, hairless mound, on to the damaged skin at the tops of her inner thighs, and over the marks on her breasts. 'They've hurt you,' he whispered. His face was full of sad incomprehension. 'I said they would. Why didn't you listen? I thought you'd got away.'

Anna eased herself up off the bed. She could speak freely now; she knew there were no cameras or microphones in these rooms. 'Frank, I came back because I have to find out why the women here are being put in these rooms and punished.' She didn't have time to explain that Frank had mistaken ecstasy for agony. She had a feeling he'd never understand. 'Your father's just taken some cells from my finger.' She held it up for him to see. 'I think this is something to do with the way the women are treated here.'

His brow knitted. He shook his head. 'The cell-extraction programme has nothing to do with these torture chambers, Anna.'

She blinked several times, amazed he knew what she was talking about, for a change. 'What is it to do with, then?'

'Making people, of course.' He laughed, amused by her naïveté.

Anna swallowed hard. When she opened her mouth, the breath came out in a rush. 'What do you know about "making people"?'

'Everything. I work in the gene bank.' He proudly stuck out his perfect chin. 'I'm the top scientist here, you know.'

'Of course you are.' She scrambled from the bed and put her dress back on. 'I have to see the gene bank, but I'd get into trouble if anyone caught me. They'd punish me again, Frank. When can we go there, alone?'

He looked at his watch. 'They'll be going to lunch. We can go now, if you like.'

Anna leant against the wall outside the gene bank, trying to catch her breath. Her heart was beating so fast she felt dizzy. Thoughts were colliding in her head. She had to get photographs, video footage – firm evidence of what she'd just seen. But her surveillance equipment was in her wrecked car. She pounded her fists against the wall. Think, she told herself. Think.

She had three priorities: collect evidence, alert Mike and do nothing to arouse suspicion until he got there. It would be almost impossible to pull off all three, but she had to try.

She tried to impress upon Frank that she really was in danger now. Making the most of the camera-less corridor, she explained that she needed him to protect her from further 'punishment'. He promised he would, telling her again that he had feelings for her – feelings that made his heart ache. If she hadn't been in such a panic, she would have been moved.

She went back to her cell, sending Frank downstairs to the labs. Five minutes later, he returned with Simon. 'Frank said you wanted me,' he leered. 'I told him I already knew that, but he insisted I came up to see you.'

Anna darted to the door, peering out of the hatch to make sure no one was there. 'Is there anyone back there?' She motioned towards the mirrored wall. Simon shook his head. 'I'll come straight to the point. You were right to be worried about the research you've been doing. I've just seen the gene bank.'

Simon's eyebrows twitched. 'The what?'

'The gene bank. It's the reason behind all those inexplicable experiments Peter's been asking you to do.' She lunged towards him, squeezing his arm to try to show him how serious this was. 'Frank works there, with Peter and Joan. I've just seen it. It's frightening, Simon.'

'Calm down,' he said.

'You wouldn't be calm if you'd seen what I have. There were rows and rows of freezers in there, packed with metal canisters. Every canister's labelled with a name and date. Inside each one there are test tubes together with descriptions: eye colour, hair colour, height, gender, intelligence, sexual preferences ... Don't you see what this means? My theory about cloning was right!' She held up her finger, showing him the scar on the tip. 'Galloway extracts cells from the staff, and then you're given the task of identifying the genes and replicating them. Once you've done that, the genetic information is documented and stored, and then ...'

'And then what?'

Annoyed, she huffed at his incredible calmness. 'I don't know what happens next. But I will find out. I've got to.'

'Why?' His eyes softened as he caressed her cheek. 'Why are you so excited about all this?'

She didn't falter. She had nothing to lose now. And

she knew she could trust him. 'Simon, I'm not who you think I am. I came here to try to find out what was going on.' He didn't seem shocked. 'Do you understand what I'm saying?'

He nodded. 'You're a spy.'

'Simon, you've got to help me. You told me yourself, cloning is illegal. Galloway's a madman if he thinks he can get away with this.'

'How can I possibly help?'

'I had a video camera. Peter caught me with it, and I don't know what he's done with it. I need it to get some evidence. Can you find it for me?'

'Of course, but . . .' He looked bemused.

'What is it?'

'I thought you liked it here. I thought you wanted to stay.'

'I do. But what Galloway's doing is wrong, Simon. He's got to be stopped.'

He nodded quickly. 'I'll find your camera.'

He left Anna alone with Frank again. 'That's phase one under way,' she muttered to herself. 'Now for phase two. Frank?' She held his hand. 'I want you to listen very carefully. You have to do something very important for me.'

When Frank didn't return, Anna began to pace distractedly. Her spirits soared as Simon came through the door, but she could tell by the coldness in his eyes that there was something wrong. When Galloway followed him in, her tiny camcorder in his hand, her hopes shattered in a thousand sharp pieces on the floor.

'I believe you want this back,' Peter smirked, holding up the video camera.

Anna looked uncertainly at Simon, but he wasn't giving her any help. His eyes were fixed on the floor.

'It's no good looking at him.' Like a wolf, Peter circled

his captive prey. His fingers were cold as they trailed across her neck. 'Simon's mine, just like you're mine.'

Anna's hand flew to her mouth, but it was far too late to recapture all the things she'd said to Simon. No wonder he wouldn't look her in the eye; he was a spy himself, Galloway's faithful servant.

'I trusted you,' she whispered sadly. 'I thought we were . . . friends.'

'And I trusted you.' Galloway's face loomed into view. 'I also told you once that, if you had questions, you should come to me for answers.'

'All right.' She jutted her chin defiantly. The game was up, but she wasn't going to go down without a fight. 'Answer this. Why did you really need my cells?'

'So that we can clone you.'

She gasped. His calmness knocked the breath out of her. 'That's illegal.'

He tilted his head in agreement. 'At the moment, it is.'

'It's also immoral, unethical . . . insane –'

He held up his hand. 'Only to those who refuse to open their minds. I thought we had finally managed to open yours, but it seems I was wrong.'

'Don't change the subject,' she hissed. 'I've another question. Why are you trying to clone people?'

He shrugged, as if to say, why not? 'At first, it was because everyone said it couldn't be done. Then it was because they said it mustn't be done. Now that we've done it, I must admit the money's looking like another very good reason.'

'But who are you doing it for? Where's the money coming from?'

'America, mainly. They've lots of money and no morals over there, you know.' He winked. 'Our research is being funded by a chain of very prominent people. Politicians, lawyers, businessmen – even the President's a donor, a very generous one, too.' He laughed at Anna's impatience. Her mind was full of questions, her mouth

241

opening and closing. 'These people don't want normal children. They want babies who'll grow up according to their grand plans. Some want blond, blue-eyed boys guaranteed free from disease and without any chance of growing up to be homosexual. Some want children who are programmed to be gay, like themselves. Others, and I believe the President is one of them, want to spawn geniuses. Some want to breed Olympic athletes. Some want children with an aptitude for music.' He spread his hands wide. 'We can give them anything they want, Anna. Blond, blue-eyed boys ... black-haired, green-eyed girls with great tits and built-in sexual perversions. They can order the perfect child, just like a takeaway.' He sneered at her disgust. 'Mail-order babies, Anna. The ultimate designer accessory for the super-rich control freak who wants more than a hand in his child's future. Oh, close your mouth, it's not so surprising. This was talked about, the day a scientist first discovered what a gene was. It was inevitable that someone would do it sooner or later.'

'It'll never work,' Anna insisted. 'Real professors say it's impossible to clone a human.'

He turned down the corners of his wide mouth. 'They can't have seen Frank, then.' Anna's mouth gaped, again. 'Not bad for our first attempt, was he? "Perfect", I think you called him.'

'That's obscene,' she gasped. 'You're insane.'

'Am I? My staff think I'm rather clever.'

Anna looked at Simon. 'You knew about this?'

Galloway answered for him. 'All my staff are fully aware of their purpose here. They're more than willing to be involved. They get to indulge their fantasies and they'll have a share of the profits when we start business. You would have been told, too, had you behaved like a normal recruit. But we knew you were different, Anna Caplin.'

It took her a moment to realise that Johnson was the

242

name she'd given in her interview. 'How long have you known who I am?'

'Not long. But, from the start, there was something different about you.' He squinted, as if he was still trying to work it out. 'You were almost too willing.'

'If you knew what I was doing here, why didn't you ask me to leave? Why are you telling me all this now?'

As if she had finally come up with a good question, Galloway nodded. 'At first, I thought you were playing along because you had to. But then I realised your desires were getting out of control. You didn't want to let go, but you couldn't help it. I was enjoying watching you fight with yourself.' He grinned salaciously. 'That's why I let you stay. And I know it's safe to tell you everything now, because you admitted there's nothing left for you in the outside world. You don't want to leave this place, Anna. You realised that not long after I did.'

'You're wrong,' she spat. 'I lied to you. And someone's on their way here now to get me.'

'A knight in shining armour?' Galloway shrugged nonchalantly. 'He won't get through the front gate.'

She could have burst into tears. She'd been so irritated by Mike's doubts, and he'd been right all along. This job had been too much for her. Galloway had seen through Anna as easily as if she'd been transparent. She'd got the answers she needed, but now it was too late to do anything with them. The only hope she could cling to now was that Frank had done what she'd asked.

'Cuff her,' Peter barked as he disappeared through the door. 'Simon, she's yours.'

Two hooded men trooped in. Working the pulleys on opposite walls, they lowered two long chains from the ceiling. They cuffed Anna's hands above her head. Pulling her ankles apart, they fastened those into thick leather bands chained to the floor. 'She's all yours,' one of them muttered to Simon as they left the room again.

Simon looked uneasily at Anna. 'I'm sorry,' he offered.

243

'Don't bother,' she snapped. His betrayal tasted bitter in her mouth.

'I had to tell him.' Tentatively, as if she was an animal who might rip off the chains and lunge at his throat, he stepped closer. 'We really thought you'd come back because you wanted to.'

Anna flinched, turning her head away as he lifted his hand. 'Don't touch me.'

He grabbed her jaw, gently forcing her to look at him. 'You liked it when I was touching you before.'

She burnt him with the hate in her eyes. Slowly, she softened and allowed him a faint, sad smile. It was hard not to like him. 'I knew which one was you. I could tell by the way you licked me.'

'Anna, if you stayed here I could make you come like that every day.'

She closed her eyes as he dropped to his knees. It didn't look like she had much choice.

Chapter Thirteen

M ike wasn't sure that Frank had understood his instructions, but he had left the gate open as planned. Parking his car outside the fence, just out of range of the cameras, Mike sat for a moment and weighed up whether he should wait for the others to arrive before going in. He knew he probably should, but the thought of Anna being in pain, as Frank had said, decided it. He went through the gate and up to the Institute's front door, which immediately opened.

'Frank?'

'Mike?'

Mike nodded and held out his hand, but Frank was already on the move. He beckoned Mike urgently towards a staircase. Mike struggled to keep up as the blond hulk took the stairs three at a time. Mike was puffing heavily by the time they reached the top floor.

Frank peered out into the corridor, then waved Mike through. They moved stealthily to the end of the passage and through a dark doorway. Another door, and then he saw her.

'Anna! Oh God . . .' For a moment, he thought the look

on her face was pain. Then, as his brain caught up with his eyes, he realised it was the opposite.

Anna was falling out of a tight-fitting red dress. It was open down the front, and her breasts were spilling out of her low-cut black bra. She had knee-length leather boots on, stockings and suspenders, but no panties – and no pubic hair. A naked man was sitting up between her open legs, licking her naked pussy. Behind her, another man was reaching round to pinch and pull her stiff nipples.

'Mike!'

The two men looked up as she cried out. One of them strode menacingly towards him. 'Who are you?'

Mike huffed. 'Who are you?'

'Peter Galloway. This is my Institute, and you're trespassing.'

Mike met his challenging glare. He wasn't about to be intimidated by a naked, fake doctor, even if he was a megalomaniac. 'I'm not trespassing, Peter. Your son Frank invited me here.' Mike jerked his head towards Anna. 'Come on, Frank, let's get her out of that thing.'

Peter watched incredulously as Mike and Frank freed Anna from her restraints. Mike heard Peter snigger as he buttoned Anna's dress up for her.

'You obviously don't know Anna very well. I think you'll find she likes to show her body.'

'How interesting. I think you'll find the police are on their way.'

Galloway's stone-cold eyes narrowed with suspicion. 'I don't believe you.'

Mike shrugged and took Anna by the hand. 'I don't give a shit what you believe. They'll be here in a minute. I left the gate open for them.'

Galloway followed them out into the corridor. On cue, a siren wailed in the distance, muffled by the building's thick walls.

'Simon – the gene bank.' Galloway grabbed Simon and they darted off down the passageway.

Anna clutched Mike's shoulder. 'They're going to destroy the evidence. Mike, for Christ's sake, we've got to stop them, now.' She jumped about, then latched on to Frank. 'Frank, listen to me. You've got to go to the gene bank and stop your father and Simon from getting in. Please, Frank, do it for me. It's very important. Go now. Run!'

Mike watched as Frank loped off down the corridor, speeding over the floor with his huge strides. 'Will he do it?'

Anna nodded. 'He'd do anything for me. He's got feelings for me, you know.'

Mike looked at her. She seemed fine, but there was something different in her eyes. He couldn't resist it; he gave her a hug. 'I'm so relieved to see you.' He squeezed her hard, making sure it really was her, and she really was safe. 'I was so worried. I hadn't heard from you since your message saying you'd call back later – and then you never did. I was already thinking about coming up here when Frank called. I got on the first plane.' He held her shoulders, peering into her beautiful green eyes. 'Looks like I got here just in time.'

There it was, that familiar smile. 'I had everything under control in there.'

'Of course you did.' He winked. 'I never doubted you for a minute.'

Her smiled dropped and she bit her lip. 'I nearly messed things up completely, though.'

She looked so serious. Perhaps she'd tell him what she meant, later – when all this was over. 'You didn't mess up, though,' he said.

They both looked up as a policeman appeared at the top of the stairs. Anna ran to meet him. 'Follow me,' she said, already running off in the direction Frank had gone. Mike waited for his film crew to pant up behind the detectives and he ran with them. 'What's the story?' the cameraman asked as they jogged along. There hadn't been time to brief anyone – when Mike had spotted his burnt-out Golf on the side of the road, he'd phoned the police and a colleague who worked on a local news programme. He didn't want to cover this story with a borrowed crew, but he didn't have much option.

'This,' he said, 'is the biggest story *Undercover* has ever done. Point the camera at the woman in the red dress.'

He watched with pride as Anna directed the police, showing them who to arrest and keeping one eye on the camera all the while. She was a natural. She would never be able to work undercover again after this, but she had a great future ahead of her as an investigative reporter. Mike admired her guts and determination. He'd been worried about sending her into the Institute, but she'd been confident all along that she'd get the story. The unmistakable fire of triumph smouldered in her eyes as she pointed the naked Galloway out to the police. There was something between the two of them that was obvious in the way Galloway smiled at her as he was being handcuffed. Under the circumstances, his expression was macabre and disturbing; but Anna smiled back, meeting the challenge in his eyes. Whatever battle had gone on between them, she had finally won it.

'Good job, Anna.' Mike smiled across at her as he started the car. Finally, the police had agreed they could leave for the night. Mike said he wanted to get her to a hotel and let her get some sleep: she'd be back early in the morning to carry on helping the detectives and to shoot some more footage for the programme. But Anna knew she wasn't going to sleep tonight.

'Are you sure about this?' Mike jerked his head towards the back seat.

Anna leant around and patted Frank's knee. 'We

couldn't let him be taken away with all the others. He's done nothing wrong.'

'Yes, but he's a . . . clone.' Mike mouthed the word, as if Frank would know what it meant.

Anna tutted. 'Where's your compassion? Even an animal bred for the laboratory deserves a decent life and a good home, with a loving owner. What was the alternative?'

'I don't know, but I hope you realise what you're taking on. Freeing a laboratory monkey is not quite the same as taking a human under your wing.'

She smiled to herself, imagining how Suzy would react when Anna introduced their new flatmate. 'Me and Suzy will look after him.'

'He doesn't know how lucky he is,' Mike murmured. 'To be getting away from that place,' he added, as Anna looked up. 'Was it really awful in there?'

She looked back over her shoulder. 'It was . . . unusual,' she said, feeling an inexplicable pang of regret as the imposing white building grew smaller. She couldn't possibly explain to Mike, or anyone else, how it had felt to be a part of the Institute. Only a few people would understand, and they were all being driven away in police vans.

'It must have been frightening, being trapped in there with that repulsive sham of a scientist.' Mike lowered his voice. 'Did it make you feel sick, having to put up with him . . . doing all those things to you?'

Sick was one thing she hadn't felt. Confused, aroused, out of control, perhaps even a little insane – but never sick. 'Peter Galloway lives by a different set of rules to the rest of us,' she murmured. 'Some would say the wrong set of rules.'

'Some? The bloke's a power-crazed madman.'

'Yes, he is.' Anna could feel Mike looking at her.

'Anna, you're glad it's all over, right?'

'Oh, yes,' she said, but she couldn't stifle a heavy sigh.

Ever since she'd made her mind up in the church, she had known her voyage of discovery was coming to an end. But a tiny part of her wished the madness could have continued – for ever. 'Can't wait to get back to normality,' she mumbled, not even managing to convince herself.

The driveway joined a narrow country lane. Mike was following a police car, and he should have kept his attention on the road, but he couldn't seem to stop himself from sneaking sidelong glances at Anna. She felt his gaze on her legs. 'One thing I'll say for Galloway,' Mike said, 'is that he's got good taste in staff uniforms.'

'Mmm,' Anna said again, leaning her head against the window.

'I think I'll bring in a uniform policy at our office.'

'Good idea,' she said, trying not to snap but wishing he'd shut up. She closed her eyes, thinking that a few weeks ago she would have savoured his attention on her body. Now, behind the refuge of her dark eyelids, it was Galloway's touch she longed for; his voice, dousing her skin; his eyes, coating her body in desire. She thought of the look on his face as she had handed him over to the police, and she felt herself getting wet.

Mike seemed to get the message that she didn't want to talk. They drove in silence for a while. He coughed before he spoke again, as if he was warning her. 'I expect it's all a bit of an anticlimax now, is it – now that your first big assignment's over?'

Anna nodded, wondering how long it would take for her to pull herself out of this anticlimax. A week? A year? A lifetime? What could ever compare?

'We'll have to find you another big challenge – something to really get your teeth into.'

Anna liked the sound of that. 'Any ideas?'

'Not at the moment. But if you come up with something . . .'

Her gaze drifted out of the window as they passed the small, innocent-looking church. A tiny part of the old Anna returned in her slowly spreading, wicked smile. 'Ever thought of doing a programme on vicars?'

BLACK LACE NEW BOOKS

Published in September

DARKER THAN LOVE
Kristina Lloyd
£5.99

It's 1875 and the morals of Queen Victoria have no hold over London's debauched elite. Young and naive Clarissa is eager to meet Lord Marldon, the man to whom she is betrothed. She knows he is handsome, dark and sophisticated. He is, in fact, depraved and louche with a taste for sexual excess.

ISBN 0 352 33279 4

RISKY BUSINESS
Lisette Allen
£5.99

Liam is a hard-working journalist fighting a battle against injustice. Rebecca is a spoilt rich girl used to having her own way. Their lives collide when they are thrown into a dangerous intimacy with each other. His rugged charm is about to turn her world upside-down.

ISBN 0 352 33280 8

DARK OBSESSION
Fredrica Alleyn
£7.99

Ambitious young interior designer Annabel Moss is delighted when a new assignment takes her to the country estate of Lord and Lady Corbett-Wynne. The grandeur of the house and the impeccable family credentials are a façade for shockingly salacious practices. Lord James, Lady Marina, their family and their subservient staff maintain a veneer of respectability over some highly esoteric sexual practices and Annabel is drawn into a world of decadence where anything is allowed as long as a respectable appearance prevails.

ISBN 0 352 33281 6

Published in October

SEARCHING FOR VENUS
Ella Broussard
£5.99

Art history student Louise decides to travel to rural France to track down a lost painting – the sensuous *Venus of Collioure* – whose disappearance is one of the mysteries of the art world. She is about to embark on another quest: one which will bring her sexual fulfilment with a number of dashing Frenchmen!

ISBN 0 352 33284 0

UNDERCOVER SECRETS
Zoe le Verdier
£5.99

Anna Caplin is a TV reporter. When her boss offers her the chance to infiltrate a secret medical institute, she grabs the opportunity – not realising the institute specialises in human sexual response. It isn't long before Anna finds herself involved in some highly unorthodox situations with Doctor Galloway – the institute's director.

ISBN 0 352 33285 9

To be published in November

FORBIDDEN FRUIT
Susie Raymond
£5.99

Beth is thirty-eight. Jonathan is sixteen. An affair betwen them is unthinkable. Or is it? To Jonathan, Beth is much more exciting than girls his own age. She's a real woman: sexy, sophisticated and experienced. And Beth can't get the image of his fit young body out of her mind. Although she knows she shouldn't encourage him, the temptation is irresistible. What will happen when they have tasted the forbidden fruit?

ISBN 0 352 33306 5

HOSTAGE TO FANTASY
Louisa Francis
£5.99

Bridie Flanagan is a spirited young Irish woman living a harsh life in outback Australia at the turn of the century. A reversal of fortune enables her to travel to the thriving city of Melbourne and become a lady. But rugged bushranger Lucan Martin is in pursuit of her; he wants her money and she wants his body. Can they reach a civilised agreement?

ISBN 0 352 33305 7

If you would like a complete list of plot summaries of Black Lace titles, please fill out the questionnaire overleaf or send a stamped addressed envelope to:

Black Lace, Thames Wharf Studios, Rainville Road, London W6 9HT

BLACK LACE BOOKLIST

All books are priced £4.99 unless another price is given.

Black Lace books with a contemporary setting

ODALISQUE	Fleur Reynolds ISBN 0 352 32887 8	☐
VIRTUOSO	Katrina Vincenzi ISBN 0 352 32907 6	☐
THE SILKEN CAGE	Sophie Danson ISBN 0 352 32928 9	☐
RIVER OF SECRETS	Saskia Hope & Georgia Angelis ISBN 0 352 32925 4	☐
SUMMER OF ENLIGHTENMENT	Cheryl Mildenhall ISBN 0 352 32937 8	☐
MOON OF DESIRE	Sophie Danson ISBN 0 352 32911 4	☐
A BOUQUET OF BLACK ORCHIDS	Roxanne Carr ISBN 0 352 32939 4	☐
THE TUTOR	Portia Da Costa ISBN 0 352 32946 7	☐
THE HOUSE IN NEW ORLEANS	Fleur Reynolds ISBN 0 352 32951 3	☐
WICKED WORK	Pamela Kyle ISBN 0 352 32958 0	☐
DREAM LOVER	Katrina Vincenzi ISBN 0 352 32956 4	☐
UNFINISHED BUSINESS	Sarah Hope-Walker ISBN 0 352 32983 1	☐
THE DEVIL INSIDE	Portia Da Costa ISBN 0 352 32993 9	☐
HEALING PASSION	Sylvie Ouellette ISBN 0 352 32998 X	☐
THE STALLION	Georgina Brown ISBN 0 352 33005 8	☐

RUDE AWAKENING	Pamela Kyle ISBN 0 352 33036 8	☐
EYE OF THE STORM	Georgina Brown ISBN 0 352 33044 9	☐
GEMINI HEAT	Portia Da Costa ISBN 0 352 32912 2	☐
ODYSSEY	Katrina Vincenzi-Thyne ISBN 0 352 33111 9	☐
PULLING POWER	Cheryl Mildenhall ISBN 0 352 33139 9	☐
PALAZZO	Jan Smith ISBN 0 352 33156 9	☐
THE GALLERY	Fredrica Alleyn ISBN 0 352 33148 8	☐
AVENGING ANGELS	Roxanne Carr ISBN 0 352 33147 X	☐
COUNTRY MATTERS	Tesni Morgan ISBN 0 352 33174 7	☐
GINGER ROOT	Robyn Russell ISBN 0 352 33152 6	☐
DANGEROUS CONSEQUENCES	Pamela Rochford ISBN 0 352 33185 2	☐
THE NAME OF AN ANGEL £6.99	Laura Thornton ISBN 0 352 33205 0	☐
SILENT SEDUCTION	Tanya Bishop ISBN 0 352 33193 3	☐
BONDED	Fleur Reynolds ISBN 0 352 33192 5	☐
THE STRANGER	Portia Da Costa ISBN 0 352 33211 5	☐
CONTEST OF WILLS £5.99	Louisa Francis ISBN 0 352 33223 9	☐
BY ANY MEANS £5.99	Cheryl Mildenhall ISBN 0 352 33221 2	☐
MÉNAGE £5.99	Emma Holly ISBN 0 352 33231 X	☐
THE SUCCUBUS £5.99	Zoe le Verdier ISBN 0 352 33230 1	☐
FEMININE WILES £7.99	Karina Moore ISBN 0 352 33235 2	☐

AN ACT OF LOVE £5.99	Ella Broussard ISBN 0 352 33240 9	☐
THE SEVEN-YEAR LIST £5.99	Zoe le Verdier ISBN 0 352 33254 9	☐
MASQUE OF PASSION £5.99	Tesni Morgan ISBN 0 352 33259 X	☐
DRAWN TOGETHER £5.99	Robyn Russell ISBN 0 352 33269 7	☐
DRAMATIC AFFAIRS £5.99	Fredrica Alleyn ISBN 0 352 33289 1	☐

Black Lace books with an historical setting

THE CAPTIVE FLESH	Cleo Cordell ISBN 0 352 32872 X	☐
THE SENSES BEJEWELLED	Cleo Cordell ISBN 0 352 32904 1	☐
HANDMAIDEN OF PALMYRA	Fleur Reynolds ISBN 0 352 32919 X	☐
JULIET RISING	Cleo Cordell ISBN 0 352 32938 6	☐
ELENA'S CONQUEST	Lisette Allen ISBN 0 352 32950 5	☐
PATH OF THE TIGER	Cleo Cordell ISBN 0 352 32959 9	☐
BELLA'S BLADE	Georgia Angelis ISBN 0 352 32965 3	☐
WESTERN STAR	Roxanne Carr ISBN 0 352 32969 6	☐
CRIMSON BUCCANEER	Cleo Cordell ISBN 0 352 32987 4	☐
LA BASQUIASE	Angel Strand ISBN 0 352 32988 2	☐
THE LURE OF SATYRIA	Cheryl Mildenhall ISBN 0 352 32994 7	☐
THE INTIMATE EYE	Georgia Angelis ISBN 0 352 33004 X	☐
THE AMULET	Lisette Allen ISBN 0 352 33019 8	☐
CONQUERED	Fleur Reynolds ISBN 0 352 33025 2	☐

JEWEL OF XANADU	Roxanne Carr ISBN 0 352 33037 6	☐
THE MISTRESS	Vivienne LaFay ISBN 0 352 33057 0	☐
LORD WRAXALL'S FANCY	Anna Lieff Saxby ISBN 0 352 33080 5	☐
FORBIDDEN CRUSADE	Juliet Hastings ISBN 0 352 33079 1	☐
TO TAKE A QUEEN	Jan Smith ISBN 0 352 33098 8	☐
ÎLE DE PARADIS	Mercedes Kelly ISBN 0 352 33121 6	☐
NADYA'S QUEST	Lisette Allen ISBN 0 352 33135 6	☐
DESIRE UNDER CAPRICORN	Louisa Francis ISBN 0 352 33136 4	☐
THE HAND OF AMUN	Juliet Hastings ISBN 0 352 33144 5	☐
THE LION LOVER	Mercedes Kelly ISBN 0 352 33162 3	☐
A VOLCANIC AFFAIR	Xanthia Rhodes ISBN 0 352 33184 4	☐
FRENCH MANNERS	Olivia Christie ISBN 0 352 33214 X	☐
ARTISTIC LICENCE	Vivienne LaFay ISBN 0 352 33210 7	☐
INVITATION TO SIN £6.99	Charlotte Royal ISBN 0 352 33217 4	☐
ELENA'S DESTINY	Lisette Allen ISBN 0 352 33218 2	☐
LAKE OF LOST LOVE £5.99	Mercedes Kelly ISBN 0 352 33220 4	☐
UNHALLOWED RITES £5.99	Martine Marquand ISBN 0 352 33222 0	☐
THE CAPTIVATION £5.99	Natasha Rostova ISBN 0 352 33234 4	☐
A DANGEROUS LADY £5.99	Lucinda Carrington ISBN 0 352 33236 0	☐
PLEASURE'S DAUGHTER £5.99	Sedalia Johnson ISBN 0 352 33237 9	☐

SAVAGE SURRENDER £5.99	Deanna Ashford ISBN 0 352 33253 0	☐
CIRCO EROTICA £5.99	Mercedes Kelly ISBN 0 352 33257 3	☐
BARBARIAN GEISHA £5.99	Charlotte Royal ISBN 0 352 33267 0	☐

Black Lace anthologies

PAST PASSIONS £6.99	ISBN 0 352 33159 3	☐
PANDORA'S BOX 2 £4.99	ISBN 0 352 33151 8	☐
PANDORA'S BOX 3 £5.99	ISBN 0 352 33274 3	☐
SUGAR AND SPICE £7.99	ISBN 0 352 33227 1	☐

Black Lace non-fiction

WOMAN, SEX AND ASTROLOGY £5.99	Sarah Bartlett ISBN 0 352 33262 X	☐

------ ✂ --------------------

Please send me the books I have ticked above.

Name ....

Address ....

....

....

.... Post Code ....

Send to: **Cash Sales, Black Lace Books, Thames Wharf Studios, Rainville Road, London W6 9HT.**

US customers: for prices and details of how to order books for delivery by mail, call 1-800-805-1083.

Please enclose a cheque or postal order, made payable to **Virgin Publishing Ltd**, to the value of the books you have ordered plus postage and packing costs as follows:
    UK and BFPO – £1.00 for the first book, 50p for each subsequent book.
    Overseas (including Republic of Ireland) – £2.00 for the first book, £1.00 each subsequent book.

If you would prefer to pay by VISA or ACCESS/ MASTERCARD, please write your card number and expiry date here:

....

Please allow up to 28 days for delivery.

Signature ....

------ ✂ --------------------

BLACK
lace

WE NEED YOUR HELP ...
to plan the future of women's erotic fiction –

– and no stamp required!

Yours are the only opinions that matter.

Black Lace is the first series of books devoted to erotic fiction by women for women.

We intend to keep providing the best-written, sexiest books you can buy. And we'd appreciate your help and valued opinion of the books so far. Tell us what you want to read.

THE BLACK LACE QUESTIONNAIRE

SECTION ONE: ABOUT YOU

1.1 Sex (*we presume you are female, but so as not to discriminate*)
Are you?

Male	☐
Female	☐

1.2 Age

under 21	☐	21–30	☐
31–40	☐	41–50	☐
51–60	☐	over 60	☐

1.3 At what age did you leave full-time education?

still in education	☐	16 or younger	☐
17–19	☐	20 or older	☐

1.4 Occupation _____

1.5 Annual household income _____

1.6 We are perfectly happy for you to remain anonymous; but if you would like to receive information on other publications available, please insert your name and address

_____

_____

_____

_____

SECTION TWO: ABOUT BUYING BLACK LACE BOOKS

2.1 Where did you get this copy of *Undercover Secrets*?
- Bought at chain book shop ☐
- Bought at independent book shop ☐
- Bought at supermarket ☐
- Bought at book exchange or used book shop ☐
- I borrowed it/found it ☐
- My partner bought it ☐

2.2 How did you find out about Black Lace books?
- I saw them in a shop ☐
- I saw them advertised in a magazine ☐
- I read about them in _____
- Other _____

2.3 Please tick the following statements you agree with:
- I would be less embarrassed about buying Black Lace books if the cover pictures were less explicit ☐
- I think that in general the pictures on Black Lace books are about right ☐
- I think Black Lace cover pictures should be as explicit as possible ☐

2.4 Would you read a Black Lace book in a public place – on a train for instance?
- Yes ☐   No ☐

SECTION THREE: ABOUT THIS BLACK LACE BOOK

3.1 Do you think the sex content in this book is:
    Too much ☐   About right ☐
    Not enough ☐

3.2 Do you think the writing style in this book is:
    Too unreal/escapist ☐   About right ☐
    Too down to earth ☐

3.3 Do you think the story in this book is:
    Too complicated ☐   About right ☐
    Too boring/simple ☐

3.4 Do you think the cover of this book is:
    Too explicit ☐   About right ☐
    Not explicit enough ☐

Here's a space for any other comments:

SECTION FOUR: ABOUT OTHER BLACK LACE BOOKS

4.1 How many Black Lace books have you read? ☐

4.2 If more than one, which one did you prefer?

4.3 Why?

SECTION FIVE: ABOUT YOUR IDEAL EROTIC NOVEL

We want to publish the books you want to read – so this is your chance to tell us exactly what your ideal erotic novel would be like.

5.1 Using a scale of 1 to 5 (1 = no interest at all, 5 = your ideal), please rate the following possible settings for an erotic novel:

Medieval/barbarian/sword 'n' sorcery ☐
Renaissance/Elizabethan/Restoration ☐
Victorian/Edwardian ☐
1920s & 1930s – the Jazz Age ☐
Present day ☐
Future/Science Fiction ☐

5.2 Using the same scale of 1 to 5, please rate the following themes you may find in an erotic novel:

Submissive male/dominant female ☐
Submissive female/dominant male ☐
Lesbianism ☐
Bondage/fetishism ☐
Romantic love ☐
Experimental sex e.g. anal/watersports/sex toys ☐
Gay male sex ☐
Group sex ☐

5.3 Using the same scale of 1 to 5, please rate the following styles in which an erotic novel could be written:

Realistic, down to earth, set in real life ☐
Escapist fantasy, but just about believable ☐
Completely unreal, impressionistic, dreamlike ☐

5.4 Would you prefer your ideal erotic novel to be written from the viewpoint of the main male characters or the main female characters?

Male ☐   Female ☐
Both ☐

5.5 What would your ideal Black Lace heroine be like? Tick as many as you like:

Dominant	☐	Glamorous	☐
Extroverted	☐	Contemporary	☐
Independent	☐	Bisexual	☐
Adventurous	☐	Naive	☐
Intellectual	☐	Introverted	☐
Professional	☐	Kinky	☐
Submissive	☐	Anything else?	☐
Ordinary	☐	_____	

5.6 What would your ideal male lead character be like? Again, tick as many as you like:

Rugged	☐		
Athletic	☐	Caring	☐
Sophisticated	☐	Cruel	☐
Retiring	☐	Debonair	☐
Outdoor-type	☐	Naive	☐
Executive-type	☐	Intellectual	☐
Ordinary	☐	Professional	☐
Kinky	☐	Romantic	☐
Hunky	☐		
Sexually dominant	☐	Anything else?	☐
Sexually submissive	☐	_____	

5.7 Is there one particular setting or subject matter that your ideal erotic novel would contain?

_____

SECTION SIX: LAST WORDS

6.1 What do you like best about Black Lace books?

_____

6.2 What do you most dislike about Black Lace books?

_____

6.3 In what way, if any, would you like to change Black Lace covers?

_____

6.4 Here's a space for any other comments:

_____
_____
_____
_____

_____

Thank you for completing this questionnaire. Now tear it out of the book – carefully! – put it in an envelope and send it to:

Black Lace
FREEPOST PAM 6899
London
W6 9BR

No stamp is required if you are resident in the U.K.